# Glenn Horowitz Bookseller

# Recent Imprints

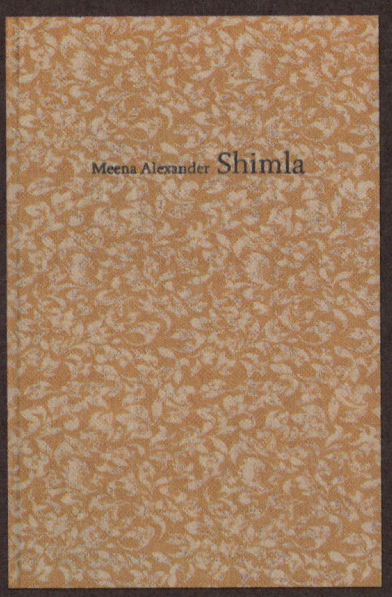

### *Shimla*
### Meena Alexander

A poem cycle reflecting on locations ranging from New York to Delhi to Japan. Includes "Lady Dufferin's Terrace," which appeared in the September 2011 issue of *The New Yorker*.

25 signed copies, printed letterpress, in patterned cloth: *$125*

125 signed copies, printed letterpress, in red handmade paper, sewn: *$40*

### *Leg City*
### Louis & Peter Begley

A new short story by Louis Begley, augmented by eighteen color paintings by his son, Peter. Includes "Cuisine," in which the artist discusses his creative process.

18 signed copies, linen bound, each slipcased with one of the original paintings reproduced in the book: *$1,500*

282 signed copies, in wrappers: *$75*

 7 West 18th Street • NY, NY 10011 • 212-691-9100
info@glennhorowitz.com • www.glennhorowitz.com

# Junot Díaz

**WINNER OF THE PULITZER PRIZE**

**RECIPIENT OF A 2012 MACARTHUR "GENIUS" FELLOWSHIP**

**FINALIST FOR THE 2012 NATIONAL BOOK AWARD**

"Writes in an idiom so electrifying and distinct it's practically an act of aggression."
(The New York Times Book Review)

"Has one of the most distinctive and magnetic voices in contemporary fiction."
(Michiko Kakutani, The New York Times)

Is "the voice of the future."
(Salon)

  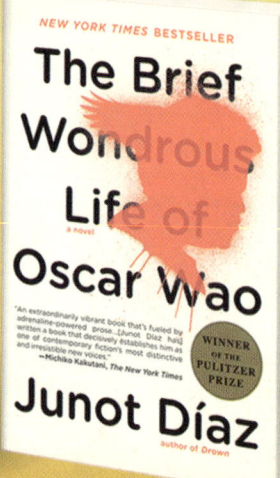

**AVAILABLE NOW WHEREVER BOOKS ARE SOLD OR AT PENGUIN.COM**
Also available as ebooks and audio books

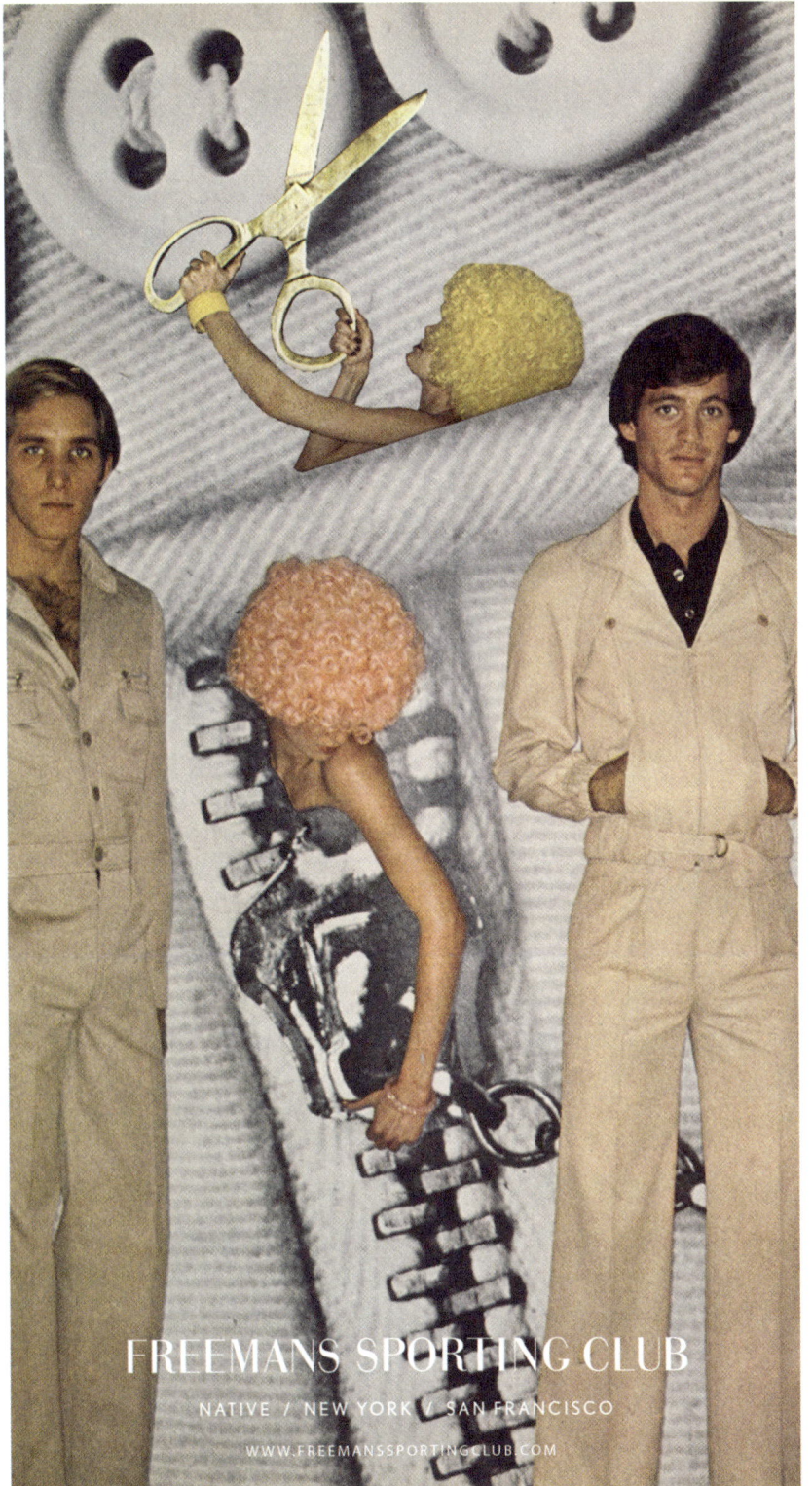

# *the* PARIS

# REVIEW

**62 WHITE STREET** *new york, new york 10013*

# LITERARY Characters

### CLIMATES
#### by André Maurois

Written in 1928 by French biographer and novelist André Maurois, CLIMATES became a best seller in France and all over Europe. The first 100,000 copies printed of its Russian translation sold out the day they appeared in Moscow bookstores.

"A valuable reintroduction to a neglected master...This lucid new translation probes the timeless complications, betrayals, and fascinations wrought by love." —*Publishers Weekly* (starred)

"A timeless tale of women on pedestals and the pain of loving not wisely, but too well." —*Kirkus Reviews*

### MONSIEUR PROUST'S LIBRARY
#### by Anka Muhlstein

"There are many ways of reading a novel as complex as IN SEARCH OF LOST TIME. I found that concentrating on Proust's literary affinities and his use of literature was one of the most rewarding approaches."
—Anka Muhlstein

"A...stimulating study that should deepen readers' appreciation of Proust and draw them back to the original."
—*Kirkus Reviews*

 Visit otherpress.com for excerpts and more information

# OTHER PRESS

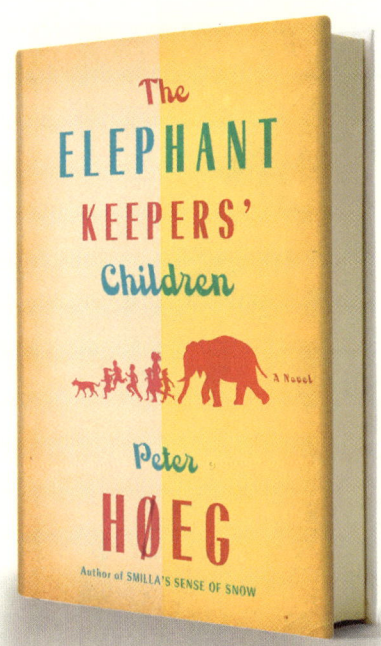

### THE ELEPHANT KEEPERS' CHILDREN by Peter Høeg

*An epic novel about faith and the magic of everyday life, from the author of SMILLA'S SENSE OF SNOW.*

"Madcap, imaginative...[this] funny, wry novel packs serious emotional truths."
—*Minneapolis Star-Tribune*

"Høeg writes prose that is as bitter, changeable, and deep-fathomed as poetry—prose that demands to be read aloud and savored."
—*The New Yorker*

"Høeg poses serious questions about neglected children, venal church officials, and the paths to intellectual and spiritual freedom." —*Publishers Weekly*

### MY ESCAPE
### A memoir by Benoîte Groult

*The autobiography of one of France's most beloved novelists and feminist pioneers.*
A VANITY FAIR HOT TYPE PICK

"Now finally the last first-generation feminist book."
—Kate Millett, author of *Sexual Politics*

"She approaches feminism...from the vibrant stance of a woman who has lived life to the full and who has fought for equal rights whilst being a mother, a wife, a grandmother, and a professional writer." —*Seattle Post Intelligencer*

twitter.com/otherpress • facebook.com/otherpress

*From the heart of a craftsman*

# Frank Clegg

www.FrankCleggLeatherworks.com

"**THE MIDDLESTEINS** had me from its very first pages."
—Jonathan Franzen, author of *Freedom*

"As blazing, ferocious, and great-hearted as anything I've read…. *The Middlesteins* will blow you away."
—Lauren Groff, author of *Arcadia*

"Wonderfully messy and layered."
—*Publishers Weekly* (starred review)

"A sharp-tongued, sweet-natured masterpiece."
—*Kirkus Reviews* (starred review)

Also available in audio and e-book formats
jamiattenberg.com

GRAND CENTRAL PUBLISHING
Hachette Book Group

THE BEEFROLL PENNY LOAFER IN HORWEEN® NATURAL CHROMEXCEL®
HANDCRAFTED IN USA

OAK STREET
BOOTMAKERS

OAKSTREETBOOTMAKERS.COM

# the PARIS REVIEW
GEORGE PLIMPTON 1927–2003

| | |
|---|---|
| Editor | Lorin Stein |
| Managing Editor | Nicole Rudick |
| Deputy Editor | Sadie Stein |
| Associate Editor | Stephen Andrew Hiltner |
| Editorial Assistant | Clare Fentress |
| Poetry Editor | Robyn Creswell |
| Art Editor | Charlotte Strick |
| Paris Editor | Susannah Hunnewell |
| Southern Editor | John Jeremiah Sullivan |
| Advisory Editors | Dan Chiasson, Meghan O'Rourke, Caitlin Roper, Frederick Seidel, David Wallace-Wells |
| Design | Charlotte Strick |
| Development & Events | Emily Cole-Kelly |
| Finance Manager | Janet Gillespie |
| Advertising & Promotions | Hailey Gates |
| Digital Assistant | Justin Alvarez |
| Interns | Samuel Fox, Emma Goldhammer, Charlotte Goldney, Graham Rogers, Thea Slotover |
| Publisher | Antonio Weiss |
| Board of Directors | Scott Asen, Clara Bingham, Jeffrey Eugenides, Stephen Gaghan, Mala Gaonkar, James C. Goodale, Lawrence H. Guffey, Drue Heinz, Bokara Legendre, Jeanne McCulloch, Terry McDonell, Sandy Gotham Meehan, Sarah Dudley Plimpton, Robert Silvers, Rose Styron, Liza Wachter, Antonio Weiss |
| Director Emeritus | Peter Matthiessen |
| Founding Editors | William Pène du Bois, Thomas H. Guinzburg, Harold L. Humes, Peter Matthiessen, George Plimpton, John P. C. Train |
| Past Editors | George Plimpton (1953–2003), Philip Gourevitch (2005–2010) Brigid Hughes (Executive Editor, 2004–2005) |
| Editors Emeriti | Maxine Groffsky, Donald Hall |
| Past Publishers | Bernard F. Conners, Ron Dante, Deborah Pease, Drue Heinz |
| Founding Publisher | Sadruddin Aga Khan |

The Paris Review (ISSN #0031–2037) is published quarterly by The Paris Review Foundation, Inc. at 62 White Street, New York, NY 10013. Vol. 54, No. 203, Winter 2012. Terry McDonell, President; William B. Beekman, Secretary; Antonio Weiss, Treasurer. Please give six weeks notice of change of address. Periodicals postage paid at New York, NY, and at additional mailing offices. Postmaster: please send address changes to The Paris Review, PO Box 23165, Jackson, MS 39225-3165. For subscriptions, please call toll-free: (866) 354-0212. From outside the U.S.: (601) 354-0384 • While The Paris Review welcomes the submission of unsolicited manuscripts, it cannot accept responsibility for their loss or engage in related correspondence. Please send manuscripts with a self-addressed, stamped envelope to The Paris Review, 62 White Street, New York, NY 10013. For additional information, please visit www.theparisreview.org. Printed in the United States. Copyright © 2012 by The Paris Review Foundation, Inc.

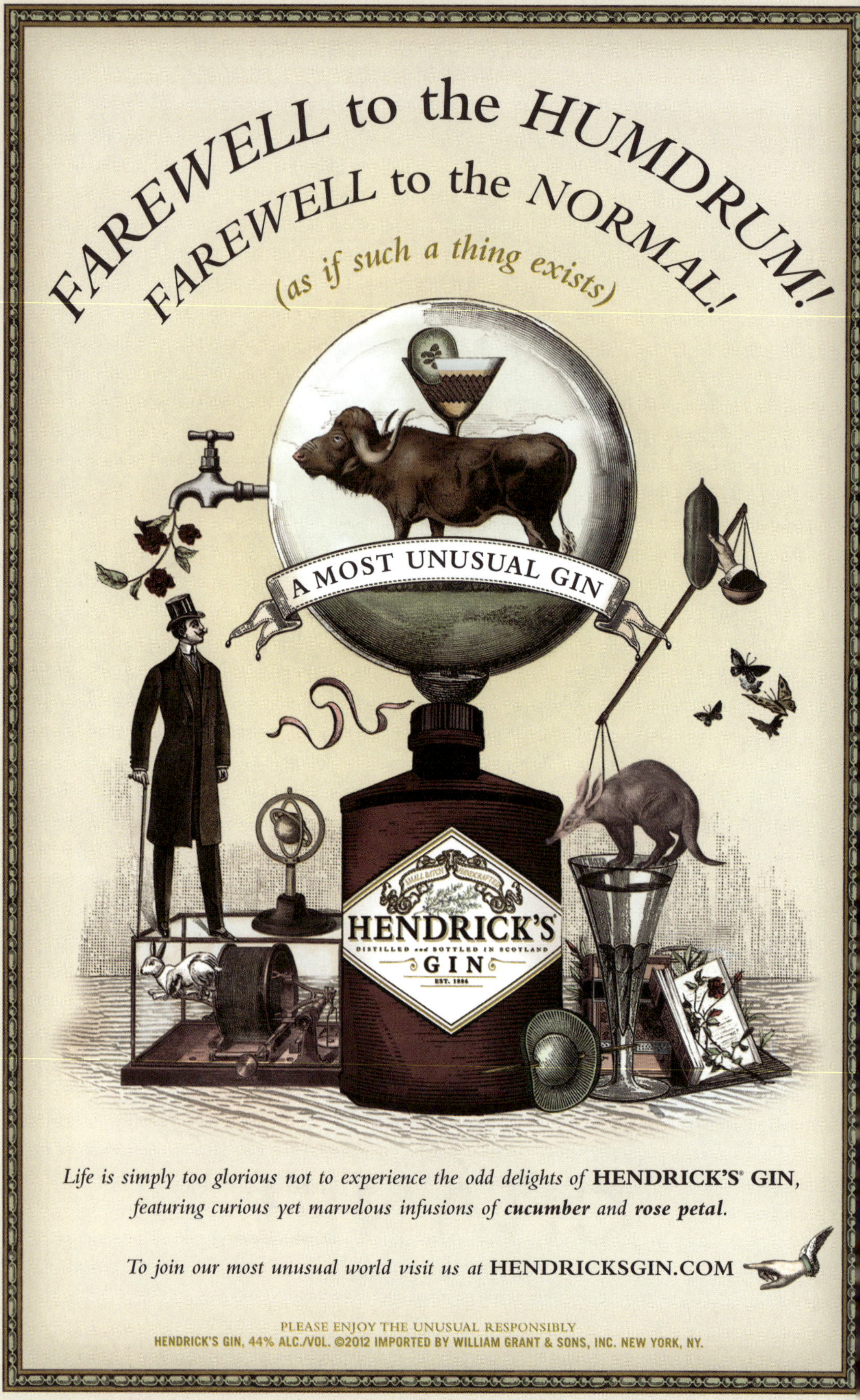

# FAREWELL to the HUMDRUM!
## FAREWELL to the NORMAL!
*(as if such a thing exists)*

**A MOST UNUSUAL GIN**

Life is simply too glorious not to experience the odd delights of **HENDRICK'S® GIN**, featuring curious yet marvelous infusions of **cucumber** and **rose petal**.

To join our most unusual world visit us at **HENDRICKSGIN.COM**

PLEASE ENJOY THE UNUSUAL RESPONSIBLY
HENDRICK'S GIN, 44% ALC./VOL. ©2012 IMPORTED BY WILLIAM GRANT & SONS, INC. NEW YORK, NY.

# TABLE OF CONTENTS

**FICTION**

James Salter, *Virginia* .................................................................. 19
Peter Orner, *The Vac-Haul* ............................................................ 89
Tim Parks, *The Tangling Point* ....................................................... 95
Sarah Frisch, *Housebreaking* .......................................................... 111
Rachel Kushner, *Blanks* ................................................................ 171
The NPR Three-Minute Fiction Contest ............................................... 233

**INTERVIEWS**

*From the Proceedings of the First Annual Norwegian-American Literary Festival* ..... 49
Susan Howe, *The Art of Poetry No. 97* ............................................... 144

**POETRY**

Devin Johnston, *Means of Escape* ..................................................... 47
Ben Lerner, *No Art* ..................................................................... 88
Linda Pastan, *Ah, Friend* .............................................................. 94
Steven Cramer, *Lackawanna* ........................................................... 110
Joshua Mehigan, *Two Poems* .......................................................... 142
Regan Good, *The Wasps' House* ...................................................... 170
Geoffrey Hill, *Three Poems* ............................................................ 216
Yasiin Bey, *One Called Trill* ........................................................... 232

**PORTFOLIO**

The Flamethrowers, curated by Rachel Kushner ..................................... 196

**NONFICTION**

J.D. Daniels, *Letter from Kentucky* ................................................... 219

Contributors ............................................................................. 239

Cover: Anders Danielsen Lie and Viktoria Winge in *Reprise* (2006), directed by Joachim Trier.
Frontispiece: William Pène du Bois, *Paris View*.

# The Plimpton Prize for Fiction

is an annual award of $10,000 given to an emerging writer whose work has appeared in *The Paris Review*. The prize is named for the *Review*'s longtime editor, George Plimpton, and reflects his commitment to discovering new writers of exceptional merit. Past recipients include Jesse Ball, Amie Barrodale, Caitlin Horrocks, April Ayers Lawson, Alistair Morgan, and Benjamin Percy.

## Get discovered.
## Submit to *The Paris Review*.

62 WHITE STREET • NEW YORK, NY 10013

# *Virginia*

## JAMES SALTER

S t. Patrick's Day was sunny and unusually mild, men were in shirtsleeves and from the appearance of things work was ending at noon. The bars were full. Coming into one of them from out of the sunlight, Philip Bowman, his eyes blinded, could barely make out the faces along the bar but found a place to stand near the back where they were all shouting and calling to one another. The bartender brought his drink and he took it and looked around. There were men and women drinking, young women mostly, two of them—he never forgot this moment—standing near him to his right, one dark haired with dark brows and, when he could see her better, a faint down along her jawbone. The other was blonde with a bare, shining forehead and wide-set eyes, instantly compelling, even in some way coarse. He was so struck by her face that it was difficult to look at her, she stood out so—on the other hand he could not keep himself from doing it. He was almost fearful of looking.

He raised his glass toward them.

"Happy St. Patrick's," he managed to say.

"Can't hear you," one of them cried.

He tried to introduce himself. The place was too noisy. It was like a raging party they were in the middle of.

"What's your name?" he called.

"Vivian," the blonde girl said.

He stepped closer. Louise was the dark-haired one. She already had a secondary role, but Bowman, trying not to be too direct, included her.

"Do you live around here?" he said.

Louise answered. She lived on Fifty-third Street. Vivian lived in Virginia.

"Virginia?" Bowman said, stupidly he felt, as if it were China.

"I live in Washington," Vivian said.

He could not keep his eyes from her. Her face was as if, somehow, it was not completely finished, with smouldering features, a mouth not eager to smile, a riveting face that God had stamped with the simple answer to life. In profile she was even more beautiful.

When they asked what he did—the noise had quieted a little—he replied he was an editor.

"An editor?"

"Yes."

"Of what? Magazines?"

"Books," he said. "I work at Braden and Baum."

They had never heard of it.

"I was thinking of going to Clarke's," he said, "but there was all this noise in here, and I just came in to see what was going on. I'll have to go back to work. What … what are you doing later?"

They were going to a movie.

"Want to come?" Louise said.

He suddenly liked, even loved her.

"I can't. Can I meet you later? I'll meet you here."

"What time?"

"After work. Any time."

They agreed to meet at six.

All afternoon he was almost giddy and found it hard to keep his mind on things. Time moved with a terrible slowness, but at a quarter to six, walking quickly, almost running, he went back. He was a few minutes early, they were not there. He waited impatiently until six-fifteen, then six-thirty. They never appeared. With a sickening feeling he realized what he had done—he had let them go without asking for a telephone number or address, Fifty-third Street was all he knew and he would never see them, her, again. Hating his ineptness, he stayed for nearly an hour, toward the end striking up a conversation with the man next to him so that if by chance they did finally come, he would not seem foolish and doglike standing there.

What was it, he wondered, that had betrayed him and made them decide not to come back? Had they been approached by someone else after he left? He was miserable. He felt the terrible emptiness of men who are ruined, who see everything collapse in a single day. He went to work in the morning still feeling anguish. It was in him like a deep splinter together with a sense of failure.

"How are you this morning?" Baum said easily, the usual overture when he had nothing particular in mind.

They talked for a bit and had just finished when the secretary came over. "There's someone on the phone for you."

Bowman picked up his phone and said, somewhat curtly, "Hello."

It was her. He felt a moment of insane happiness. She was apologizing. They had come back at six the night before but hadn't been able to find the bar, they couldn't remember the street.

"Yes, of course," Bowman said. "I'm so sorry, but that's all right."

"We even went to Clarke's," she said. "I remembered you said that."

"I'm so glad you called."

"I just wanted you to know. That we tried to come back and meet you."

"No, no, that's all right, that's fine. Look, give me your address, will you?"

"In Washington?"

"Yes, anywhere."

She gave it and Louise's as well. She was going back to Washington that afternoon, she said.

"Do you … what time is the train? Do you have time for lunch?"

Not really. The train was at one.

"That's too bad. Maybe another time," he said foolishly.

"Well, bye," she said after a pause.

"Good-bye," he somehow agreed.

But he had her address, he looked at it after hanging up. It was precious beyond words. He didn't know her last name.

In the great vault of Penn Station with the light in wide blocks coming down through the glass and onto the crowd that was always waiting, Bowman made his way. He was nervous but then caught sight of her standing unaware.

"Vivian!"

She looked around and then saw him.

"Oh. It's you. What a surprise. What are you doing here?"

"I wanted to say good-bye," he said and added, "I brought you a book I thought you might like."

Vivian had had books as a child, she and her sister, children's books, they had even fought over them. She had read Nancy Drew and some others, but to be honest, she said, she didn't read that much. *Forever Amber*. Her skin was luminous.

"Well, thank you."

"It's one of ours," he said.

She read the title. It was very sweet of him. It was not something she would ever expect or that boys she knew would do or even grown-ups. She was twenty years old but not yet ready to think of herself as a woman, probably because she was still largely supported by her father and because of her devotion to him. She had gone to junior college and gotten a job. The women she knew were known for their style, their riding ability, and their husbands. Also their nerve. She had an aunt who had been robbed in her home at gunpoint by two black men and had said to them cooly, "We've been too good to you people."

The Virginia of Vivian Amussen was Anglo, privileged, and inbred. It was made up of rolling, wooded country, beautiful country, rich at heart, with low stone walls and narrow roads that had preserved it. By the straight, two-lane blacktop it was less than an hour's drive to Washington and the downtown section where Vivian worked. Her job was more or less a formality, she was a receptionist in a title office, and on weekends she went home, to the races or thoroughbred sales or hunts through the countryside. The hunts were like clubs, to belong to the best one, the one she and her father were members of, you had to own at least fifty acres. The master of that hunt was a judge, John Stump, a figure out of Dickens, stout and choleric, with an incurable fondness for women that had once led him to attempt suicide upon being rejected by a woman he loved. He threw himself from a window in passion but landed in some bushes. He had been married three times, each time, it was observed, to a woman with bigger breasts. The divorces were because of his drinking, which befitted his image as a squire, but as master of the hunt he was resolute and demanded perfect etiquette, one time halting the field when they'd done something wrong and giving them a ferocious dressing-down until someone spoke out,

"Look, I didn't get up at six o'clock to listen to a lecture."

"Dismount!" Stump cried. "Dismount at once and return to the stables!"

Later he apologized.

Judge Stump was a friend of Vivian's father, George Amussen, who had manners and was always polite but also particular regarding those he might call a friend. The judge was his lawyer and Anna Wayne, the judge's first wife, who was narrow chested but a very fine rider, had for a time before her marriage gone with Amussen, and it was generally believed that she accepted the judge when she was convinced that Amussen would not marry her.

Judge Stump pursued women, but George Amussen did not—they pursued him. He was elegant and reserved and also much admired for having done well buying and selling property in Washington and in the country. Even tempered and patient, he had seen, earlier than others, how Washington was changing, and over the years had bought, sometimes in partnerships, apartment buildings in the northwest part of the city and an office building on Wisconsin Avenue. He was discreet about what he owned and refrained from talking about it. He drove an ordinary car and dressed casually, without ostentation, usually in a sport jacket and well-made pants, and a suit when it was called for.

He had fair hair into which the gray blended and an easy walk that seemed to embody strength and even a kind of principle, to stand for things as they should be. A gentleman and a figure of country clubs, he knew all the black waiters by name and they knew him. At Christmas every year he gave them a double tip.

Washington was a Southern city, lethargic and not really that big. It had atrocious weather, damp and cold in the winter and in the summers fiercely hot, the heat of the Delta. It had its institutions apart from the government, the old, favored hotels including the Wardman, familiarly called the riding academy because of the many mistresses who were kept there; the Riggs Bank, which was the bank of choice; the established downtown department stores.

The war changed it all. The hordes of military and naval personnel, government employees, young women who were drawn to the city by the demand for secretaries—in two or three years the sleepy, provincial town was gone. In some respects it clung to its ways, but the old days were vanishing. Vivian had come of age during that time. Though she appeared at the club in shorts that were in her father's opinion a little too brief and wore high heels too soon, her notions were really all from the world she had been a girl in.

Bowman wrote to her, and almost to his disbelief she wrote back. Her letters were friendly and open. She came to New York several times that spring and early summer, staying with Louise and even sharing the bed with her, laughing, in pajamas. She had not yet told her father about her boyfriend. The ones she had in Washington worked at State or in the trust department at Riggs and were in many ways replicas of their parents. She did not think of herself as a replica. She was daring, in fact, taking the train up to see a man she had met in a bar, whose background she did not know but who seemed to have depth and originality. They went to Luchow's, where the waiter said *guten Abend* and Bowman talked to him for a moment in German.

"I didn't know you spoke German."

"Well, until recently it wasn't a great thing to do," Bowman said.

He had taken German at Harvard, he explained.

"At the time I thought I wanted to be a scientist. I went back and forth between a number of things. I thought for a while I might teach. I still have a certain yearning for teaching. Then I decided to be a journalist, but I wasn't able to get a job as one. I heard about a job as a reader then. It was pure luck or maybe destiny. What do you think of the idea of destiny?"

"Hadn't thought about it," she said casually.

He liked talking to her and the occasional smile that made her forehead shine. She was wearing a sleeveless dress and the roundness of her small shoulders gleamed. Her little finger was curled and held apart as she ate a bite of bread. Gestures, facial expressions, way of dressing—these were the revealing things. He was imagining places where they might go together, where no one knew them and he would have her to himself for days on end, though he was uncertain of how it might happen.

"New York's a wonderful place, isn't it?" he said.

"Yes. I like coming here."

"How do you know Louise?"

"We were in boarding school, in the same class. The first thing she ever said to me was a dirty joke. Well, not exactly dirty but … you know."

He told her about the time the letters *ES* on the big sign above the Essex House had gone out and there it was, forty stories up, shining in the night. He went no further. He didn't want to seem coarse.

At the end of the evening, at the front door, he was prepared to say good night but she acted as if he were not there, unlocking the door and saying nothing. Louise was gone for the weekend to visit her parents. Vivian was nervous, though she did not want to show it. He went upstairs with her.

"Would you like a cup of coffee?" she asked.

"Yes, that would be … No," he said, "not really."

They sat for a few moments in silence and then she simply leaned forward and kissed him. The kiss was light but ardent.

"Do you want to?" she asked.

She did not take everything off—shoes, stockings, and skirt, that was all. She was not prepared for more. They kissed and whispered. As she slid from her white panties, a white that seemed sacred, he barely breathed. The fineness of her, the blondish fleece. He could not believe they were doing this.

"I don't … have anything," he whispered. There was no answer.

He was inexperienced, but it was natural and overwhelming. Also too quick, he couldn't help it. He felt embarrassed. Her face was close to his.

"I'm sorry," he said. "I couldn't stop it."

She said nothing, she had almost no way to judge it.

She went into the bathroom and Bowman lay back in awe at what had happened and feeling intoxicated by a world that had suddenly opened wide to the greatest pleasure, pleasure beyond knowing. He knew of the joy that might lie ahead.

Vivian was thinking along less heady lines. There was the chance of her becoming pg though she had, in truth, only an inexact idea of how likely that was. At school there had been a lot of talk, but it was only talk and vague. Still, there were stories of girls who got that way the first time. It would be just her luck, she thought. Of course, it hadn't been entirely the first time.

"You make me think of a pony," he said lovingly.

"A pony? Why?"

"You're just beautiful. And free."

"I don't see how that's like a pony," she said. "Besides, ponies bite. Mine did."

She nestled against him and he tried to think along her lines. Whatever might happen, they had done it. He felt only exaltation.

THEY SPENT THE NIGHT TOGETHER when he came to Washington that month and drove to the country the next day to have lunch with her father. He had a four-hundred-acre farm called Gallops, mostly given over to grazing. The main house was fieldstone and sat on top of a rise. Vivian showed him around, the grounds and first floor, as if introducing him to it and, in a way, to her. The house was lightly furnished in a manner that was indifferent to style. Behind a couch in the living room Bowman noticed, as in seventeenth-century palaces, were some dried dog turds.

Lunch was served by a black maid toward whom Amussen behaved with complete familiarity. Her name was Mattie and the main course came in on a silver tray.

"Vivian says you work in publishing," Amussen said.

"Yes, sir. I'm an editor."

"I see."

"It's a small house," Bowman went on, "but with quite a good literary reputation."

Amussen, picking at something near his incisor with his little finger, said,

"What do you mean by literary?"

"Well, books of quality, essentially. Books that might have a long life. Of course, that's the top end. We publish other books, to make money or try to."

"Can we have some coffee, Mattie?" Amussen said to the maid. "Would you like some coffee, Mr. Bowman?"

"Thank you."

"Viv, you?"

"Yes, Daddy."

As they drank coffee, Bowman made a last attempt to cast himself favorably as an editor, but Amussen turned the subject to the navy, Bowman had been in the navy, was that right? There was a neighbor down the road, Royce Cromwell, who had gone to Annapolis and been in the same class as Charlie McVay, the captain of the *Indianapolis*. Bowman hadn't run into him in the navy, by any chance?

"No, I don't think so. I was only a junior officer. Was he in the Pacific?"

"I don't know."

"Well, there was a big Atlantic fleet, too, for the convoys, the invasion, and all that. Hundreds of ships."

"I wouldn't know. You'd have to ask him."

Almost without effort he had made Bowman feel as if he were prying. The lunch had been one of those meals when the sound of a knife or fork on a plate or a glass being set down only marks the silence.

Outside, as they walked to the car, Bowman saw something moving slowly with undulant curves into the ivy bed along the driveway.

"There's a snake, I think."

"Where?"

"There. Just going into the ivy."

"Damn it," Vivian said, "that's just where the dogs like to sleep. Was it big?"

It had not been a small snake, it was thick as a hose.

"Pretty good-sized," Bowman said.

Vivian, looking around, found a rake and began furiously running the handle of it back and forth through the ivy. The snake was gone, however.

"What was it? Was it a rattler?"

"I don't know. It was big. Do they have rattlesnakes around here?"

"They sure do."

"You'd better come out of there."

She was not afraid. She ran the handle through the dark, shiny leaves a final time.

"Damned thing," she said.

She went to tell her father. Bowman stood looking at the thick ivy, watching for any movement. She had stepped right into it.

Driving back that day, Bowman felt they were leaving a place where not even his language was understood. He was about to say it, but Vivian commented,

"Don't mind Daddy," she said. "He's like that sometimes. It wasn't you."

"I don't think I made a very good impression."

"Oh, you should see him with Bryan, my sister's husband. Daddy calls him Whyan, why in hell did she pick him? Can't even ride, he says."

"You aren't making me feel much better. I can sail," he added. "Can your father sail?"

"He's sailed to the Bahamas."

She seemed ready to defend him, and Bowman felt he should not go further. She sat looking out of the window on her side, somewhat removed, but in her leather skirt, hair pulled back, face wide, with a thin gold chain looped around her neck, she was the image of desirability. She turned back toward him.

"It's like that," she commented. "You sort of have to go through the mud room first."

"Is your mother anything like that?"

"My mother? No."

"What's she like?"

"She's a drunk," Vivian said. "That's the reason they got divorced."

"Where does she live? In Middleburg?"

"No, she has an apartment in Washington near Dupont Circle. You'll meet her."

Her mother had been beautiful but you couldn't tell it now, Vivian added. She started in the morning with vodka and rarely got dressed until afternoon.

"Daddy really raised us. We're his two girls. He had to protect us."

They drove for a while in silence and near Centerville somewhere he glanced over and saw that she was asleep.

FREELY, AS THEY SAT OR ATE OR WALKED he shared with her his thoughts and ideas about life, history, and art. He told her everything. He knew she didn't think about these things, but she understood and could learn. He loved her for not only what she was but what she might be, the idea that she might be otherwise did not occur to him or did not matter. Why would it occur? When you love you see a future according to your dreams.

In Summit, where he wanted his mother to meet Vivian, to see and approve of her, he took her first to a diner across from City Hall that had been there for years. It had actually been a railroad car with windows all along the side facing the avenue. Inside, the floor was tile and the ceiling pale wood that curved down into the wall. A counter where customers sat—there were always one or two—ran the length of the place. It was more crowded in the morning; the railroad station, the Morris and Essex line that went to the city, was just down the street. The tracks were low and out of sight. At night the lights of the diner were the only lights along the street. You entered by a door opposite the counter and there was another door at one end.

It was here that Hemingway placed his story "The Killers," Bowman said.

"Right here, in this diner. The counter, everything. Do you know the story? It's marvelous. Fabulously written. If you never read another word of his, you'd know right away what a great writer he is. It's in the evening. Nobody's in the place, there are no customers, it's empty, and two men in tight black overcoats come in and sit down at the counter. They look at the menu and order, and one of them says to the counterman, This is some town, what's the name of this place? And the counterman, who's frightened of course, says, Summit. It's right there in the story, Summit, and when the food comes they eat with their gloves on. They're there to kill a Swede, they tell the counterman. They know the Swede always comes there. He's an ex-fighter named Ole Andreson who double-crossed the mob somehow. One of them takes a sawed-off shotgun from beneath his coat and goes into the kitchen to hide and wait."

"Did this actually happen?"

"No, no. He wrote it in Spain."

"It's just made up."

"You don't believe it's made up, reading it. That's what's so incredible, you absolutely believe it."

"And they kill him?"

"It's better than that. They don't kill him because he doesn't show up, but he knows they're after him, they'll come again. He's big, he was a boxer, but whatever he did, they're going to kill him. He just lies in bed in the rooming house, looking at the wall."

They began to read the menu.

"What are you going to have?" Vivian asked.

"I think I'll have eggs with Taylor ham."

"What's Taylor ham?" she said.

"It's a kind of ham they have around here. I've never really asked."

"All right, I'll have it, too."

He liked being with her. He liked having her with him. There were only a few other people in the diner, but how colorless they seemed compared to her. They were all aware of her presence. It was impossible not to be.

"I'd like to meet Hemingway," he said. "Go down to Cuba and meet him. Maybe we could go together."

"Well, I don't know," she said. "Maybe."

"You have to read him," he said.

Beatrice Bowman had been eager to meet Vivian and was also struck by her looks, though in a different way, the freshness and naked, animal statement. How much one knows from the first! She had bought flowers and set the table in the dining room where they seldom ate, usually using a table in the kitchen, one end of which was against the wall. The kitchen with shelves but no cabinets was the real heart of the house together with a sitting room where they often sat in front of the fireplace talking and having a drink. Now there was this girl with somewhat stiff manners. She was from Virginia, and Beatrice asked what part, Middleburg?

"We really live nearer to Upperville," Vivian replied.

Upperville. It sounded rural and small. It was, in fact, small, there was one place to eat but no town water or sewage. Nothing had changed there for a hundred years and people there liked it that way whether they lived in an old house without heat or on a thousand acres. Upperville in the country and beyond, was an exalted name, the emblem of a proud, parochial class of which Vivian was a member. You could not stay there, you had to live there.

"It's beautiful country," Bowman said.

Beatrice said, "I'd love to see it. What does your family do there?"

"Farm," Vivian said. "Well, my father farms some but also he puts his fields up for grazing."

"It must be big."

"It's not terribly big, it's about four hundred acres."

"That's so interesting. Apart from farming, what is there to do?"

"Daddy always says there's lots to do. He means looking after the horses."

"Horses."

"Yes."

It was not that she was difficult to talk to, but you immediately felt the limits. Vivian had gone to junior college, probably at the suggestion of her father to keep her out of mischief. She had a certain confidence, based on the things she absolutely knew and which had proved to be enough. Like all mothers though, Beatrice hoped for a girl like herself, with whom she could speak easily and whose view of life could almost perfectly be combined with her own. Among her pupils, she could think of girls who were like that, good students with natural charm that you admired and were drawn to, but there were also others not so easily understood and whose fate you were not meant to know.

"Didn't Liz Bohannon come from Middleburg?" Beatrice asked, bringing up a name, a horse and society figure of the thirties, always photographed with her husband aboard some ship sailing to Europe or in their box at Saratoga.

"Yes, she has a big place. She's a friend of my father's."

"She's still around?"

"Oh, very much around."

There were a lot of stories about her, Vivian said. When they first bought their place, Longtree—that was the name then—she used to ride in from the hunt and let the dogs come right into the house. They'd jump up on the table and eat everything. After she got divorced, she calmed down a bit.

"Oh, you must know her, then?"

"Oh, yes."

Vivian was eating somewhat carefully, not like a girl with a genuine appetite. The flowers, which Beatrice had moved to the side, were a lush backdrop for her, some young pagan goddess who had cast a spell over her son.

When he told his mother he hoped to marry her, Beatrice, though afraid it would prove nothing, protested how unalike the two of them were, how little they had in common. They had a great deal in common, Bowman a little defiantly said. What they had in common was more vital than similar interests—it was wordless understanding and accord.

It was love, the furnace into which everything is dropped.

In New York at a restaurant called El Faro where the prices were low, in back, beneath the darkened walls, Vivian said, "Louise would love this. She's mad about Spain."

"Has she been there?"

"No. She's never even been to Mexico. She was in Boston last weekend with her boyfriend."

"Who's that?"

"His name's Ted. They went to some hotel and never got out of bed the whole time."

"I didn't know she was like that."

"She was so sore she could hardly walk."

The place was full, there was a crowd at the bar. Beyond the single window, across the street were second and third floors with large, lighted rooms where a couple might live. Vivian was drinking a second glass of wine. The waiter was squeezing past tables with their order on a tray.

"What is this? Is this the paella?" she asked.

"Yes."

"What's in it?" she said.

"Sausage, rice, clams, everything."

She began to eat.

"It's good," she said.

The crowded tables and talk around them gave it an intimacy. He knew it was the time, he must say it somehow.

"I love it when you come up here."

"Me, too," she said automatically.

"Really?"

"Yes," she said and his heart began wildly.

"What would you think," he said, "about living here? I mean, we'd be married, of course."

She paused in her eating. He couldn't tell what her reaction was. Had he misstated something?

"There's so much noise in here," she said.

"Yes, it's noisy."

"Was that a proposal?"

"It was pitiful, wasn't it? Yes, it's a proposal. I love you," he said. "I need you. I'd do anything for you."

He'd said it, just as he meant to.

"Will you marry me?" he said.

"We'll have to get Daddy's permission," she said.

An immense happiness filled him.

"Of course. Is that really necessary?"

"Yes," she said.

THE LUNCH WAS AT GEORGE AMUSSEN'S CLUB in Washington. Amussen was already seated when the steward showed Bowman in. Across a number of tables he could see his prospective father-in-law reading something. Sitting alone, hair combed straight back, at his ease, he looked at that moment like a figure from the war, even someone who had been on the other side, some commander or Luftwaffe pilot. It was noon and the tables were just filling up.

"Good morning," Bowman said as a greeting.

"Good morning. Nice to see you," Amussen replied. "I'm just looking at the menu here. Sit down. I see they have shad roe."

Bowman picked up the menu himself, and they each ordered a drink.

The waiter came to take their order.

"How is the shad roe, Edward?" Amussen asked.

"Jus' fine, Mistuh Amussen."

"Do you have two orders of it?" he asked. "If you'd like to have it," he said to his guest.

Bowman assumed it was a Southern dish.

"Do you do any fishing?" Amussen said. "Shad is bony, generally too bony to bother with. The roe is the best part."

"Yes, I'll have it. How do they make it?"

"In a pan with some bacon. They brown it. That's right, isn't it, Edward?"

It was at the end of lunch, when they were being served coffee, that Bowman said, "You know, I'm in love with Vivian."

Amussen continued stirring his coffee as if he had not heard.

"And I think she's in love with me," Bowman went on. "We would like to get married."

Still Amussen showed no emotion. He was as calm as if he were alone.

"I've come to ask for your permission, sir," Bowman said.

The "sir" seemed a little courtly but he felt it was appropriate. Amussen was still occupied with stirring.

"Vivian's a nice girl," Amussen finally said. "She was raised in the country. I don't know how she'd take to city life. She's not one of those people."

He then looked up.

"How do you plan on providing for her?" he said.

"Well, as you know, I have a good job. I like my work, I have a career. I earn enough to support us at this point, and whatever I have is hers. I'll make sure she's comfortable."

"She's not a city girl," Amussen said again. "You know, from the time she was just a little thing, she's had her own horse."

"We haven't talked about that. I suppose we could always make room for a horse," Bowman said lightly.

Amussen seemed not to hear him.

"We love one another," Bowman said. "I'll do everything in my power to make her happy."

Amussen nodded slightly.

"I promise you that. We're hoping for your permission, then. Your blessing, sir."

There was a pause.

"I don't think I can give you that," Amussen said. "Not and be honest with you."

"I see."

"I don't think it would work. I think it would be a mistake."

"I see."

"But I won't stand in Vivian's way," her father said.

Bowman left feeling disappointed but defiant. It would be a kind of morganatic marriage then, politely tolerated. He was not sure what attitude to take about it, but when he told Vivian what her father had said, she was not disturbed.

"That's just Daddy," she said.

The minister was a tall man in his seventies with silvery hair who couldn't hear very well, having fallen from a horse. Age had taken the edge from his voice, which was silken but thin. At the prenuptial meeting he said he would ask them three questions, the ones he always asked couples. He wanted to know if they were in love. Next, did they want to be married in the church? And lastly, would the marriage last?

"We can definitely answer yes to the first two," Bowman replied.

"Ah," the minister said, "yes." He was absentminded and had forgotten the order of the questions. "I don't suppose it's so important to be in love," he admitted.

He hadn't shaved, Bowman noticed, there was a white stubble on his face, but he was more presentable at the wedding. Vivian's family was there, her mother, sister, brother-in-law, and some others Bowman had never met and also friends. There were fewer on the groom's side. It was a bright, cool morning, then afternoon, passing in an excitement that made it hard to remember. He was with his mother beforehand and could see her during the ceremony. He watched with a sense of victory as Amussen brought Vivian down the aisle. He put any misgivings aside, it was like a scene from a play. During the vows he saw only his bride, her face clear and shining, and in back of her Louise smiling, too, as he heard himself say, With this ring, I thee wed. I thee wed.

Beatrice had wept at the church. She had embraced Vivian and in return felt a dutiful response. It had all been like that, dutiful, restrained, with only smiles and polite talk.

She was bidding good-bye to her son. She had a chance to embrace him and to say with all her heart,

"Be good to one another. Love one another," she said.

Vivian was happy. She was wearing a white wedding gown, she had yet to change, and though she was not yet used to the idea, she was a married woman. She'd married at home, with her father's blessing, more or less. It had happened, she had done it.

Bowman was happy or felt he was, she was his, a beautiful woman or girl. He saw life ahead in regular terms, with someone who would be beside him. In the presence of her family and friends he realized that he knew only one side of her, a side that attracted him but that was not her entire or essential self. Behind her as he looked was her unyielding father. Across the room, smiling and alcoholic, was her mother. Vivian caught his eye and perhaps his thoughts and smiled at him, it seemed understandingly. The unsettled feeling disappeared. Her smile was loving, sincere. We'll leave soon, it said. That night though, having driven to the Hay-Adams Hotel in Washington, wearied by the events of the day and unaccustomed to being a wedded couple, they simply went to sleep.

IT SNOWED BEFORE CHRISTMAS but then turned cold. The sky was pale. The country lay silent, the fields dusted white with the hard furrows showing where they had been plowed. All was still. The foxes were in their dens, the deer bedded down. Route 50 from Washington, the road that had been originally laid out in almost a straight line by George Washington when he was a surveyor, was empty of traffic. On the back roads an early car with its headlights came along. First the trees, half-frosted, were lit, then the road itself, and finally the sound as the car passed.

They had Christmas at George Amussen's, and the next day was to be dinner at Longtree, Longtree Farm, more than a thousand acres running almost to the Blue Ridge. Liz Bohannon had gotten Longtree in the divorce. The house, that had burned down and been rebuilt, was named Ha Ha.

Late in the afternoon they drove through the iron gates that were posted with a warning that only one car at a time could pass through. The long driveway led upward with evenly spaced trees on either side. At last the house appeared, a vast facade with many windows, every one of them lit as if the house were a huge toy. When Amussen knocked at the door there was a sudden barking of dogs.

"Rollo! Slipper!" a voice inside cried and then began cursing.

In a mauve, flowered gown that bared one plump shoulder and impatiently kicking at the dogs, Liz Bohannon opened the door. She had been a deity once and was still beautiful. As Amussen kissed her, she said, "Darling, I thought it was you." To Vivian and her new husband, she said, "I'm so glad you could come."

To Bowman she held out a surprisingly small hand that bore a large emerald ring.

"I was in the study, paying bills. Is it going to snow? It feels like it. How was your Christmas?" she asked Amussen.

She continued pushing away the importuning dogs, one small and white, the other a Dalmatian.

"Ours was quiet," she went on. "You haven't been here before, have you?" she said to Bowman. "The house was built originally in 1838, but it's burned down twice, the last time in the middle of the night while I was sleeping."

She held Bowman's hand. He felt a kind of thrill. "What shall I call you? Philip? Phil?"

She had beautiful features, now a little small for the face that for years had allowed her to say and do whatever she liked, that and the money. She was loved, derided, and known as the most dishonest horsewoman in the business, banned at Saratoga where she had once bought back two of her own horses at auction, which was strictly prohibited. Keeping Bowman's hand in hers, she led the way in as she talked, speaking to Amussen.

"I was paying bills. My God, this place costs a fortune to run. It costs more to run when I'm away than when I'm here, can you believe that? No one to watch. I've just about made up my mind to sell it."

"Sell it?" said Amussen.

"Move to Florida," she said. "Live with the Jews. Vivian, you look so beautiful."

They went into the study, where the walls were a dark green and covered with pictures of horses, paintings and photographs.

"This is my favorite room," she said. "Don't you like these pictures? That one there," she said pointing, "is Khartoum—I loved that horse—I wouldn't part with it for anything. When the house burned in 1944, I ran out in the middle of the night with nothing but my mink coat and that painting. That was all I had."

"Woody won't eat!" a voice called from another room.

"Who?"

"Woody."

A man with his hair combed in a careful wave came to the doorway. He was wearing a V-neck sweater and lizard shoes. He had a look of feigned concern on his face.

"Go tell Willa," Liz said.

"She's the one who told me."

"Travis, you don't know these people. This is my husband, Travis," Liz said. "I married someone from the backyard. Everybody knows you shouldn't, but you do it anyway, don't you, sweetheart?" she said lovingly.

"You mean I didn't come from a rich family?"

"That's for certain."

"Perfection pays off," he said with a practiced smile.

Travis Gates was a lieutenant colonel in the air force but with something vaguely fraudulent about him. He'd been in China during the war and liked to use Chinese expressions, *Ding hao*, he would say. He was her third husband. The first, Ted Bohannon, had been rich, his family owned newspapers and copper mines. Liz had been twenty, careless and sure of herself, the marriage was the event of the year. They had already slept together at a friend's house in Georgetown and were wildly in love. They were invited and traveled everywhere, to California, Europe, the Far East. It was during the Depression and photographs of them in the papers, on shipboard or at the track, were an anodyne, a reminder of life as it had been and might be. They also went a number of times to Silver Hill to visit Laura, Liz's younger sister, who worked as a club singer, usually on a small stage in a white or beaded dress, and was also an alcoholic. She took the cure at Silver Hill every few years.

One night during the war, the three of them were stranded in New York when there was trouble with the car. The hotels were all full but because Ted knew the manager they were able to get a room at the Westbury. They had to sleep three in the bed. In the middle of the night Liz woke up to find her husband doing something with her sister who had the nightgown up under her armpits. It was the tenth year of the marriage that had begun to be stale anyway, and that night marked the end.

Meanwhile the telephone was ringing.

"Shall I get that, Bun?" Travis said.

"Willa will get it. I don't want to talk to anyone."

She had picked up Slipper and was holding her cradled against her breasts as she showed Bowman the view from the window, the Blue Ridge Mountains far off with only one or two other houses in sight.

"It's starting to snow again," she commented. "Willa! Who was that?"

There was no response. She called again.

"Willa!"

"Yas."

"Who was that on the phone? What are you, going deaf?"

A lean black woman appeared in the doorway.

"I'm not going deaf," she stated. "That was Mrs. Pry."

"P-R-Y?"

"Pry."

"What did she say? Are they coming?"

"She say Mr. Pry afraid of coming out in this weather."

"Is Monroe back there in the kitchen? Tell him to bring out some ice. Come on," she said to Bowman and Vivian, "I'll show you some of the house."

In the kitchen she paused to try to coax words out of a mynah bird that was missing some tail feathers. It was in a big bamboo cage where it had made a kind of hammock for itself. Monroe was working at an unhurried pace. Liz took an all-weather coat from a hook.

"It's not that cold," she said. "I'll show you the stables."

AMUSSEN WAS SEATED on a large upholstered couch in the living room, leafing through a copy of *National Geographic* and occasionally reading a caption. A young girl in jodhpurs and a sweater came in and sat carelessly down at the far end of the couch.

"Hello, Darrin," Amussen said.

She was named for an uncle but didn't like the name and preferred to be called Dare.

"Hi," she said.

"How are you feeling?"

She looked at him and almost smiled.

"Screwed out," she said, stretching her arms lazily.

"You always talk like that?"

"No," she said, "I do it for you. I know you like it. Did my father call?"

"I don't know. Anne Pry called."

"Mrs. Emmett Pry? Graywillow Farm? I went to school with her daughter, Sally."

"I guess you did."

"I rode all her horses and the grooms rode her."

"How's your momma?" Amussen said, changing the subject. "She's a sweet woman. Haven't seen her for ages."

"She's feeling better."

"That's good," Amussen said, putting down the magazine. "I see that you're feeling fine."

"Up every morning, no matter what."

"How old are you now, Darrin?"

"Why are you calling me Darrin?"

"All right. Dare. How old are you?"

"Eighteen," she said.

He rose and got a glass from a bar that was among the bookshelves. He continued looking for something.

"It's in the cabinet underneath," Dare said.

"How's your daddy?" Amussen asked as he found the bottle he was looking for.

"He's fine. Fix me one, too, will you?"

"I didn't know you drank."

"With some water," she said.

"Just branch water?"

"Yes."

He poured two drinks.

"Here you are."

"Peter Connors is here, too. You know him, don't you?"

"I don't know if I do."

"He's my boyfriend."

"Well, good."

"He follows me around. He wants to marry me. I can't think what he imagines that would be like."

"I guess you're old enough."

"My parents think so. I'll probably end up marrying some forty-year-old groom."

"You might. I don't think it would last long."

"No, but he'd always be grateful," she said.

Amussen made no comment.

"That's a nice sweater," he said.

The sweater was not snug, but still.

"Thank you," she said.

"What is it, silk? It looks like the things they used to have in that little shop over in Middleburg. You know, the one Peggy Court ran, what's the name?"

"Patio. You've probably bought a lot of things there."

"Me? No. But your sweater looks like Patio."

"It is. It was a gift."

"Oh, yes?"

"But I prefer Garfinkle's," she said.

"Well, you don't always get to choose where a gift comes from."

"I generally do," she said.

"Dare, now you behave."

They sat drinking. Amussen looked down at his glass but could feel her eyes on him.

"You know, my daughter Vivian is older than you are," he remarked.

"I know. And my father's going to call here, probably, and want me to be getting home."

"I guess you'll have to do that."

"I wish Peter's father would call him."

Amussen looked at her, the riding pants, her calm face.

"Where are you in school, now?" he said.

"I've quit school," she said.

He nodded a little, as if agreeing.

"You knew that."

"No, I didn't," he answered.

"Daddy's after me to go back, but I don't think so. It's a waste of time, don't you think?"

"I didn't get that much out of school, I guess. Want a refill?" he asked.

"Are you trying to get me drunk?"

"I wouldn't do that," Amussen said.

"Why not?"

Her boyfriend, Peter, who had red lips and crinkled blond hair came into the room just as she spoke, and smiled as a kind of admission of interrupting. He was a student at Lafayette and headed for law. He could sense that Dare was somehow annoyed. He knew little enough about her except for the difficulties she presented.

"Uh, I'm Peter Connors, sir," he said, introducing himself.

"Nice to meet you, Peter. I'm George Amussen."

"Yes, sir, I know."

He spoke to Dare. "Hi," he said, and confidently sat down beside her. "It looks like it's snowing."

It was snowing, harder now, blowing along the fence rows, and the light was beginning to fade.

IN THE MASTER BEDROOM with its oversize bed, medicines, and jewelry on the night table and clothes draped over the backs of chairs, Liz was talking to her brother, Eddie. The radio was playing and all the lights including the bathroom lights were on. Written in pencil on the wallpaper above the night table were various names and telephone numbers, first names for the most part, but also doctors and Clark Gable. Eddie lived in Florida, it was the first time she'd seen him since her marriage to Travis. He was her older brother, three years older, and had the handsome face of someone who had never done much. He had bought and sold cars.

"You're getting gray," she said.

"Thanks for the news."

"It looks good."

He glanced at her and didn't reply. She reached over and rumpled his hair affectionately. There was no response.

"Oh, you're still beautiful. You're as good-looking as when you got all dressed up in your tuxedo for the DeVores' party, remember that? You were there on the steps smoking a cigarette and hiding it in case Daddy was looking. You were hot stuff. That big car."

"George Stuver in his daddy's LaSalle."

"I was so jealous."

"The Stuvers' LaSalle. I was with Lee Donaldson in the backseat that night."

"Whatever happened to her?"

"She had a hysterectomy."

"Oh, Christ. I hate doctors."

"You can't tell the difference from the outside. You have anything to drink up here?"

"No, I try not to have it around. I don't want it to become a problem."

"Speaking of that, where's the flyboy? And how'd you get involved with him?"

"Sweetheart, don't start on that."

"He's a prize. Where'd you meet him?"

Eddie had liked Ted Bohannon, who he felt was his kind of man.

"We met in Buenos Aires," she said. "In the embassy. He was the attaché. It just happened that he came along. I was lonely, you know I don't like living alone. I was down there for three months."

"Buenos Aires."

"I got so sick of South America," she said. "Nothing is clean there, no matter where you go. They're so lazy, those people. It just burns me up to see the money we're throwing away down there. They have enough money of their own, my God, they have money. You should see the ranches, they have a thousand people working for them. You have to see it with your own eyes. They told us that Perón made off with over sixty million. And then they ask us for money."

She was silent for a moment.

"The man I really wanted to marry was Aly Khan," she said, "but I never got close. I'd have been perfect for him, but he married that Hollywood cunt. Anyway, promise me something. Promise me you'll try and get to know Travis. Will you promise that?"

Outside the window the snow was pouring down in the early darkness. The room was comforting and secure. She was reminded of feelings of childhood, the excitement of snowstorms and the joy of Christmas and the holidays. She could see herself in the mirror in the bright room. She was like a movie star. She said so.

"Yeah, but a little older," Eddie said. "Promise me about Travis," she ordered.

"Yeah, but there's something you could do for me."

He was a little short of money, it being Christmas and all. He needed something to tide him over.

"How much?"

"Tit for tat," he said pleasantly.

AT DINNER WHERE THEY SAT rather far apart at the big table the talk was about the storm that was raging and roads being closed. There was plenty of room for all of them to stay over, though, Liz said. She took it as a given that they would.

"There's plenty of bacon and plenty of eggs."

Eddie was talking to Travis.

"I've looked forward to meeting you," he said.

"Me, too."

"Where are you from?"

"California, originally," Travis said. "I grew up in California. But then the war, you know. The army. I was overseas for a long time, almost two years, flying the Hump."

"You flew the Hump? What was that like?"

"Rugged, rugged." He smiled like a poster. "Mountains five miles high and we were flying blind. I lost a lot of good friends."

Willa was serving. Monroe had been sent upstairs to make beds.

"Do you still fly?" Eddie asked.

"Oh, sure. I fly out of Andrews at the moment."

"I hear you have a nigger general in the air corps," Eddie said.

"It's the air force now," Travis said.

"I always heard it called the air corps."

"They changed it. It's the air force now."

"Does it really have a nigger general?"

"Darling, shut up," Liz said. "Just shut up."

Willa had gone back to the kitchen, closing the door behind her. "It's hard enough keeping good help," Liz said.

"Willa? Willa knows me," Eddie said. "She knows I'm not talking about her."

"What branch were you in, Eddie?" Travis asked him.

"Me? I wasn't in a branch. The army wouldn't take me."

"Why was that?"

"Couldn't pass the physical."

"Ah."

"I rode in the Gold Cup, that's what I did," Eddie said.

Afterward they went in to have coffee by the fire. Liz sat back on the couch with her bare arms along the top cushion and kicked off her shoes.

"Slipper me, darling," she said to Travis.

He stood up without a word and got them for her but stopped short of putting them on her feet. She bent with a slight groan to do it herself.

"You are the limit," she said to Eddie.

"What do you mean?"

"You're the limit."

Peter Connors, who had said very little during dinner, managed to speak briefly, alone, with Amussen. He was hesitant about it, he needed some advice. It was about Dare, he was in love with her but couldn't be sure of where he stood.

"You were talking to her this afternoon, I mean she got quiet when I came in. I wonder if it was about me. I know she looks up to you."

"We weren't talking about you. She's a spirited girl," Amussen said, "they can be hard to manage."

"How do you go about that?"

"I expect she'd let you know if she didn't want you around. I'd say be patient."

"I don't want it to seem I don't have any backbone."

"Of course not."

In a way, that was the impression he was afraid he gave, at odds with his hopes and desires. And dreams. He didn't imagine anyone having dreams like his. She was in them, they were about her. She was naked and sitting in an armchair, one leg thrown carelessly over an arm. He is near her in a cotton robe that has fallen open. She seems indifferent but accepting, and he kneels and puts his lips to her. He lifts her and holds her up by the waist, like a vessel, to his mouth. He can see himself as they pass a dark silvery mirror, her legs dangling, beginning to kick as he hardens his tongue. She is leaning backward as in one smooth movement he sets her, in the dream and to an extent in life, on his unholy hard-on and as he does, comes in a flood.

After a while, except for Liz and Travis who were playing cards, they had all gone to bed. The snow went on falling though sometime in the early hours it stopped and stars appeared in the black sky. Also it became even colder.

IN THE MORNING THROUGH WINDOWS that were half covered with frost the great white expanse of fields could be seen, not a footprint on them, not a flaw. The whiteness reached into the distance, into the sky. Two of the dogs had gotten outside and were flying over the snow, throwing up a white trail like comets as they ran.

One by one they all came down to breakfast in the dining room. Liz and Dare were among the last. Bowman and Vivian were just finishing. Amussen was still at the table.

"Good morning," he said.

"Good morning." Liz's voice was a little hoarse. "Look at the snow," she said.

"It finally stopped. That was a real storm. Don't know if the roads will be open. Good morning," he said to Dare as she took a seat.

"Morning." It was almost a whisper.

"Your daddy already called," Willa told her as she brought coffee.

They sat eating bacon and eggs. Travis joined them. Peter was the only one who didn't appear.

A terrible thing had happened during the night. After everyone had gone to bed and it was finally quiet, Peter, who had waited as long as he could, stepped out into the hall in his pants and undershirt, carefully closing the door behind him. The light was subdued. All was silent. Quietly he walked to Dare's room and put his face close to the doorjamb. He whispered her name.

"Dare."

He waited and whispered again, more intently.

"Dare!"

He was afraid she was asleep. He called again and then, overcoming his fear, knocked lightly.

"Dare."

He stood there, despite himself.

"I just want to talk to you," he was going say.

He knocked again. Just as he finished, his heart leapt as the door opened slightly and revealed George Amussen, who said in a low, authoritative voice, "Go on to bed."

LIZ ALL MORNING had been on the phone deciding whether or not to go to California. She wanted to go to Santa Anita and was asking about the weather there and if her horse would be running. Finally she decided.

"We're going."

"You're sure, Bun?"

"Yes."

Eddie watched it all without comment. Later he said, "He won't be around for long. She'll marry someone else."

It would not be Aly Khan, who had been divorced and was planning to marry a French model when he was killed in a car crash. Liz read it in the paper. She had never really stopped thinking about being married to him. It was always a fond dream. They would be in Neuilly in the morning, watching the horses train, the early mist still in the trees. He'd be in Levi's and a jacket and they would walk back together to have breakfast at the house. She'd be the wife of a prince and converted to Islam. But Aly was dead, Ted had gone on to marry someone else, and her second husband had moved to New Jersey. Still she had lots of friends, some made one way, some another, and she rode.

Vivian had liked Christmas and being home. Liz, she could see, took to Philip, and even her father, who was in an amiable mood that morning, seemed to accept him more. They all said good-bye, Amussen to Liz and then to Dare, whose boyfriend wasn't feeling well, rubbing a bit of egg from the side of her mouth as they talked briefly. He did it with his napkin in a fatherly way.

"Is Liz Bohannon really your father's cousin?" Bowman asked afterwards.

"They just call each other cousin, I don't know why," Vivian said.

The world was still white as they drove back to Washington, snow rushing across the road like smoke. Currently twenty-two degrees in downtown Washington, the radio said. The highway was disappearing in bursts of wind. The fur was up around Vivian's face in the cold, the smooth miles passing soundlessly beneath. Good-bye to Virginia and the fields and strange feeling of isolation. He was taking Vivian home—in fact that was not what he was doing but it was what gave him the sensation of happiness.

# Devin Johnston

MEANS OF ESCAPE

The courtroom, clad in wood veneer,
could be a lesser pharaoh's tomb
equipped for immortality.
A civil servant drags her broom
around the bench and gallery
as jurors darken a questionnaire.

One coughs against the courtroom chill.
One drums her fingers atop the bar.
One finds escape through Stephen King,
as through a window left ajar.
One talks and talks, a reckoning
of who got sober, who took ill.

The talker seeks me out at lunch,
a bond of passing circumstance.
He slides the food around his tray
disdainfully and looks askance
at those nearby, as if to say,
*In here, you can't expect too much.*

Across the hall, five years ago,
the talker fought for custody
and lost, his daylight blotted out.
He'd spent the decade carelessly
and sucked a mortgage up his snout.
He never sees his daughter now.

They meet online for *Realms of Ra*
as siblings, cat-like humanoids,
survivors from the Hybrid Age;

or Foxen riding flightless birds
across the plain, a scrolling page
above which two moons light their way.

They gather gold coins as they roam,
and relics, sometimes holy ones.
They seldom map attentively,
but swing their swords and have some fun.
They chat—back-channel strategy,
but not of school, her friends, or home.

Last night, they entered a castle keep
infested with the living dead,
whose breath abruptly turned the air
to crackled glass. A pop-up read,
*Initializing Griffin's Lair:*
*Please wait*, and soon he fell asleep.

Of course, he can reboot the game
tonight, with nothing lost or missed.
Meanwhile, a case of larceny
awaits, from which we'll be dismissed
(we both have too much history).
I wish him well in his campaign.

*From the Proceedings of the First Annual Norwegian-American Literary Festival*

---

This fall, two editors of *The Paris Review*—John Jeremiah Sullivan and the undersigned—were invited to Oslo to take part in the first annual Norwegian-American Literary Festival. This was the brainchild of Frode Saugestad, a sometime DJ, musician, Diesel franchise manager, extreme athlete, and competitive chain-saw operator who recently completed a teaching fellowship in comparative literature at Harvard. His idea was to give Norwegians an introduction to current trends in American writing. Our fellow panelists were Donald Antrim, Elif Batuman, Graywolf publisher Fiona McCrae, the Norwegian filmmaker Joachim Trier, Lucas Wittmann of *The Daily Beast*, and *New Yorker* book critic James Wood.

Our talks took place over three days, mainly at the Litteraturhuset in central Oslo, a café and writers' loft across the street from the royal palace. The one exception was an hour-long public lecture on the novelist Knut Hamsun, delivered by Wood at the invitation of Hamsun's publishing house Gyldendal. As a group, we urged Wood to decline the honor (one of us compared him to a Norwegian lecturing on Mark Twain at the Mark Twain Center, in Hannibal, Mo., without any grasp of English).* In the event, he drew a standing-room-only crowd. When he concluded, several Norwegians were heard to yell bravo.

The NALF lacked many of the usual trappings of a literary conference. There was no Web site and no printed program. There were no name tags. The entire promotional budget seems to have been spent on a stack of postcards. It is not clear to whom these were sent. There was no theme. The audience was made up as much of students and the merely curious as of professional writers. Yet their close attention unlocked several lively discussions on the arts of cinema and writing. I am grateful to Trier, Batuman, Sullivan, and Antrim, and to Saugestad, for letting us publish them here.

—*Lorin Stein*

---

### ON LITERATURE AND FILM

*Joachim Trier is the director of two feature films:* Reprise *(2006) and* Oslo, August 31st *(2011). These have received honors at Toronto, Milan, Cannes, and other festivals and have made Trier, at thirty-eight, one of the most celebrated independent filmmakers of his generation.*

INTERVIEWER

*Reprise* is the best movie I've seen about young writers today. What inspired you to make your first film about two novelists?

TRIER

I've always admired writers, maybe because I feel that I'm not a good writer myself. I always write with my good friend Eskil Vogt, who is much better

---

* To perform this experiment, one would first have to locate a Norwegian who did not speak shamingly fluent English.

on the page. So I feel honored, but also slightly nervous, to be talking about a movie with literary people. Mind you, this may be a Norwegian thing. In Norway we have a great tradition of writing literature, whereas cinema … historically this is not our strength. A Norwegian friend of mine interviewed Don DeLillo and asked him, "What do American writers talk about when they hang out casually?" DeLillo said, "We talk about movies." I felt so proud!

When Eskil and I began writing *Reprise*, I was finishing my studies in London at the National Film and Television School. I had been making short films that were more formally oriented and less about character and psychology, drama, relationships, stuff like that. Eskil and I were hesitant to admit that this would be our first feature. It was too close to our lives. It was about people we knew, it was about the cultural specifics of an environment that we'd grown up in. Also, someone had said to me, "Don't start out your career by making your version of *8 ½*." The self-portrait of the artist—it's risky territory.

INTERVIEWER

So *Reprise* is a self-portrait?

TRIER

Well, to us it's kind of shameful to make a film that's too close to home, so we transferred the story onto writers rather than filmmakers and based it on writers we knew. This gave us a way to tell a story about ambition and friendship. There was also a fanboy quality that we wanted to capture. I felt at the time that there were a lot of good movies about boys and girls. I wanted to make a film about guys who are friends. Writing with Eskil, we could lean on our own friendship and draw on that as we were working.

INTERVIEWER

How do you and Mr. Vogt divide up the work of writing?

TRIER

At the beginning, and especially when working on *Reprise*, Eskil and I would sit and write continuously together, and I was always slower than he was, and he always had to rewrite my stuff anyway. Now we've found our balance, I think. When we made *Oslo, August 31st*, we structured the film together, we discussed the content of the scenes, then Eskil wrote them. Then I would

Anders Danielsen Lie and Espen Klouman-Høiner in *Reprise*.

read them, and edit and add to the dialogue. Often we'll go back and forth on one scene four or five times in a single day.

INTERVIEWER

Some of the most revealing moments in your films happen without dialogue. For example, in *Oslo*, there's a moment Anders—the main character, played by Anders Danielsen Lie—has just said good-bye to his friend Thomas. And he puts his hands in his pockets and just raises his chin in that Obama-esque way he has. Tears spring to your eyes. And nothing has happened! Did you write the script knowing that moment would be a turning point?

TRIER

If we are clear thematically in the script, then I find that we are not smart enough not to repeat ourselves. So you might have several places where you want some turning point, some emotion to happen. Then when you edit, you sift out the repetitions.

You see, I look at a script as a working tool. It's got to be an okay read so that people will want to get involved with it, but in the end it's just a tool. Like a *partiture* in music. The actors change the pacing, and then you edit the film and you change it again. How the emotions are preserved is a strange mystery to me. I have never figured it out. Often the feeling ends up very much the same, but it always has to go on a big detour, which you can't foresee. The script is only a starting point.

There's an anecdote I love. Samuel Fuller wanted to shoot a film with an arguing couple, and he's out at this farm, and while they're waiting to set up the next shot he discovers a chicken out in the yard chasing a cat around in circles. He sees this and says to his cinematographer, This is the perfect metaphor for the arguing going on inside—we shoot this, then we pull back into the room and see the actors. They do it and it's perfect. And if you'd written that in the script, the producers would have said, We've got to train a chicken to chase a cat? That's going to be expensive.

INTERVIEWER

And possibly cheesy.

TRIER

Exactly. Sometimes seeing is believing—a moment that seems too obvious in writing only works when you actually see it. My motto is always "Luck favors the well prepared." If it rains when you need the sun, you've got to deal with it. You wanted the melancholy of a Terrence Malick magic hour, so how will you express that with a gray sky and rain? Sometimes you're fortunate and it works out, sometimes not.

With *Reprise* the wonderful seasonal changes in Norway were an advantage. Here's another example of a happy accident. When you have a film with many temporal layers, it's kind of embarrassing that they all happen at the

"If we are clear thematically in the script, then I find we are not smart enough not to repeat ourselves." Anders Danielsen Lie in *Oslo, August 31st*.

same time of year. The viewer thinks, Why do these guys relive all of their memories in the summertime? It's an embarrassing thing. So we had this one moment when the two guys, Erik and Phillip, are kind of stalking the old writer, Sten Egil Dahl, the recluse. And one day he comes out of the house, and they chase him around Frogner Park, which you should go and see—it's a wonderful park. The day we were shooting that scene it suddenly started snowing in the morning. So we got that flashback with snow. The next day we were back in the more linear part of the story in present-day autumn, and the snow was gone. That's Norwegian weather. It's painful to live with but okay to shoot in.

INTERVIEWER

Some American viewers associated that scene with a scene in the novel *The Savage Detectives*, where two young poets stalk Octavio Paz in a park. I imagine that's coincidental.

TRIER

It is. I'm aware of the book, but I haven't read it. You know what's funny about this made-up writer, Sten Egil Dahl? We created a backstory for him in a documentary style that we hoped would look half-believable, and at the premier of the film a Polish journalist told us how happy he was that we had included Sten Egil Dahl, whom he so admired. He thought he had read some of his books. In a perverse way I found that very satisfying. We had added to the canon, so to speak.

INTERVIEWER

When I first saw *Reprise*, I remember thinking that I had never seen a movie dramatize depression quite the way you managed to do—depression and the charisma that a certain kind of brilliant depressed person can have. Mr. Lie's performance was riveting. In *Oslo* you cast the same actor, not in a similar role, exactly, but in a similar predicament.

TRIER

Eskil and I wrote *Oslo* for Anders. I felt that he'd grown older, and that something had happened to him, that he was ready to show more of his abilities. It seemed to me that there was even more texture and subtlety to his performance in *Oslo*.

INTERVIEWER

Even my sister agreed. She's a much tougher critic than I am. We were both nervous that the second time round you would screw up.

TRIER

So was I! No doubt some people think I did. These things are very subjective. At the outset I thought the two movies would be very different, because Anders was the only thing they had in common. I said, It's not going to be about different time layers, it's going to be about one day. It's going to be linear, focusing on one character only this time.

"A documentary style that we hoped would look half-believable." *Reprise*.

The thing is, you're not able to change yourself. I thought I was making a different movie and people keep pointing out that, structurally, there are a lot of similarities. And the same themes. You're always biting yourself in the ass.

INTERVIEWER

In one scene, the sound track is made up entirely of overheard conversations. Did you plan that from the beginning?

#### TRIER

This is a part of the script where we were hoping for happy accidents. Parts of the sound track are simple documentary, parts are slightly improvised, some of it is completely scripted. In that scene there's a girl who reads out forty things she wants to do before she dies. A bucket list, I think you call it in America. What happened is, I was listening to the radio and I heard a story about a girl who had made one of these lists. The reporter had discovered that these lists show up on the Internet a lot at the moment, all around the world, thousands of them. And one of the things that is

Anders Danielsen Lie and Viktoria Winge in *Reprise*.

repeated in all these lists is the wish to swim with dolphins. I just thought that was sweet. I thought we should call the film *Swimming with Dolphins*. I was thinking about this dark, intellectually tough guy sitting there listening to this—

#### INTERVIEWER

Cheesy, chicken-chasing-a-cat bucket list.

TRIER

There you go! So we got in touch with the girl, and she gave us the list. I wouldn't have been able to write it myself. I would have started structuring, trying to be smart, trying to put in something allegorical. As I was shooting, I kept thinking, What the hell? Am I making children's television or are we doing something of interest? I had no clue.

INTERVIEWER

You're going to make your next movie in the States. I'm worried that we're going to cramp your style.

TRIER

So am I. I'm always worried. I'm tremendously anxious whenever I do any work. And I'm interested in cultural specifics, so having grown up on Philip Roth and Woody Allen—and being one-sixteenth Jewish, believe it or not, somewhere back in my Danish ancestry—I'm taking a frightening leap.

INTERVIEWER

Will the movie be based on a book?

TRIER

No, it's not, but I think of it as literary, perhaps because it's a family drama and structured around a lot of different characters. It's called *Louder Than Bombs*. Everyone thinks this is a reference to the Smiths album, which it is, but it's also a quotation from Elizabeth Smart, the poet. From *By Grand Central Station I Sat Down and Wept*, which is a wonderful poem.

INTERVIEWER

"Louder than bombs" comes from *By Grand Central Station I Sat Down and Wept*?

TRIER

Morrissey loved that poem.

INTERVIEWER

For our Norwegian friends, *By Grand Central Station I Sat Down and Wept* is a book-length prose poem. It has to be one of the more operatic books of the last century.

                              TRIER

Now you know what I read. But actually, this question of literariness is something I think a lot about. The vocabulary of cinema, at least mainstream cinema, hasn't changed tremendously since the time of D. W. Griffith, especially not when compared to the experiments of, let's say, Faulkner, Woolf, or Joyce. And yet if you look at how the French nouveau roman influenced French movies—I'm thinking of *Hiroshima Mon Amour*, written by Marguerite Duras, or *Last Year at Marienbad*—you see how the novel actually opens up space for cinema, so that it can be, paradoxically, even more cinematic.

    I'll give you an example. You're not supposed to use voice-overs. It's considered bad form—

                          INTERVIEWER

Because it's old-fashioned?

                              TRIER

Because it moves away from the theatrical tradition. You are supposed to use action and dialogue to tell your story. But if you look at the way Terrence Malick uses voice-over, it very often liberates the images to do something else. The images are not enslaved, for lack of a better expression, by narrativity in the classical sense. Thanks to voice-over, the images can be something other than just plot or story. The film opens up to something that could be beautiful, tactile, phenomenological, an observation of the world, a different kind of narrative.

                          INTERVIEWER

What's another technique you think of as being "literary"?

                              TRIER

In cinema you have a famous dichotomy between continual time and space—when you film something with no cuts—and montage, when images are put together in some kind of suggestive way. In a Hollywood movie, you see a young couple drinking, laughing, kissing, and you feel that, between these images, you experienced the whole evening. So these two methods are very often contrasted, and virtuous film craft is supposed to lean on the continuation of time and space, not on montage.

But to me there's something interesting about montage, about jumping between different times and places. Literature does this seamlessly. Think of Proust. The narrator may think of this or that, which will make him think of his aunt when he was little, and then we come back to the present day—it doesn't matter, you just follow the voice.

Viktoria Winge in *Reprise*.

I think montage can do something similar in movies. Now, I'm talking about my ambitions. I'm not saying this is something I've achieved. But Eskil and I have spent a lot of time discussing these things. In *Reprise*, we'll follow a train of thought the way you sometimes see in comedies—in *Sex and the City*, for example. Let's say Carrie Bradshaw refers in a voice-over to something she did last week—she met someone on a street corner—and suddenly we're at the street corner. Woody Allen does this a lot. In *Hannah and Her Sisters* or *Annie Hall*, he does it very cleverly but almost always in comedic ways.

But why not use montage in a more serious way, to get inside and show the thoughts of your characters? In *Reprise*, when Erik is going to break up with his girlfriend, he thinks of his mother and pornography. He thinks about going to the Steiner School [*laughter from audience*], which some of you probably went to as well. All these things about guilt, they're thrown in there as montage elements, and then he ends up not being able to break up with his girlfriend, Lillian. A sequence like that is tricky. When people read that in a script, they say, That's confusing. They say, I'll be taken out of the film. Which is the biggest crime in the world. So it's tricky stuff, whereas in literature it's just obvious. It's what you do all the time.

"But why not use montage in a more serious way, to get inside and show the thoughts of your characters?" Espen Klouman-Høiner amd Silje Hagen in *Reprise*.

INTERVIEWER

And we never see Lillian's face. Not until—

TRIER

Not until the end. She surprised you, at least I hope so.

INTERVIEWER

Indeed. In your movies, you teach us to notice the beauty of the characters—men and women both—in an unusually "realistic" way. Their beauty often surprises us. For example, when the editor, Johanne, strips down to her bathing suit, it's not a nudge-nudge hubba-hubba moment. You don't play it for laughs, still the audience thinks, Holy mackerel.

TRIER

There is shame about looking at beauty, I think, at least in the Protestant culture of Norway. If something is beautiful, it's called refinement, ornament.

INTERVIEWER

*Oslo* begins with a very tender montage of the city, only tangentially related to the story. I wonder what you wanted to conjure about this place.

TRIER

I used to feel ashamed about being too navel-gazing and too subjective. Now I've learned to say fuck it. If you want to add to some larger tradition, your own experience is what you have to bring. In these movies Oslo is something that I care about, that I see, that I want to show.

Mind you, I come from a skateboarding background. For us every part of the city was named for some curb or staircase. Then sometimes those places would disappear. Like the CC Bank—the old supermarket Cash & Carry had a wonderful loading dock, like a bank, we could jump off. Then suddenly it was gone. But I filmed it. I have it on tape. It existed. It was there. We were there. I have friends here tonight who skated that spot with me, and this sounds trite and banal and nostalgic, but to us that mattered. When you're filming your own city, you can, on a very basic level, document stuff. I can document that café across the road. I'm almost ashamed to go there now because the people there know I made that film. Now I'm the guy who made the movie. Still, there's something satisfying about that documentation, in itself.

AUDIENCE

You adapted *Oslo* from a book, *Le feu follet*, the same one that Louis Malle adapted in *The Fire Within*. What attracted you to that book?

TRIER

Something thematic, something about the characters—that's what attracts me. *Reprise* was loosely based on a Henry James novella called *The Lesson of the Master*. Please laugh. It sounds very pretentious. As the film is today, it has nothing to do with that short story. But Henry James is wonderful when he writes about the dilemma of writers choosing between the bourgeois life of family and their commitment to the free life of the artist. Now, how many people do I know who smoke pot and go to Berlin to write a novel and come back with nothing, and talk about how "free" they were. It's such a cliché, but that novella treats the cliché with great complexity.

INTERVIEWER

Can you say what part was the germ of *Reprise*?

TRIER

In most of James's short fiction, right at the end, when you think you know where the story is leading, he takes things in a last, unexpected direction. You see it in "The Beast in the Jungle" and *The Aspern Papers*, and a lot of the others. By the end of *The Lesson of the Master*, James leaves you with a sense of an impossible choice, and yet the story has reached a dramatic conclusion. That ending shows the continuing doubt of the writer bumping up against the complexity of love. To me it has great authority. It's sort of like *Vertigo*—you have a conclusion that makes sense, but the dilemma, the feeling, lingers on.

But to go back to the earlier question, with *Le feu follet* what inspired me is probably the main character and the theme, rather than the narrative. In general, you take a theme or a concept and use it as a Dumbo feather. You know, Dumbo can fly when he has that feather—and even when he loses it, he may be able to keep flying. He just needs help taking off.

---

## ON FALSE STARTS

*A scholar of Russian literature by training, Elif Batuman began a second career as a reporter and essayist in the first issues of* n+1 *in 2005. Since then she has become a staff writer at* The New Yorker. *Her essays were collected in* The Possessed: Adventures with Russian Books and the People Who Read Them.

*John Jeremiah Sullivan is Southern editor of* The Paris Review. *He is a contributing writer at* The New York Times Magazine *and has published two books:* Blood Horses: Notes of a Sportswriter's Son *and the collection* Pulphead. *His essay "Mister Lytle" won* The Paris Review *a National Magazine Award in 2011.*

INTERVIEWER

I've seen each of you report a story—then take months, or even years, to actually write it. Why does that happen?

"There is shame about looking at beauty… If something is beautiful, it's called refinement, ornament." Rebekka Karijord in *Reprise*.

BATUMAN

It happens because life tends to just hand you a big pile of stuff, and often it isn't obvious what the story is. I think it's true that we experience our lives in terms of narrative, and certain elements of a story, certain questions or juxtapositions or moods, are already basically there in the experience. But it can be really hard to organize those elements and to decide what kind of meaning you want to give them.

"Thanks to voice-over, the images can be something other than just plot or story." *Oslo, August 31st.*

For example, when I was a graduate student, I went to a Russian literature conference at Tolstoy's house in Yasnaya Polyana, near Tula. We were presenting papers in the house where Tolstoy wrote *Anna Karenina* and *War and Peace* and where he led this psychically, psychotically intense life, with the disciples and his marriage and the peasants. On the last day of the conference, we took a field trip to Chekhov's house, just randomly, because it was on the way back to Moscow. That was the whole week.

I wanted to write about it, but it took me ages to find the story. I knew it involved the question of what you learn when you go to a writer's house. I mean, you do learn *something*, right? The table next to Tolstoy's bed, in Tolstoy's house, clearly has a closer relationship to Tolstoy than this table [*points to table*], which Tolstoy never saw. But what is that relationship, and what do I learn from seeing the table?

The place I eventually found the story was actually in the application for the grant to get the money to go to the conference. There were two kinds of grants you could apply for—one was for presenting a paper, which was what I was actually doing, and the other was for field research. The field-research grant was more money, so when I was applying, I started asking myself, What's a question you can only answer by going to Tolstoy's house?

One night I was watching *The Daily Show*, and there was a segment about someone doing a CT scan of King Tut's mummy to determine his cause of death. Jon Stewart was like, "Did King Tut die of natural causes?"—and then he turned around with a flashlight under his chin and said, "Or was he … *murdered*?" That was when I started wondering, Did Tolstoy die of natural causes—or was he … *murdered*? It was a joke at first, and I didn't have any plan to write about it. But the whole time I was there, part of me was looking for clues. And the thing is, when you look at anyone's life—

INTERVIEWER

May I interrupt, just for one quick moment? Could you remind us how old Tolstoy was when he died?

BATUMAN

Eighty-two.

INTERVIEWER

I'm sorry. You were saying?

BATUMAN

Well, the murder mystery turns out to be a really useful frame for a literary conference at Tolstoy's house. The situation is similar—you're in a country

*Oslo, August 31st.*

house full of stuff belonging to a dead man, and you have to figure out from that stuff who he really was. Your observations aren't just random anymore. Now they're *clues*.

It was after I started thinking about Sherlock Holmes that Chekhov finally fit into the picture, instead of being some weird detour. It suddenly seemed really obvious to me that Chekhov was Dr. Watson—the doctor next door, the admiring apprentice, the rationalist who's always on the wrong track, the one who fights death but always loses. In any case, having the model of a detective story informed what I could put in and what I could leave out of the piece.

INTERVIEWER

How long did this take to write?

BATUMAN

I went to the conference in 2005 and the piece came out in 2009.

INTERVIEWER

So it took you three or four years to figure out—even though, looking back, it was as if you had come up with this ridiculous proposal in order to write the piece. John, can you top that?

SULLIVAN

I can't top that. I can extract something from it, though. Elif just said, What is the question that can only be answered in Tolstoy's house? That's a perfect example of what nonfiction has to do if it's going to work. It has to find a task for itself, it's always prosecuting a task of some kind. A lot of its power comes from that, because where you have a task, you have a story. Do you want the answer to a question, to find out how something works or what happened on a specific day? Then already, just in your moving from a state of greater to lesser ignorance, there's an implication of narrative, chronology, conflict, everything you need. People talk about the importance of curiosity or obsession in good nonfiction, but you can't just let it sit there on the page and circulate. It has to be moving, has to itself be feeling the pull of the task.

INTERVIEWER

Can you remember a time when you went off and reported without knowing what the task was?

SULLIVAN

I don't have to look further than what's in front of me right now, the article I was supposed to turn in last night. I had an assignment to go to Cuba and write about the changes under Raúl Castro, the new leader of Cuba. But I had another task happening: my wife and six-year-old daughter were with me. My wife is Cuban American, so the six-year-old was going to meet her Cuban relatives for the first time, and in some cases—because they're old—probably for the only time. Going into the assignment, I thought of all that as something that was just happening incidentally. I was there to get the Story. So I did tons of reading and a few interviews with the kind of likely characters you'd interview for a piece like that. We got home from Cuba, and I had this mass of stuff, this shapeless mass—and it's like that game where somebody holds a bunch of threads, and they all look the same length, but one of them is going to come all the way out when you pull it. There's one thread that's going to take you all the way through to the end of the piece, and for me it often takes false starts and mistaken choices to find it. In this case I had to accept that the stuff I saw in connection with the family trip was more interesting, or at least was the thing that really interested me. It had given me access to more revealing moments and images, concerning what's happening in Cuba, than a bunch of interviews with Party officials could do. Or so I felt.

INTERVIEWER

Can you give an example?

SULLIVAN

Meeting with my wife's family in this small town where they live, in the interior of the island, and listening to them talk. Drinking and smoking with them, frankly. I've been there three times now and every time there's a bottle of Havana Club and some cigars when I walk into the house. They start hustling to get these things as soon as they hear we're coming, and it takes months. But the reason I bring it up is that they talk to me in a candid way about how difficult and, in some respects, awful things are there. It gets dark, and it gets sad, and I kept thinking, This beats the crap out of anything I'll get from the government. We were outside the zone of political rhetoric, pro-Cuba or anti-. It didn't matter—we were where people live. But it's funny, I didn't want the essay to go there, partly because I'm tired of using myself as material. I was hoping to get out of the first person, to just have an empirical experience and not think of it as material. A casualty of constantly cannibalizing your life for a living is that you're always fouling the nest, the boundaries blur. But the piece didn't care. It wanted me to tell the family story.

INTERVIEWER

John mentioned false starts. Elif, do you make fewer of those, as you gain experience? Why does a writer make false starts in the first place?

BATUMAN

I wish I knew. My editor at *The New Yorker* was like, Why don't you just skip the whole part where you do all the wrong things and just do the right thing?

SULLIVAN

Thank you. Thank you, editor.

BATUMAN

And then he was like, Of course I'm just joking. He wasn't joking! I don't think I make fewer false starts now than I did before. Maybe I get faster at recognizing them.

INTERVIEWER

How do you recognize a false start? Does it give you a particular feeling?

BATUMAN

Yeah, but not right away. I think any start has to be a false start because really there's no way to start. You just have to force yourself to sit down and turn off the quality censor. And you have to keep the censor off, or you start second-guessing every other sentence. Sometimes the suspicion of a possible false start comes through, and you have to suppress it to keep writing. But it gets more persistent. And the moment you know it's really a false start is when you start ... it's hard to put into words.

SULLIVAN

When you start pushing it forward?

BATUMAN

Exactly! When you start pushing.

SULLIVAN

And you feel the slight exertion, like your tires just hit sand.

BATUMAN

And you have some line of dialogue that doesn't look as funny as you thought it would, so you try to add something funny after it. That's always bad.

SULLIVAN

Only, just as your realizing it's a false start, you're also realizing it has some really good *writing* in it. Maybe even, like, some of the best writing you're going to do—

Anders Danielsen Lie and Espen Klouman-Høiner in *Reprise*.

BATUMAN

In your whole life!

SULLIVAN

So you keep going, but it's already a phantom thing at that point. You know nobody's ever going to see the stuff, but you have to write through it. You're just trying to satisfy some grim, barren mandate. There's probably a German word for that.

INTERVIEWER

How about the long threads—the useful starts? Do they tend to have anything in common?

SULLIVAN

A lot of times it's humiliating, because the long thread ends up being the simplest way in—what to another person might have seemed the most obvious thing to do. What a child would have seen. But as a writer you must first chop through all kinds of illusions you had about how the piece would go, aggrandizing visions of what it would be.

BATUMAN

It is humiliating. When I was in graduate school, I went to Samarkand, in Uzbekistan, for two months to prepare for a job that, for bureaucratic reasons, it then turned out I was not legally qualified for. So for two months I was in Samarkand learning the Uzbek language for no reason, and that was an experience I did nothing with for years and years. I'd been taking notes the whole time, because it was super interesting. But it was also really hot and difficult and painful. It's hard to learn the Uzbek language in two months! There was a lot of pressure because I was the only student in the whole program, so all of my classes were one-on-one, with teachers who were looking me in the eyes the whole time like, You're it. Anyway, the story turned out to be about being somewhere for two months for no reason, which is so like life.

SULLIVAN

You'd been trying to figure out how to fight off the pointlessness of it, and that turned out to be the story. Your task was to capture the feeling of no task.

Elif, have you noticed that it helps, and is hard, to stay mindful of the—I've never tried to articulate this before, so it'll sound abstruse—the *materiality* of a piece? The fact that, in the end, it is going to be made of language, of words and sentences, and even paper?

BATUMAN

Yes! Every single time, there's a moment when you realize it's going to be made of words, and you think, Can't I just remember that for next time?

SULLIVAN

Right? You'll be typing away and—

INTERVIEWER

Excuse me. Could one of you explain what you're talking about?

SULLIVAN

In the beginning, a piece doesn't seem to be made of sentences and pages, it seems to be made of colors and textures and thought clouds, and you're running around in a field, manipulating tones. You might be thinking of a character's dialogue, for instance. But at first, you're not quite hearing the sequence of syllables, the thing itself. You're receiving the meaning they're meant to convey, pure and without ambiguity, on a totally different sensory channel, like ants communicating chemically or something—

BATUMAN

And then you're like, Oh wait, yet again, it's just going to be a pile of words. Just like it was last time.

INTERVIEWER

I want to ask about a specific article that John published recently in *The New York Times Magazine*, about the tennis stars Serena and Venus Williams. As I understand it, John, you had only a few hours with each of the Williams sisters, but everyone who read the article noticed how at ease they seemed to be answering your questions. So I wonder, if it takes so long to figure out the story, how do you get your subjects on board in such a little space of time?

Often you can't, and that's one of the reasons this kind of piece has waned in quality, a decline from which I by no means absolve myself. *The New Yorker* is one of the only magazines that can still do it right on a regular basis, or that even tries. That has to do, partly, with the political economy of the thing, the way *The New Yorker* can leverage what it has to offer, a career-enhancing profile in exchange for a lot of someone's time. Not many magazines can do that anymore. The subject tends to feel like, Why should I give you access to my deeper self, why should I expose that part of myself to your judgment? And there's rarely a good answer.

In this case I had a feeling, setting out, that we were probably not going to get Venus and Serena until the very end, and indeed the interview with Venus happened four days before the piece had to go off to the printer, which was just gut-wrenching. But because I knew it was probably going to happen that way, I started doing tons of reading and video watching, making a lot of phone calls to other family members and people who'd known them. Not even to use, necessarily, but so that I would have real questions—things I needed to know—when I got in the room with the sisters. And subjects do respond to that, to the depth of your questions, even subjects who aren't particularly deep themselves, which doesn't apply to the Williams sisters—their self-actualization, which seemed fairly hard-won, was one of the most surprising and compelling things about them. We can sense in a primate way when there's actual urgency beyond somebody's question. I was coming to them and saying, I'm deeply fascinated by your family. I don't think they've ever been written about in a satisfying way, and I need you to tell me this stuff. What is real? What really happened? To the extent that it wasn't luck—which I'm not sure is not a very great extent—it was because of that.

### BATUMAN

I always feel a sense of belatedness with reporting. As you're writing, you realize more and more what the story is, and at the end I always wish I could go back and report that story, now that I know what it is. That's why I like fact-checking, actually, because you get a second shot. You can ask a few more questions.

SULLIVAN

Fact-checking is underrated as a tool of writing itself.

INTERVIEWER

[*To the audience*] In Norway, is the fact-checker a fact of magazine life?

AUDIENCE

We don't check facts.

INTERVIEWER

You are a truth-telling people. Maybe Elif or John can explain what a fact-checker is.

BATUMAN

It's someone who gets on the phone and calls every single person you spoke to and verifies every word that you wrote.

SULLIVAN

A good fact-checker has learned how to mistrust sentences that seem beyond doubt, that look obviously, unassailably true and factual. The fact-checker is trained to go, Really? It's your better brain. *The New Yorker*, where Elif writes, has a famously rigorous and passionate fact-checking department. They'll go to cemeteries to check the spelling of somebody's name on a tombstone. This does something to the way you read the magazine, and to the magazine itself. It charges the prose with a certain energy, because the reader can actually feel—in the carefulness of the diction, maybe?—different minds having worried about whether this was correct.

INTERVIEWER

Lately various writers have challenged the use of fact-checking, of factual accuracy, in nonfiction. They've asked, Why can't there be nonfiction that doesn't get the facts right?

SULLIVAN

My trouble with that whole discussion, as it's happened in America over the last couple of years, is that it seems to take place so many levels of complexity below where the actual problems lie for a writer. The argument that nonfiction can never be purely nonfiction, can never get all the way to absolute factual accuracy, is of course totally solid. We could even have a separate conversation about whether a "fact" is anything but a social construct at the end of the day, since "facts" change. But the great nonfiction writers, or the ones whose work speaks most deeply to me, respond to that abyss of ambiguity with a determination to be as right as they can be, and not with a kind of prankish desire to push the ambiguity in the reader's face, announcing as a discovery something that everyone already concedes. When you do that, you're ripping the net right out of the tennis match, since nonfiction derives so much of its power—finds its task, to go back to that—in the striving toward fact.

INTERVIEWER

But there's a long tradition of fudging stuff in nonfiction. You're the one who made me read Defoe's *Journal of the Plague Year*. If someone wants to write a nonfiction account that isn't strictly accurate, what's the problem?

SULLIVAN

Take the case of Ryszard Kapuściński. It came out very late in his life that a lot of the stuff in his work, including in his masterpiece, *The Emperor*, had been invented. Okay, a person can say, he was an artist, he did that in the service of the story, or whatever. But when you go back to the book knowing these things, it simply is weaker. The reading experience itself has been diminished, not because the book is any less beautifully written, but because he's put the reader in this very distracting situation of constantly having to guess whether he's making it up, whether a particular sentence is true or "true." I think that's a cautionary tale.

AUDIENCE

How important is it to know that a story you're reading is fiction or nonfiction?

BATUMAN

*The Emperor* example suggests that it's important. It is interesting that the direction matters, too. If you read something thinking it's true, and then find out it isn't, you feel offended, but if you were to read something thinking it was fiction, and then found out it really happened, I don't think you'd feel the same sense of letdown.

SULLIVAN

You'd think, How gutsy. You could have claimed it as real and you didn't even do that. You didn't even need to do that.

INTERVIEWER

A story we published in *The Paris Review* was submitted as nonfiction, but eventually the author, Kerry Howley, decided to invent a few very minor details and call the whole thing fiction.

BATUMAN

Why?

INTERVIEWER

Because she wanted to throw attention onto the voice. As soon as it was fiction, the reader concentrated on the person telling the story, and why she was telling the story. It created a mystery.

AUDIENCE

Do you think that the use of other media, like video and sound and photos, adds to or subtracts from a written piece?

BATUMAN

I was once writing for *The New York Times Magazine* about a seventy-year-old woman in Tel Aviv, the daughter of Max Brod's secretary, who was maybe hoarding some unpublished manuscripts by Kafka in her dead mother's apartment, together with more than a hundred cats. The thing that everyone kept telling me about this woman was, She used to be a great beauty, she used to be a great beauty. I was like, Okay, so she was a great beauty. Then the photographer, an Israeli guy, somehow talked her into giving him an old

Following spread: "You wanted the melancholy of a Terrence Malick magic hour, so how will you express that with gray sky and rain?" *Oslo, August 31st.*

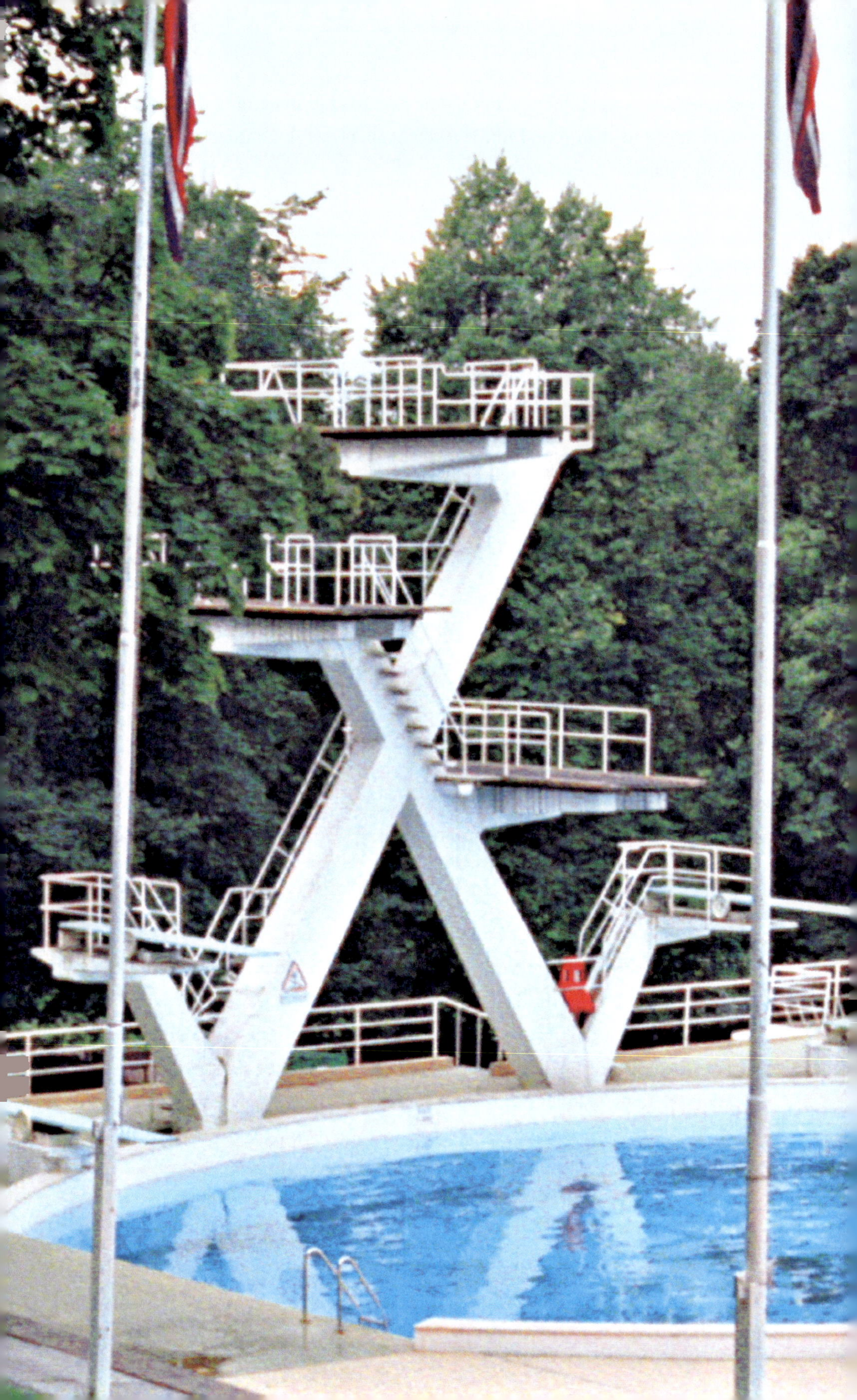

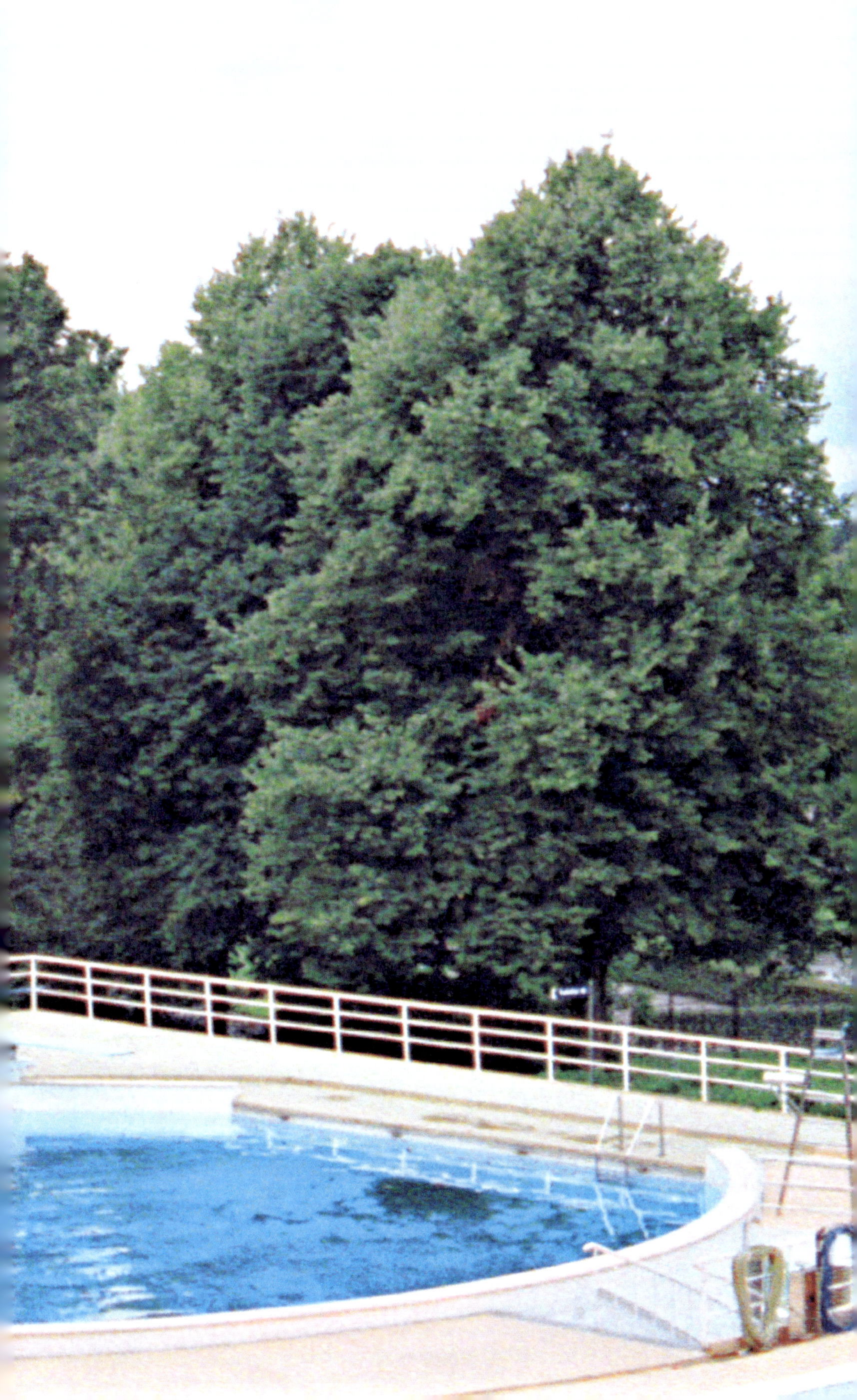

photo—I think she was wearing a flight attendant's uniform in it—and I saw it for the first time in the magazine. And *she was a great beauty*.

SULLIVAN

So that sentence you had written—

BATUMAN

The sentence became true.

---

## ON THE FANTASTICAL

*Donald Antrim is the author of three novels*—Elect Mr. Robinson for a Better World, The Hundred Brothers, *and* The Verificationist—*and a memoir,* The Afterlife. *He published his first story in* The Paris Review *in 1993 and has since become a frequent contributor to* The New Yorker. *Antrim's work has yet to be translated into Norwegian.*

INTERVIEWER

You've written three novels that are often described as "fantastical," but over the past few years you've been publishing stories in *The New Yorker* that are, for lack of a better word, realistic. I'd like to discuss this evolution in your work, but since the books aren't available in Norway, maybe you could begin by describing them.

ANTRIM

It seems strange to talk without the books here—no one's read them. Can I take a minute to give some context? Would that be all right?

I could begin by saying that, many years ago, when I began writing in earnest, I wrote stories, story after story, that were modeled on the kind of stories I thought I *should* write. The stories were about my family, mainly, about my alcoholic mother and about being her son, but they weren't succeeding. They were dutifully written, and they failed. They were dead. And later on, right around the time I was thirty or so—because I started late—I went into a depression over this. I didn't know what to do. I got out of the funk, eventually, through the fantastic, through making up other worlds. I felt at the time that since no one was paying me to write, since my family didn't want me to write, I had to have pleasure in writing.

[*To the audience*] It's difficult for me to say, in response to Lorin's question, what I think the novels are about. For me, they are maybe *about* the experience and the pleasure of writing them. It took me a while to understand that in building another world through the fantastic I was making a set of rules that had to be observed, a logic that had to be carried through—that I was in some ways obeying the premise of the very opening line, and that each book would make itself out of itself as time went on.

"If you want to add to some longer tradition, your own experience is what you have to bring." Viktoria Winge in *Reprise*.

It's a fairly slow process. The books are not long. For me, content—the premise itself, the subject matter of the books—is less important than the process. There's no particular message, no particular thematic unity, except that each novel features—each is carried out, you might say—by a narrator who is fundamentally a dangerous character, who in his attempts to do well by others, and to do well in the world, causes damage and destruction.

So perhaps I was writing a kind of encrypted autobiography, a story of my own family, my own childhood. Over time, after the death of my mother, I recognized that I would write about her, that I would write about her in realistic terms, and I wrote a memoir. And this was a very stressful thing to do. I felt quite guilty, quite ashamed as I did it, and I'm an anxious person, so my anxiety was very, very high while I was writing. But I wrote and published and came to feel, eventually, after several years of regretting ever having begun to write at all, that I was learning. So when I began to write short stories again, after some twenty years, I wanted to learn what short stories were. I wanted to learn how to write in a much more compressed and frankly realistic, or realistic-seeming, manner.

But what can I talk about in this setting? The books aren't here. How can I speak in some way that would be worth hearing?

INTERVIEWER

Will you talk a little bit about the novel you're working on now, *Must I Now Read All of Wittgenstein?*

ANTRIM

My ambivalence about all of this—about writing, about books in general—is fairly pronounced. My father was an English professor, and I grew up in a house full of books, and yet our house was not a particularly happy place. My father was a T. S. Eliot scholar, and he wrote a brief study called *T. S. Eliot's Concept of Language.* He wrote this monograph when I was a teenager, and I carried it around for years after I left home. I could never read it. I don't know whether anybody here has a father or mother who has written something. I'd open the first page of my father's book, and I would just go white in my brain. I couldn't see it. I couldn't read it. But many years later, literally while reaching for another book on a high shelf, it fell out onto the floor. I had forgotten I even had it. I picked it up, and because this wasn't premeditated, because I wasn't prepared to read it, I was able to, and I began to read this thing that he wrote. Several things struck me right away. One was that it was good. Another was that it was composed—[*casement window flies open in a gust of wind: loud crash*] Whoa! Hi, Dad.

AUDIENCE

[*Apologetically*] This is happening very often.

ANTRIM

It was composed, syntactically, in a language that I recognized and aspired to, a language that I shared with him, to some degree, without ever having known it. The structures of the sentences and paragraphs seemed very familiar to me, not just because I recognized *him*, but also because I recognized his language in my own writing. It occurred to me then that something could be made of this. I had no idea what, because, at that time, I hadn't yet written the memoir, and I wasn't quite prepared to deal with the material of my own family and upbringing, but it seemed to me that something could be made out of the idea of a son trying to write the story of the father—because my father was something of a mystery to me—with that study of T. S. Eliot as his primary document. The situations and characters and events that made the actual substance of my book would be fictional, but the Eliot monograph would be the source for what is made up.

It's been slow going.

INTERVIEWER

Do you remember the first sentence?

ANTRIM

By now I probably do [*recites*].

> My father, whose work in radical orthopedics was for many years disparaged in the journals and professional letters devoted to shoe design for the congenitally disabled, was also (I should say *is* also)—and it may come as a surprise to followers of H. T. Antrim's theories concerning his first wife's (my mother's) "psychosomatic" clubfoot—the author of a brief yet quite readable study of T. S. Eliot's poetic development, from "The Love Song of J. Alfred Prufrock" to *Four Quartets*, with special attention paid to the influence on the young Eliot of the neglected English metaphysician F. H. Bradley, whose *Appearance and Reality* helped set the stage not only for a great amount of literary and artistic contrarianism in the early twentieth century, but also—by way of Eliot—for my father's often intense relationships with people's feet.

That's the framework out of which this thing must grow, and it's been growing. All of my novels have begun with one sentence. It's been a great pleasure for me to work that way, but it has its limitations. You aren't going to write a large historical novel that way. You aren't going to write a saga. Each of my novels is a bit of a house of cards. They are all made up and held together by themselves, as it were, and each has been a laboratory, really, for exploring the technical demands of maintaining the suspension of disbelief inside the fantastic.

INTERVIEWER

You compare your books to a house of cards, but many writers, some of them quite popular in America, use a wacky premise to write wildly inventive books that leave me cold within the first half page. Yours never do. I wonder if you can talk a little about the technical difficulties of writing outside "realism."

ANTRIM

Part of what's required, for me, is speed. Speed is a function of, among other things, fast transitions. The books are devoted to a kind of momentum. There are no chapters, no section breaks. This maybe shows insecurity on the writer's part—the fear, my fear, that if a reader were to put the book down in the middle, he or she might not go back. So psychologically and emotionally the books don't really *get* put down. They carry through. It's difficult to talk about technique without something in front of us, without the audience having read any of these books. Enough to say, maybe, that the technical and mechanical demands that I was trying to learn as I went along were substantial. I think that what I've been learning over, oh, God, it's been almost three decades now, is how to hurt myself—how to hurt myself enough to give something through the book.

INTERVIEWER

Hurt yourself?

ANTRIM

Even works of the fantastic must be grounded in the world as we know it, or in some world that is concretely substantial. The challenge for me has been to bring forward a greater and greater emotional gesture, as it were. For instance, my second novel is about one hundred brothers and a night that they spend in a room, a library, in a mansion. It's possible to imagine this as a work of artifice entirely, but in fact that premise asks that the writer find a way to deliver some kind of emotion, to deliver selfhood—I'm not sure that that's a good way to put it—and to communicate. This is what we want when we read. We want a communication that can be felt. I think what I'm trying to say here—in this contextually strange conversation in which I'm explaining myself to these very welcoming people—is that it's taken me a long time to come to terms, or to begin to come to terms, with what I think is actually demanded of a writer. So when I say "hurt myself," what I mean is that stories and novels are, for me, ways to make more and more of a communication, not just of affect but of real feeling. That's been a hugely challenging proposition.

INTERVIEWER

But why? Why isn't it easy to hurt yourself, to feel shame? These are things we all feel in the course of a day. Why can't it happen on the page?

ANTRIM

The hurt and shame are not contained in statements about hurt and shame. For me, as I've said, the books are not *about* what they're about. They're made to give an experience. It took me a long time to conceptualize this, to feel it as a goal, and I still feel very much like I'm beginning, just starting, to get a handle on what I mean by it. But I look back now and see that I've been learning mechanics and technique in order to find a way to communicate the palpable and physical realities of shame, of depression and breakdown, of psychosis, of psychotic anxiety. The characters in these fabrications experience these things. The question is, How will the writer communicate these characters' experiences in such a way that they can be felt in the reading, not just heard?

AUDIENCE

When you talk like this, I think of Kafka's short stories.

---

Following spread: "You have a conclusion that makes sense, but the dilemma, the feeling, lingers on." *Oslo, August 31st.*

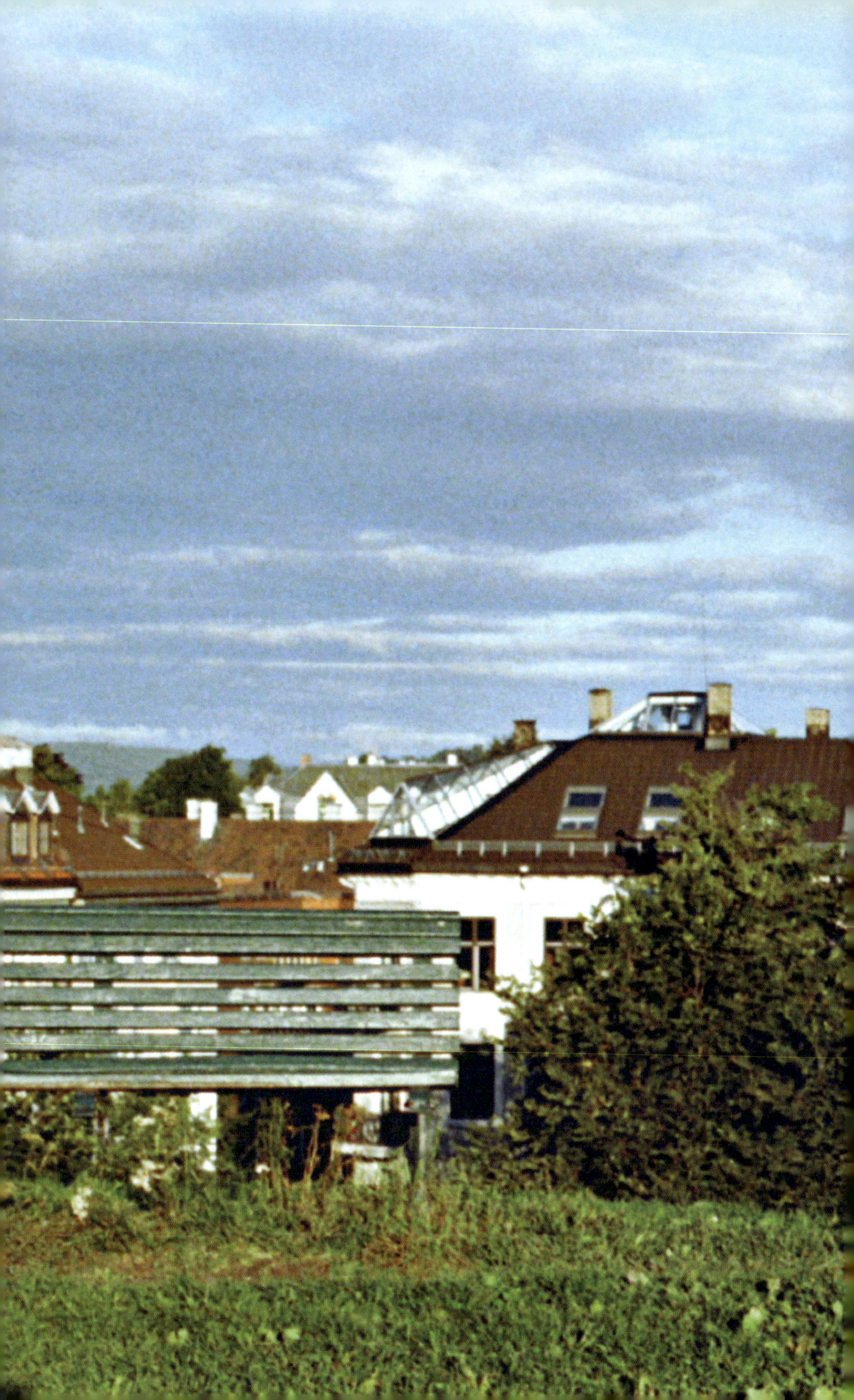

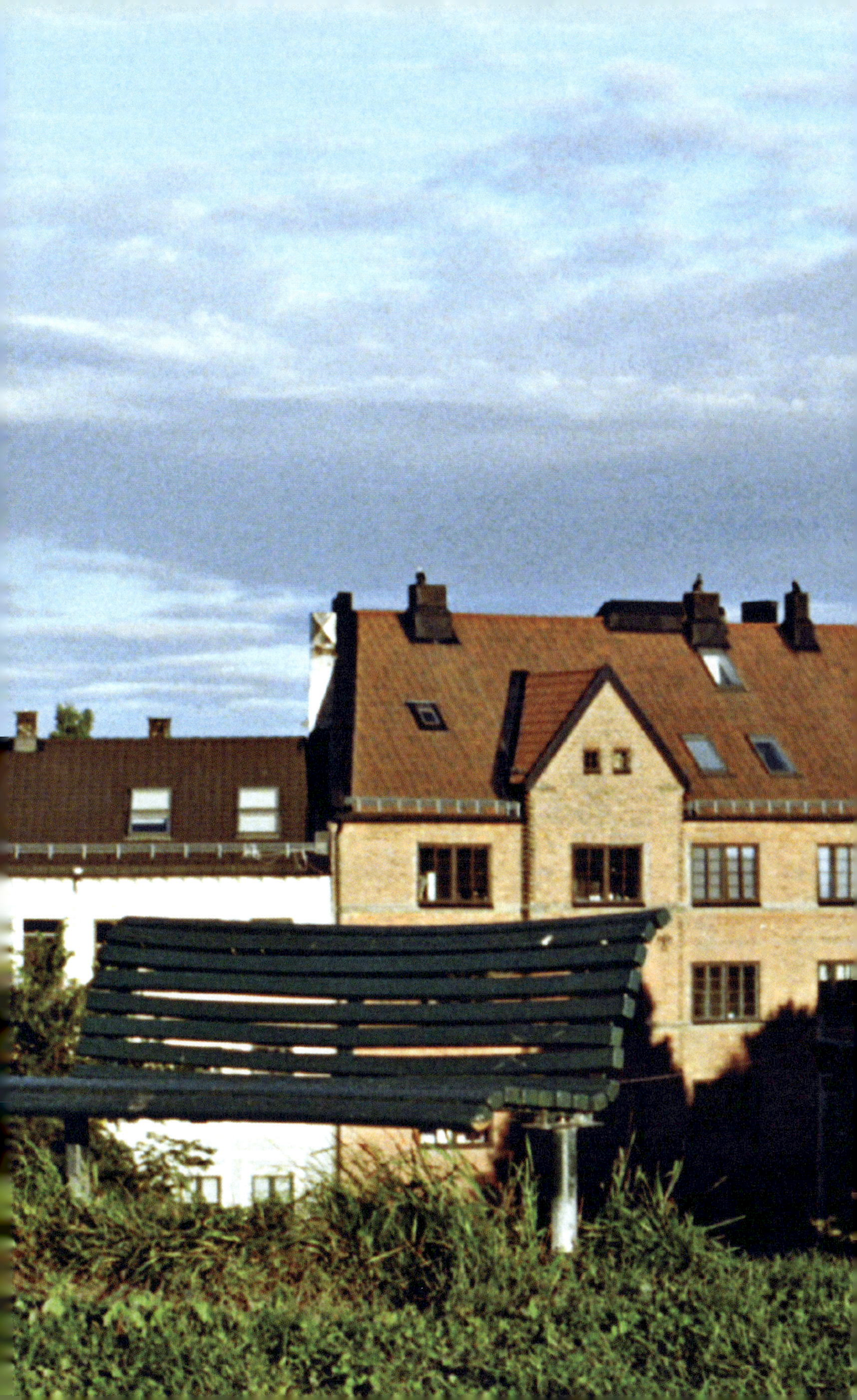

ANTRIM

In what way?

AUDIENCE

This transposition of the feelings of shame into a form that's quite strange. I haven't read you, but that's what I think of. Does it make sense?

ANTRIM

Yes, it does. Think about *The Metamorphosis*. It is fantastic insofar as the absurd premise is managed not as a poetic metaphor, but as a hard reality. And this is done through a very concrete and grounded observation of the physical realm. This is a very powerful work, a fantastic one, and it transcends the idea of the fantastic and brings us into a sense of ourselves and our own lives, our own psychological, emotional, and maybe unconscious reality. To produce that in writing, in words and paragraphs, is an almost inconceivably big job, right? One pushes that way and tries this way, but I go back again and again to the feeling that so far I've only just been able to touch this possibility—the possibility of making a work of art.

AUDIENCE

I am interested in your point about the communication of real feeling. How do you know when you have found the right voice? When can you say, I am going to communicate such and such a feeling through the particular voice of this man, or woman, or child?

ANTRIM

I've always had a hard time thinking in terms of a voice that one *makes* and then checks for feelings or some sense of rightness, as it were. For me, voice mainly comes down to a lot of waiting. When I think about voice, I don't think, Now we're in New York, or Now we're down South—what would this character sound like? It's not a matter of developing or constructing an idea about the way a character sounds and speaks. Instead, it's a matter of waiting to discover or feel the logic of a premise, and an idea, and a situation as it unfolds into contingencies. So even when I'm teaching, I never really talk about voice.

AUDIENCE

How do the South and New York influence you in your writing?

ANTRIM

I'm from the South, and my family is a Southern family—my father's from Virginia, my mother's from Tennessee, and they wound up in Florida, where I was born. So my whole childhood took place in a kind of Presbyterian-Episcopal South, and when I left home, a long time ago, I wound up in New York, though without any clear idea what I would do there. I wasn't even really writing yet. I thought I would be in the theater. Writing became the way that I was able to use myself—to use more than I thought I even had. Even though I've been in New York for thirty years, and I recognize that I've spent most of my life there, and feel like a New Yorker, I also have to recognize that I carry within me a Southern tradition or experience that doesn't get acted out, these days, by, say, living in the mountains or on a farm, as I did as a child. I don't really know where home is. Maybe that's also part of what this is all about, being homeless and having a home, finally, in the act of writing, in those hours when the world goes away, and you're just a tiny bit immortal, you know? That, along with lots of other things, saved my life. That, along with lots of therapeutic intervention [*laughs*], became the way I was able to begin to make a home.

# Ben Lerner

NO ART

Tonight I can't remember why
everything is permitted or,
what amounts to the same thing,
forbidden. No art is total, even

theirs, even though it raises
towers or kills from the air,
there's too much piety in despair,
as if the silver leaves behind

the glass were politics
and the wind they move in
and the chance of scattered
storms. Those are still

my ways of making and
I know that I can call on you
until you're real enough
to turn from. Maybe I have fallen

behind, am falling, but
I think of myself as having
people, a small people
in a failed state, and love

more avant-garde than shame
or the easy distances.
All my people are with me now
the way the light is.

# The Vac-Haul

## PETER ORNER

For hours we listened to it on the radio, and not once did Larry Phoebus say a word. A woman walked into a classroom of a school a couple of towns over and started shooting. She killed an eight-year-old boy and wounded five other kids. She'd also, the radio said, left homemade bombs at other schools, including a school just a few blocks from where Larry Phoebus and I were parked. I could hear the frantic sirens like crazed, amplified mosquitoes. Now the radio was saying that the police had confirmed that the woman had fled across the street from the school where she'd shot the boy and was holed up in a house with a hostage. This was in 1988, when things like this still had capacity to shock. I was sitting there with Larry Phoebus, looking out the windshield of the truck, staring at the Chicago and North Western tracks, at the tall weeds that grew up between the ties, listening to all this on WBBM.

I was home from my first year at college. It was July. I'd wandered across that year, as I'd wandered across much else, incurious, biding my time. Waiting for what, I couldn't say. My stepfather, who was mayor of our suburb, found me a job in the Streets and Sanitation Department. For a few weeks, I was proudly blue-collar. Work—who would have thought I would take it? I worked for Streets as a jackhammerer. I destroyed curbs with erotic abandon. I will make this corner handicap accessible if it's my last act on earth. I wore a sweaty red bandanna. Rudimentary biceps were beginning to rise between my shoulders and elbows like little loaves. I'd be uptown, standing on the street, encircled by a little ring of pylons, smoking, and I would tell the imaginary pom-pom girls who thronged around me that I can't talk right now. Look, can't you see I'm a workingman?

Then I was late three mornings in a row and the crew boss, Miguel, said, I'm taking you off Streets. You're with Larry Phoebus now.

No, Miguel, no—please—

And don't run to your dad. He knows all about it. In fact, he said to go ahead and fire you, but I figure, why not let you quit on your own? Won't be long now.

He's not my dad.

Turn in your gloves, Hirsch. You won't be needing them again. *Ever*.

LARRY PHOEBUS WORKED on the Sanitation side. He drove an enormous white truck with an enormous, bulbous hose attached to the end of it. It was called the Vac-Haul. It was rumored to have cost the taxpayers of Highland Park two million dollars. My stepfather was very proud of it. The Vac-Haul was designed to suck up major sewage backups without the need to send "manpower down the manhole," as my former Streets partner, Steve Boland, explained it. The truck was Larry Phoebus's baby. He was long past retirement age. He'd worked for Sanitation for something like fifty years and was now refusing to leave. It was said that he didn't trust another living soul with the Vac-Haul and when it was time for him to die he was going to drive that two million dollars straight into Lake Michigan.

Also, Larry never spoke. It was said around the lunch table that Larry Phoebus had pretty much given up communing with the rest of the human race in the 1960s, when the world, his world, everybody's world, went so haywire. Yet the precise reason for his total silence was a mystery nobody was especially interested in solving. Only Steve Boland speculated at all. He liked to hold forth in the lunchroom. Love, Boland said, what else is new under the sun? Only a woman could numb a guy like that. I hit the mute button myself for a couple of years after my first divorce. She took all my money, the house. Even then I had to sell the boat to pay her monthly. So I mean, answer me this, you're living by yourself in some dump-ass rented apartment in Highwood and you think you're going to want to converse?

"What the hell are you yattering about?" Miguel said.

"I'm talking about alone," Boland said. "Do any of you even know what it means?"

LARRY PHOEBUS HIMSELF never appeared in the lunchroom. He ate in the Vac-Haul. At lunch, he'd glide the Vac-Haul into its special parking place in the garage and pull out a sandwich from his jacket pocket. We'd watch him up there in his cab, slowly chewing, looking down at us, but not seeming to see very much.

Being Larry Phoebus's assistant was the worst job in either division, and they usually gave it to one of the illegal Mexicans who'd come in looking for a day's work, but that day, the day I was late a third day in a row, none of those guys were around, and so I became Larry's new boy.

The Vac-Haul needed two people to operate it. One to guide the hose into the hole, the other to flick the switch in the cab.

The worst part of the worst job was that the Vac-Haul was rarely put to use. No question that it was a great monument to the progress of modern sewage engineering, but the town's system apparently functioned just fine. Yet in order for Larry Phoebus to be paid (and for the department and the town to justify the expense), the Vac-Haul had to leave the garage. And so every morning and every afternoon, Larry Phoebus would parade that truck around town for a while and then park behind the White Hen Pantry to wait out the hours listening to the news on the radio. And so maybe to Larry Phoebus that day was no different than any other day. Maybe the voices on the radio were a little more hysterical than usual, but it all amounted to the same never-ending drone that was life outside the cab.

*WBBM News Time: 3:26. In Winnetka this hour, SWAT teams and hostage negotiators have descended upon the three hundred block of...*

Swelling hot in the cab. Larry Phoebus never rolled the windows down, and he didn't run the air conditioner, either. I listened to the old man's wheezy breathing in the stagnant air. I watched the side of his gaunt face and tried to think of something to say. Things must have been so different when you were a young kid, huh, Larry? How were things when you were young, Larry? Let's turn off the radio and talk, Larry. You and me. Tell me your life, Larry. I'll listen. Who'd you love, Larry? You must have loved somebody? Steve Boland says—

Larry Phoebus watched the railroad tracks, the weeds. Finally, I got down out of the cab and went in the White Hen and bought some doughnuts—a box, an assortment. Back in the truck, I held the box out to Larry Phoebus and in my memory, my ceaselessly lying memory, Larry Phoebus turns to me and, though he doesn't exactly speak, his eyes look at me and say, No, but thank you.

Maybe I thought the doughnuts would provide a little fellowship, break some bread at a time like this. A time like what? What was that time like? I sat there with my doughnuts. Every once in a while I took a bite out of one and put it back in the box. I figured I'd sample the whole assortment. What the hell. I seem to remember maple frosting was a new, radical flavor then. You're dead, Larry. Even you would have to be long dead by now. The Vac-Haul is probably not such a marvel anymore, either. Probably everybody in the department is allowed to drive it. You were a man I sat next to, a man who for hours and hours I sat next to.

When I think of that time, and I often do, I think of the tenacity of that man's breathing.

Of course, I think of her sometimes as well. She grew up not far from where I did. Like me, she was a suburban Jewish kid from just outside Chicago. We are legion; we hail from a place called the North Shore, a place on the bluffs of Lake Michigan where nothing ever happens, a safe, beautiful place to raise your kids. I never knew her, she was about eight or nine years older, but I did go to high school with her cousin. She—we don't like to say her name out loud—went to college in Madison, like my brother, like my father. She was a member of the same sorority that my grandmother was a founding member of in 1926.

A lot has been said over the years about what happened that day. Books have been written. All the details. She tried to kill her ex-husband with an ice pick. She slept in her car. People said she smelled. How separate she was from other people. Even as a child, how isolated she always was—

Valerie Bertinelli played her in the TV movie.

For hours, we listened to it on the radio, Larry Phoebus and me. The radio said a shot fired. The radio said SWAT teams. The radio said the house surrounded.

We were still in the truck, in the parking lot, waiting out the hours before the Vac-Haul could go home to the garage, when the radio announced another shot, a lone one. The empty parking lot, the train tracks, the tall weeds growing up through the ties. I thought something should change, that at least the light should change. But it was July in the Midwest and the sun refused to sink. Only the radio voices were moving. I gripped my doughnuts. The heat in the cab rising with every breath Larry Phoebus took. The side of his motionless face. The radio said stormed the house. Was he hearing any of this? His sharp, jutting chin, pebbled with gray hair. A strong chin, ready chin. Even hiding in the parking lot, Larry Phoebus never slouched. In the event of a catastrophic sewage emergency, Larry Phoebus would be there, on the scene. Flash-flood warnings called to him in dreams. The radio said hostage in critical condition. The radio said suspect shot herself in the mouth. The guy from the White Hen came out with a huge bag of garbage and launched it, shot-put style, to the top of the already heaping dumpster.

# Linda Pastan

## AH, FRIEND

in the black hood,
come! Pierce
my heart

with the sharp ring
of the doorbell;
throw pebbles

at my window
with the perilous sound
of hail on a tin roof.

No more of these
odd hints: a petal
of blood here,

a shadow, the size
of a thumbprint,
on an X-ray there.

I will never be more ready
than I am now,
as I sit

peeling a tangerine
and turning the brittle pages
in the long book

of my life. I won't
even need to pack
for the journey.

# *The Tangling Point*

## TIM PARKS

Before the dinner, my wife told me that her boss's daughter was obsessed by dogs. Her parents were worried about it, more than worried. In fact, they had asked whether I might be able to help. I remarked that I had never heard that a love for animals constituted a pathology. My wife sighed and explained that the young woman, Eleonora, had a job teaching biology in a local school, but couldn't be persuaded to leave home, claiming she needed all her extra money for her dogs.

"How many does she have?"

"Only two of her own. It seems she's a dog savior. She drives all over Europe saving dogs."

My wife had finally returned to work after many years as a housewife and mother. I was anxious that the job go well and that she be happy there. Our marriage had run out of steam many years ago, the last child was leaving home, and there was the prospect that we would be able to separate without too much trauma. A good job—she was PA to the director of a busy pharmaceutical concern—could only facilitate this, giving my wife something to rebuild her life around. Hence, when she said her boss had invited us to dinner, I agreed at once, hoping this indicated an investment on both sides in their new work relationship.

"I think he partly invited us so as to talk to you about her. He seemed very interested when I said you were a therapist."

We had arrived at the house, an attractive villa on the hills to the north of town. The automatic gate swung open, a yellow light flashing above one of the posts.

"What do you mean, 'saving dogs'?" I asked.

"It seems people alert her when they hear of a dog being mistreated, and she goes and rescues the creature and finds it a good home."

"Sounds rather noble," I said.

"Think if one of our kids were doing that," my wife snapped back. "Be serious." It was a while since we had spent an evening together.

Signor Fanna was a tall, bulky man, rather sloppy by Italian standards, but he greeted us energetically and with evident pleasure, rather as if he might be a big playful dog himself. Behind him, his wife leaned forward from a wheelchair; in her early sixties, she was dryly polite and wore an elegant green silk blouse. "*Buona sera*, Dr. Clarke," she greeted me. I was struck by her lean wrists, braceleted in gold but evidently powerful as she spun her wheelchair around and led the way to the dining room.

We went through the usual social rigmaroles, drinking something white and sharp. I was pleased to see that Signor Fanna was on easy and respectful terms with my wife, and she, too, seemed to have the measure of him, coming across as both sociable and sensible. For a few moments they talked about work and the arrangements for a conference in Germany that he was to be attending the following week.

"At which point I shall be left alone with the mad dog woman," his wife remarked coolly to me.

It seemed a curious thing to say for someone who must rely heavily on domestic help. Shouldn't Signora Fanna be glad to have her daughter around? I noticed that they did have an elderly Asian maid doing the cooking. Wearing a simple black dress that may or may not have been a uniform, this small, quiet woman brought in a plate of mixed hors d'oeuvres and laid it on the glass table.

"I hear your daughter is something of an activist," I smiled.

"A terrorist, Dr. Clarke."

I laughed. "I see no bomb damage."

"Because we clean up afterward."

Swallowing a vol-au-vent, Signor Fanna turned toward us and sighed. "You've studied psychology, Dr. Clarke. Perhaps you could tell us what would induce a young woman to sacrifice everything to dogs. Is there anything we can do?"

It is one of the comedies of being a mental-health therapist that people imagine you have magical powers of divination.

"Evidently she likes her dogs more than the things she is supposedly giving up," I said. "Why is it such a worry for you?"

"Honestly, she's driving us crazy," Signor Fanna began, but stopped. "You tell him, Elvira."

The woman in the wheelchair, who must have been a beauty in her day, pursed her lips and frowned. "Five or six years ago, we were expecting Eleonora to marry and leave home. She had a nice boyfriend she'd been seeing for some time. They'd lived together on and off. A young lawyer. Then it fell through because he couldn't put up with having dogs constantly lodged in his flat and even sleeping on his bed. It was sad—we'd actually become good friends with his parents, excellent people from Bologna. After the breakup, she started bringing the dogs here. Every weekend she's off in the car, driving hundreds, even thousands, of kilometers, either to fetch dogs who've been abandoned or to take the strays she's gathered to some new home. Every afternoon after school all she does is feed and walk the dogs, then get on the Internet to plan her next 'raid.' That's what she calls them."

"She was so smart at school," Signor Fanna said. "Got an excellent degree in molecular biology from Milan. We had expected her to go into research. Instead, she settled for work as a replacement teacher on the local school circuit. Now she's thirty-four and seems to have no plans beyond saving dogs."

"Last week she brought back a three-legged, leprous creature from Bari or thereabouts. It cost a fortune just in petrol. Then there are veterinary expenses."

"Not to mention problems with the law. If she sees a dog kept on a short chain, she simply steals it. Goes at night with a chain cutter. There've been two summonses. We had to put down bail."

My wife said to me, "Think if one of ours started doing that kind of thing, Ted!"

I looked around. "There are no dogs in here," I observed.

"Because we've insisted that this side of the house be kept dog-free."

"Ah."

"But if we took you round the back, you'd need a gas mask. I've set up a firewall of air fresheners," Signora Elvira explained with a pained smile.

I thought about it. "I must say, I rather like dogs. They're always friendly. And hardwired for obedience."

"We all like dogs," both of them wailed rather louder than was necessary. "Everybody does, but not scores of them, and not dogs with sores and wounded paws and pus in their eyes."

As I wondered what to say next, my wife shot me a glance to remind me that these were not any old friends, and certainly not my clients. People want a therapist's advice for their nearest and dearest but are not eager to find their own assumptions under scrutiny. Fortunately, a tureen of smooth asparagus soup was served, and we sat at table to eat. A fifth place had been set, I noticed—at the head of the table, too—but no attempt had been made to call Eleonora. Perhaps the couple wanted the benefit of my advice before she arrived. Rather deliberately, I changed the subject to pharmaceuticals, and Signor Fanna, a jowly, expansive man, spoke happily of his work and the rather special situation, as he put it, in Italy, where the industry faced the combined problems of a certain level of anarchy, a lot of petty corruption, and of course the Church doing everything possible to hinder the distribution of all products connected with contraception.

Signora Elvira seemed bored and left half her soup in her bowl.

"I've been given special instructions for how to speak to right-to-life lobbyists," my wife confirmed cheerfully.

Then Eleonora walked in, and the evening got interesting.

I had expected a loser, the dog craze covering up a young woman's fear of starting her own life away from home. Or a polemical young woman playing committed radical to her parents' bourgeois complacency; a do-gooder, a bore. Instead, Eleonora banged open the door and strode in smiling, apologizing for being late. "I never make it anywhere on time," she laughed. She was wearing a gray wool dress on a shapely, freshly showered body of medium height, feminine but healthily solid, and if her face was on the plain side, it nevertheless had plenty of character and presence. "No, don't get up," she protested. "You must be Marta, and you're the English husband."

"Ted."

"Right, the shrink."

Why had the girl been told that?

We talked for twenty minutes or so without any mention of dogs. The main dishes were brought by the discreet maid, who seemed to be from the Philippines or thereabouts, and I noticed that Eleonora's plate did not have meat on it, though she made no attempt to draw attention to her vegetarianism. She was a confident, outgoing young woman happy to discuss the school she worked in and her attitude to her teacher's role: "I try to give Papà a hand," she laughed, "telling the girls to get on the pill and the boys to use condoms."

Yet her parents were evidently unhappy with her. The mother in particular frowned constantly. Perhaps Signora Elvira was a devout Catholic, I reflected, and didn't approve of these allusions to sex and contraception. Her husband had become cautious after his daughter's arrival, as if picking his way through a minefield. I suspected he could have got on with her if the mother were not present. As it was, all his attentions seemed aimed at getting my wife and his to talk together, about recipes and clothes and shopping centers. Perhaps her PA's responsibilities were to include keeping the boss's invalid wife company while he was away.

"I hear you are a dog lover," I said as the tiramisu was placed before us.

"That's right," Eleonora agreed amiably. She concentrated on spooning up the mascarpone.

There was an expectant silence. I couldn't decide whether the Fannas wanted me to make some kind of effort to explore the dog thing or not. I was trying to be helpful.

With a dour smile, Signora Elvira said, "Eleonora's going up to Holland this weekend, aren't you, love?"

The "love" was unexpected, and unexpectedly respectful. Eleonora nodded. "I thought we'd agreed not to talk about dogs anymore, Mamma."

"It's not every weekend one drives to Holland," Signor Fanna said.

My wife threw in a few enthusiastic remarks about Amsterdam in the spring and what wonderful people the Dutch were. "So liberal. No problems selling pharmaceuticals there!"

Eleonora put her spoon down. "Too liberal sometimes."

"How so?" I asked.

She hesitated, shot a glance at her parents. "There are no laws against deviant sexual behavior in Holland. They let men rape dogs. This usually leads to the animals' death, through internal bleeding."

"God!" My wife raised her napkin to her lips.

Signora Elvira's face was a mask of severity.

"Special brothels exist to provide dogs to an international clientele. Like the cafés where you can smoke dope. This weekend there will be a big animal-rights demonstration. We're planning to free as many dogs as we can." She turned to her father who was looking a little queasy: "Do you mind if I take the SUV, Papà?"

Some time later, as we were preparing to leave, I said, "I'd love to see your dogs, Eleonora."

We were standing in the hallway. Signor Fanna had gone to get some papers he wanted my wife to deal with first thing the following morning. Signora Elvira had cheered up as the evening drew to a close and was evidently enjoying my wife's company. Perhaps Signor Fanna always introduced his PAs and their husbands to his wife to prevent suspicion that there might be any illicit intimacy developing.

Eleonora assented readily enough and led the way down the hallway, through a door that crossed a spacious kitchen, then another door that led to a generous extension on the back of the house. At once there was a strong doggy smell, but nothing excessive, or not for those of us who've been brought up with dogs. The girl crouched down to greet a fine Border collie that came scampering up to her, then stretched an arm to welcome a pretty beagle waggling behind. As she crouched, her wool dress tightened. The collie licked her face, which she turned smilingly from side to side under his long, wet tongue. Her thighs were strong and her back pleasantly full. The beagle yelped and pawed. Both dogs were beautifully glossy, in the pink of canine health, and the more Eleonora played with them, the more attractive her youth and evident good nature became.

"What my parents wanted you to pronounce on, though," she broke off, "is this."

Suddenly businesslike, she stood up and led me through the extension and out of a back door into the garden. Immediately, from a low building at the far side of the lawn, an excited barking began. It was no more than a large garden shed, half-hidden behind low bushes. Eleonora took a flashlight hanging under the eaves and pointed it through the window. Here, there were ten or a dozen dogs all falling over one another to thrust their snouts against the window, yapping and snuffling and scratching. I could see at once that these were not such healthy specimens. One had an eye missing. One limped and whimpered.

"I always find homes for them in the end. It just takes a little time."

"That's very impressive," I said. "It must be hard work."

"There's a group of us, called Puppy Love."

She turned toward me. Because we had been peering in at the small window, we were quite close to each other. It was impossible not to be aware of her body in the fresh dark, her lips faintly illuminated by the flashlight.

"Maybe you'd like to make a donation. We're not a registered charity yet, but I can guarantee that every cent would be spent on the dogs' welfare."

We began to walk back to the house.

"I've worked out that each dog I save and rehouse costs on average around four hundred euros, just over a quarter of my monthly salary."

"Let me think about it."

"Of course. Take your time. I ask everybody I meet. Otherwise we wouldn't be able to do what we do."

I felt excited.

"How would I contact you, if I did decide to give?"

She mentioned a Web site. The name was easy to remember. There was a contact box. But before we crossed the threshold back into the house, she stopped me. "Tell me something, though. I mean, you being a shrink. Why does it bother my parents so much? Especially Mamma. Why is she so hostile?"

I took a deep breath. This was tempting; an alliance against her parents would be an easy way to intimacy. I resisted.

"I suppose they wanted something different for you. As parents tend to do. They no doubt have some more conventional narrative of their daughter, happy in her middle-class marriage with a professional career that they can talk to their friends about." I hesitated. "Probably what makes it harder is that what you're doing is obviously generous and good. I mean, if one has to choose between dog rapists and dog rescuers, one plumps for the rescuers. On the other hand, we'd all be happier not to think about such disturbing things at all. I suspect you confuse them. They're not sure how to behave. And of course," I smiled, "they could probably do without the barking in the garden. And the dog shit, no doubt."

As I spoke and she watched me, standing a fraction closer than people ordinarily stand to each other, I sensed that very soon we would become lovers and I would be dedicating substantial sums of money to the salvation of Europe's abused dogs.

So it was. Eleonora was arrested in Holland. My wife told me that Signor Fanna had canceled his trip to Germany to go to the Italian consulate in The Hague. Signora Elvira, on the other hand, had kept her, my wife, on the phone for hours, expressing her indignation that her husband had allowed his daughter to get in the way of his work; she was all for leaving the girl to languish in a police cell. That way, she'd be forced to wake up and take life seriously.

I wondered who fed and walked the dogs while Eleonora was away. My wife said she had no idea.

"Ask."

She looked puzzled. "Why?"

"Just curious. I find the whole setup rather intriguing."

"I thought you'd come to the conclusion that she was a nice girl with a good cause and the parents were making too much fuss."

"Just curious," I repeated. "By the way, do you know how Signora Elvira ended up in the wheelchair?"

My wife had no idea. Signor Fanna had never talked about it.

"He's extremely devoted to her," she said with a hint of bitterness.

The following week, Eleonora appeared on the regional TV news. She had been released with a caution. Quizzed by an interviewer on her return to Verona, she said, "I just don't like to think of animals being mistreated. Especially not to satisfy perverts. It's ugly and I want the world to be beautiful."

Watching, I was struck by how at ease she was with the questions and the camera; there was no shrillness, no preaching or proselytizing. As someone who spends hours every day in conversation with conflicted and unhappy people, I rarely see this: a young woman entirely at home with herself and her choices. It made her extremely desirable. The closing shots showed Eleonora crouching down to greet her collie and beagle on arriving home. It was a replay of the scene I had witnessed after our dinner, except that now she was wearing jeans and a T-shirt. The collie pushed its wet nose into her breasts.

I would send her four hundred euros a month, I wrote in the Web site contact box, on the condition that I be allowed to see the dogs my money was helping. A few days later we met outside her school, and she took me to a veterinary clinic where an obese black Labrador was sedated on a drip. He had been found half-dead in a ditch.

The vet, in his late forties, greeted Eleonora with a warm embrace; she ruffled his hair, he tweaked her nose, and I understood at once that they had been lovers and that this was why he was willing to offer her his services for no more than the cost of the drugs. He greeted me and smiled, explaining that it was a daily occurrence in Verona for dogs to be found poisoned, either by dog haters who left spiked meatballs around or by their owners who were fed up with them. In Italy it is illegal to put a healthy animal down. "So they fake a poisoning and take care to remove the dog's collar and identification, in case it survives."

Eleonora stroked the creature, which was stretched out on a surgical table. "Come and say hello, Ted," she said in a low voice. I went to stand beside her and put a hand on the dog's matted fur. It twitched and a muscle shifted under the skin. She put her hand next to mine. It was actually quite strange to feel this threatened animal life beneath my fingers; the Labrador's bulk and odorous canine presence took on an unexpected solemnity—here were fifty kilos of sensitive suffering flesh that could not easily be ignored—and I knew it was the woman beside me who had made me feel this. Her hand invited mine to linger and to get to know the creature. Sitting in the car again we looked at each other and kissed.

Signora Elvira had fallen off a horse, my wife told me. "Twenty years ago."

"Ah."

I wondered aloud what her husband did about sex.

"Trust you," she grumbled, "it is possible for people to love each other without constant sex, you know."

It went unspoken that my wife and I hadn't made love for months, if not years.

Eleonora had a more interesting version of events. Her mother, a successful doctor at the time, had been eager to get her daughter into horse riding; she went around with a rather snobbish Rotary Club crowd. "One holiday, in Umbria, she hired these two horses and at a certain point mine took off. I couldn't control it. She was quite expert and galloped after me. Then I fell and she had to hit the brakes not to trample me. The horse crashed her into a wall."

"So it was your fault."

"She never actually said that."

Her mother was the one serious worry in Eleonora's life. "What can I do to make her happy," she moaned, "or at least to get her off my back? Why is she constantly asking me when I plan to get real and move out of the house? She's obsessed."

We met once a week and made love in my studio. Often Eleonora brought a dog to show me, ostensibly the one my money was helping. The animals did not always take kindly to our embraces. Sometimes she invited me on reconnaissance missions: I had to wander into a farmyard in some outlying village to see if it was true that a German shepherd was being kept up to its knees in slime. On another occasion I was asked to drive a bull terrier to its new owner in Genova while she went to deal with an emergency in Trieste. As I drove, sacrificing a whole Sunday in the process and wondering how I would explain to my wife about the doggy smell in the car, I realized that this must be how all her relationships went. Men fell in love with her enthusiasm around dogs, her warmth, affection, and contagious sense of purpose. It was impossible not to want to be touched and loved by this generous animal woman. Then they grew offended that the dogs always came first, and the relationships cooled and died—after which ex-lovers might become occasional helpers, taking the dogs out for walks when she was away on a mission, perhaps getting a kiss or two as a reward, or maybe more. Eleonora was not a stingy girl. She had a finely developed sense of give and take.

As far as I was concerned, though, it was rather convenient that the dogs came first. After three children, I had no interest in serious commitments with a young woman. And watching Eleonora, I was beginning to understand her motivation and her gift: again and again she made you feel the individuality and irrefutable physical presence of each animal. However sick or crippled or aggressive or stinking they might be, these creatures couldn't be wished away; they really were there, living and suffering and snuffling at your crotch. Eleonora's response to their vitality brought out the animal in her, too; she radiated life. I never minded when a promised session on my studio sofa was cancelled for a trip to some dog refuge with a carload of cheap feed. She liked my big Audi because it carried more than her old

Vectra. And she was appreciative of my patience. "I'll make it up to you, darling," she whispered. This could go on forever, I thought.

But there was one animal Eleonora couldn't get rid of. She'd had a Doberman for a year and more and despaired of finding a home for it. Paralysed in one hind leg, abandoned by its owner when no longer able to run along a fence barking madly at every passerby, this ex–guard dog was frustrated and irritable, snapping at the other dogs in the shed and making sure that there was a constant din in the garden, which of course gave Signora Elvira every excuse for insisting that the situation was unsustainable. On two occasions this grumpy creature had made the journey to generous adoptive families in distant country estates, but each time, after a week or so, these good people had asked to be relieved of the animal. So the Doberman—Kenny, he was called—was brought back, not without expense and effort, and the strife began again. He nipped the other dogs' heels and necks, they yelped and barked. The paralysis also seemed to have affected his bladder. He peed in the shed. The stink was getting worse.

"You take him," Eleonora eventually said.

Yes, this is how she gets rid of her men, I thought, with an impossible test of love.

"Let me mull it over," I told her, and I noticed that when we made love that afternoon she was particularly generous with her caresses. Sex was never easier or more affectionately physical than with Eleonora. She made you feel how fortunate you were to be alive and in possession of all your senses. In my midfifties, I had clearly lucked out.

On the other hand, Kenny was one hell of an ugly dog.

"Signora Elvira phoned me today," my wife said. My wife had been in a better mood since she had started working again, so much so that I had begun to think that, what with the affair I was enjoying and this new pleasantness at home, perhaps after all there would be no need to make major changes.

"She asked if you would be willing to see her."

"She didn't say why?"

"I thought it might be unwise to ask."

I drove over the following morning and found Signora Elvira smartly if sternly dressed in a black jacket and cream blouse.

"I never thought it would come to this," she said without any preamble, "but I was wondering if you would accept me for therapy, or analysis, or whatever it is exactly you do."

This was tricky. Ethically, it must be wrong for me to become the therapist of my lover's mother. On the other hand, I could hardly state the impediment.

"I wonder if that's a good idea," I said, "with my wife being your husband's PA."

"Nonsense," she declared.

There was a prickliness about the woman that was intimidating and endearing. I hesitated.

"Dr. Clarke," she said determinedly, "I need to learn how to stop being so unpleasant to my daughter, who after all helps me in all kinds of ways, something that is actually quite important for a woman in a wheelchair. The truth is, I don't really understand why she irritates me so much. I was hoping you could guide me."

Intrigued, I stayed to listen. The truth is that inhibitions, and even professional vetoes, have less force as one grows older. I thought, Why not?

Needless to say, my wife was horrified when she found Kenny in the garden. The creature barked and bared its teeth. He had shat on our small lawn, a steamy, liquid shit.

"Take it right back! At once. Whatever were you thinking?"

I explained that as I had come out of one of my sessions with Signora Elvira (since she was wheelchair bound, I had made the unusual concession of seeing her at her house rather than my studio), Eleonora had buttonholed me and begged me, simply begged me, to take the Doberman.

"Just temporarily, until she finds a permanent home. A good deed," I said. "Apparently it's the dog that most gets under her parents' skin."

"You're going soft," my wife told me. But that evening she looked at me in a way she hadn't for some time.

I sat outside on a garden chair, something I never do, reading and talking to Kenny and trying to pat him whenever he came close. Already the neighbors had complained about the loud barking every time they opened and closed their front door. All day Kenny dragged his bad leg back and forth from the hedge on one side of the garden to the fence on the other, occasionally stopping to growl at me in between.

"How goes it, old pal?" I asked. "How does it feel to have a territory to defend again?"

Now after making love, Eleonora gave me tips for winning the dog's confidence and imposing a minimum of discipline. She enjoyed getting me to pretend I was the Doberman and she was me. We laughed and tussled. I pretended to bite her fingers and she yelled, "Heel! Bad boy!" But there was also a new caution about Eleonora these days. She hadn't expected that I would take on Kenny. Even less that I would keep him. Perhaps she feared what I might ask in return. She certainly hadn't expected that I would become her mother's therapist.

"God knows what secrets you're learning," she fished.

"If you only knew!" I teased.

Nearly a year on it was still enormously exciting making love to Eleonora. It had cheered me up no end. Walking Kenny on the lead every evening, waiting while he dragged his bad leg, picking up his stinking shit in a plastic bag, pulling him away from the other dogs he was always determined to attack, I kept repeating, "I'm not doing this for you, you know, old mate. I'm doing it to keep a certain lady in my bed."

But Kenny didn't seem upset by this deviousness. He had started to lick my fingers and to sit when I told him to. My wife was impressed.

"I'd have never imagined you had it in you," she said, and she, too, crouched down to stroke him. Kenny growled, but softly. My wife looked up and our eyes met: this was a very unusual occurrence.

"By the way," she said then, "Signor Fanna seems rather nervous about your talks with his wife. He hadn't realized she was planning to go into analysis."

"I hope you reassured him that I never talk to you about my patients."

"Of course."

On another occasion I asked her, "Do you ever get the impression that Signor Fanna is a big shaggy dog? It's what I always think when I see him."

More and more often, Signora Elvira's husband was contriving to be around when our therapy sessions ended. He would appear in the hallway smiling nervously like an expectant father and never failed to ask me how things were going.

My wife reflected. "Not a menacing dog," she said. "Not a Kenny." She hesitated. "Maybe one of those bouncy, friendly things that don't know what to do with their energy and always try to put their snouts in your crotch."

"So he has made a pass at you!"

"No!" she shook her head. "You know I didn't mean that." Very unusually, she smiled.

Having now guessed the Fanna family's unhappy secret, my problem—but it was also an interesting challenge as a therapist—was how to play it to everyone's advantage, my own included.

"Why do you think Eleonora's so fixated with these situations where people abuse dogs sexually?" Signora Elvira demanded. "You're a bit slow for an analyst, aren't you?"

As it turned out, my lover was now involved in a campaign to ban Web sites that showed men having sex with animals.

I sighed and smiled. If she wanted to bring it out in the open she would have to say it herself.

"We had such a great love life," Signora Elvira sighed, "Gianni and I, and then of course it all ended very suddenly. I was bedridden for more than a year. And Eleonora had just turned twelve."

I listened. It was up to her.

"The fact is, he still dotes on me. It's as if he's afraid that if he has sex with anyone else he'll lose me."

I nodded.

"I'm always telling him to find a pretty young PA who knows the ropes. Then what does he do? He employs someone like your wife and invites her here *with her husband*!"

So often the best policy for a therapist is simply to nod sympathetically.

"I wish I could help him, but I can't," she wailed. She cast around. It was as if she was furious that I wouldn't tell her what she needed to tell me. "If only Eleonora would find a man who would take her away. But she deliberately chooses people who can't or won't marry, or if they will she chases them off by giving them some impossible dog to look after."

Did she know about us? How similar to her father was I?

"What's the solution?" she asked. "Gianni is dying of guilt without really being guilty," she added.

"Nobody dies of guilt," I told her. Actually, of the three of them I had the distinct impression that only Signora Elvira was suffering. The others were troubled only in so far as she was unhappy. That week Eleonora was interviewed on the radio about her campaign: "It's incredible," she said, "the lengths the Church goes to to stop people using contraceptives and day-after pills, while doing nothing to prevent this monstrous abuse of dogs."

To me, out of the blue, she said, "The problem with Dad is he lives in the past. He always treats me like I am twelve years old. You know he doesn't even close the loo door when he pees?"

Her mother had already told me this.

At home, my wife had become friendly with Kenny, who now greeted her more enthusiastically than he did me. He even wagged his tail. She was buying him treats from the supermarket, a kindness she had once shown to me.

"It seems someone's given Eleonora the money to set up a dog refuge of her own," I told my wife a few months later. "She'll even have a place to live, over the shop, as it were. In Quinzano."

The small house was just out of town. I had had my eye on it for a while.

"But that's fantastic," she said. "Really fantastic. Signor Fanna will be so pleased. They've been dying for her to get out."

"I'm surprised he didn't tell you."

Having a heart to heart with Kenny after she had left for work, I told him, "Kenny, mate, you and I are now approaching what, with my clients or lovers, I always call the tangling point."

The dog growled, tugging on a rubber bone I was holding; I yanked one way and he yanked the other. As any dog lover knows, it's a game that can go on for quite a while.

"What I mean, Kenny, is the point where it will be impossible to tell the story of your life without telling the story of mine. And vice versa of course. Impossible to talk about Dr. Clarke without mentioning Kenny."

Since I refused to let him win, the dog suddenly let go of the bone and barked fiercely. At which I actually fell off my chair. I couldn't believe it. I came crashing off my chair and cracked my head on the bottom shelf of the bookcase. It hurt like hell, a really sharp crack on the temple. Yet as I came to my senses I found I was laughing. Crumpled on the floor, my legs caught in the chair, I was laughing and sobbing together. It was strange. I was overcome with an emotion I still can't begin to explain. Meantime, slobbery, red mouth and stinking breath only inches from my face, the dog was barking and barking and barking, and in his excitement piss had begun to dribble out from his hindquarters onto our best rug. I lunged up, grabbed his head and pulled it down squealing and growling next to mine.

"Thanks, Kenny," I told him as the creature fought like mad to get loose. "Thank you so much."

# Steven Cramer

## LACKAWANNA

My brain had been swiped clean.
I couldn't love
songs I loved; friends came

nameless as mailmen.
A loaf of dough
forbidden to rise,

I'm slid into the hollow magnet.
Din of dozen arcade games, but louder.
The MRI finds no sign

of stroke; the EEG, no fried circuitry.
Short-Term Temporal Lobe Seizure.
I'm told: forget it.

Forget my state of forgetfulness …
Was *Dismal Harmony* my childhood
wildlife preserve?—near tracks

where *Lackawanna* means
two streams meet and divide
in the tongue of an obliterated tribe.

# *Housebreaking*

## SARAH FRISCH

*Nothing is lost, and all is won, by a right estimate of what is real.*
　　　　　—Mary Baker Eddy, *Science and Health with Key to the Scriptures*

Seamus lived in Wheaton, Maryland, in the last house on a quiet street that dead-ended at a county park. He'd bought the entire property, including a rental unit out back, at a decent price. This was after the housing market crashed but before people knew how bad it would get—back when he was still a practicing Christian Scientist, still had a job and a girlfriend he'd assumed he would marry. Now, two years later, he was single, faithless, and unemployed. The money his mother had loaned him for a down payment was starting to look more like a gift, as were the checks she'd been sending for the last year to help him cover the mortgage. His life was in disrepair, but for the first time in months he wasn't thinking about any of that: he was sitting out back on a warm spring day with a woman. Her name was Charity, and she was a stranger.

Earlier that afternoon Seamus had been weeding by the driveway, and she'd stopped to ask him if the cottage in the backyard was available to rent. It was already rented, but soon they were on his deck, talking and sharing a six-pack Charity had been carrying and that she confessed she'd planned on drinking alone.

She wore cutoffs and a backpack—a faded green thing cinched around her waist. She had yellow hair, dark eyes, and a broad, easy smile that made it seem as if she would be perfectly comfortable anywhere but was especially pleased to find herself there, with him. He wasn't a drinker, but in her presence he drank one beer and then another. By the third beer, he both wanted her desperately and suspected that no good could come of it—that to hunger for what you could touch was to invite disaster.

Charity lived in Arlington, with her ex-boyfriend and his aging mother. They'd been together ten years, she said, and the breakup was a rough one. She was trying to find a place as far away from them as possible but still on the Metro. "I just need to be out of that house," she said, offering Seamus the last beer.

He said he was already drunk.

"You're pretty tall for that," she said. "You must not drink a lot."

"I used to be a Christian Scientist." He regretted the words as soon they were out of his mouth. People mixed Christian Science up with Scientology, or said things like, Is that the religion where you don't believe in doctors?—as if he had refused to acknowledge doctors' very existence.

Charity said that she'd had a Christian Science friend in high school; the religion had always reminded her of Buddhism. Buddhism had always reminded Seamus of Christian Science, and he said so. "Only Christian Science is unrelentingly positive. The world's a harmonious place."

"I imagine that's a hard view to maintain," Charity said, "once you start looking around."

Yes, he said, it was.

Even after Seamus stopped taking care of his house, he had kept up the exterior for his tenants. Now, in the late-afternoon light, he could see how pretty the backyard looked: the little brick pathway that led to the blue and white cottage tucked back among the trees, beyond that the woods, shimmering green and gold in the late-afternoon sun.

"My ex's house has the gravitational pull of a black hole," Charity said. "I can't believe I'm still here."

"Congratulations," Seamus said. Then he asked her to stay for dinner.

For months Seamus's friends had been telling him he was depressed, and as soon as he stepped into his kitchen he saw what they meant: shades drawn, empty takeout boxes piled in the trash, the refrigerator looming in the dim light like a grimy white thumb. A year ago, he used to cook every night, but now all he could find was a package of ground beef rotting in the crisper and a can of pumpkin sitting inexplicably on the bottom shelf. In the freezer he located a month-old chicken and a stick of butter that he had bought one afternoon in a bout of hopefulness so brief that it had passed by the time he got home.

He defrosted the chicken in the microwave, sliced butter and stuffed it under the skin, and slid the whole thing into the oven to roast. When he turned around, Charity was standing so close behind him that he almost jumped. She had on her backpack. "I should leave."

"Don't."

"I'm kind of a mess right now. You don't need that."

"Don't tell me what I need," he said, surprised by how forceful he sounded. She looked surprised, too, but when he reached out and pulled her toward him, she grinned.

He almost cried when he saw her body. He was dizzy with longing and something that felt like fear. Afterward they lay in the dimming light of the room, her arm across his chest, her breathing slowing until he thought she was asleep. It occurred to him that for all those years when he'd believed there was no life in matter, he'd never had to contend with something that felt this good.

They lay in silence until her phone rang. She dug it out of her cutoffs and silenced it. "I don't want to go back to that hellhole," she said.

"Stay here till you find a place," Seamus heard himself say.

"I didn't mean it like that." She looked embarrassed, as if he had accused her of something.

"Everybody needs help."

"It seems like a bad idea," she said, quietly.

Seamus said he was trying to be more open to bad ideas.

When she accepted, it was with such obvious relief that he wished he'd offered the instant they'd met. Soon the smell of roast chicken filled the house, and they got dressed and returned to the kitchen, where they tore apart the bird and finished off the last of the beer, piling the bottles, sweaty with chicken fat, into the recycling.

On the couch after dinner, they talked about real estate. Seamus said he wasn't comfortable being a landlord because he didn't like living off somebody else's work. His tenants—Irene and Claudia, a lawyer and her ten-year-old daughter—were rarely at home, and he hated charging a single mom to rent a place she didn't use. He said that his mother was helping with the rest of the mortgage while he looked for work, and he'd begun to dread their weekly phone conversations because he found it so hard to admit, yet again, that he hadn't found a job. His mother would tell him what she always did: he was secure in the arms of unconditional Love; the Lord would provide. When her checks arrived in the mail, he put them immediately into envelopes so he didn't have to stare at the numbers, or her signature, or the Bible verses she always wrote in the memo lines.

His mother was a third grade teacher, and he knew that the money was most likely coming from her new husband, a Republican who owned rental property all over Honolulu. He didn't tell Charity about the husband.

"It's been humbling taking money from other people," he said.

Charity said she thought it was nice that he could admit that—that there was a time when Greg and his mother had provided for her, and she'd also found it humbling, especially because she'd been on her own for a few years by then.

She had her bare feet up on the coffee table. There was a streak of dirt on her calf that he hadn't noticed in bed. She told him she'd grown up in Bridgeport, Connecticut. Her mother had died when she was twelve. She'd gone to live with an aunt, then at fifteen moved to D.C., where she'd lived with her father for six months before he'd gotten a job as a construction worker overseas. A year later she met Greg at the restaurant where she waited tables. He was twenty-four at the time and had initially acted as both a boyfriend and mentor. He'd encouraged her to move in with him and his mother, pushed her to quit her job, to finish high school and then college.

They became her replacement family, she said. Sometimes they still made her feel like a child. "It wasn't until the last couple of years that I realized how overbearing he was. He was furious when I decided to go to business school, and even madder when I took the job in public relations."

"You work in PR?"

"It's an exclusive firm. We only take clients who can demonstrate a total absence of social conscience."

"That's not what I expected," he said, suddenly awkward. "I imagined you were a teacher or an artist."

"You're looking at Weekend Charity. Wait till you see me in a suit."

He asked why she'd chosen to work with her company, and she shrugged and said that she'd mostly taken the job to piss off Greg. "We do PR for the Chamber of Commerce, the biggest lobbying group against climate-change legislation. He can't stand that."

"He's an environmentalist?"

"He calls himself 'pro–Earth life.' He says either you're for humans living on the planet or you're against it."

She crossed her feet. Outside the sky was dark, a single light on in the cottage.

"Half our clients are scrapping the planet for parts," she said.

"That's terrible."

"But the people aren't all bad, and I enjoy a lot of the work. Plus it's not like there's anything else out there."

"Tell me about it," Seamus said.

Charity said she'd turned down only one project. Her boss had asked her to write a press release for Halliburton after the news broke that a group of its employees gang-raped a coworker and locked her in a shipping crate. "I said no way, and they gave it to another woman. Now she's a VP. She's so smug about it I could punch her in the face."

That night they slept together in his bed, the window cracked open, the smell of the woods carried in on the wind: dampness and new growth, the early spring. Seamus drifted off with Charity's head on his shoulder and woke sometime before dawn to find her sleeping heavily on her stomach, her arms out and back bare and pale in the gray light, the white sheet twisted around her waist as if she'd lashed herself to the bed.

HIS LAST JOB HAD BEEN in the tech department at a human-rights nonprofit in D.C. He was still a practicing Christian Scientist at the time, but even then he struggled to understand how so much suffering could exist in a world governed by a set of harmonious natural laws. He tried not to dwell on the stories his coworkers told, but sometimes he'd come home too upset to even pray. He would feel better only after going to church, or on the rare occasions his girlfriend convinced him to attend a Wednesday testimony meeting.

He'd been with the organization for a couple of years when his boss asked if he would go on a trip to Pakistan to document civilian deaths from U.S. drone attacks. The videographer had come down with shingles. Seamus had always assumed his first trip out of the country would be somewhere in Europe—visiting castles, staying in hostels, sleeping on trains. "I have some experience in video," he said.

"I don't know how much you'll be able to film," his boss said. "But given the area we think it's probably a good idea to have a man along."

Three days later Seamus found himself sitting in a row of blue vinyl airport seats on a layover in Doha, Qatar, a city he'd never heard of in a country he'd never heard of, his Bible and *Science and Health* stashed in his carry-on along with the Islamabad travel guide.

The woman he was traveling with was in her midfifties, with silver hair cut bluntly at the jaw, so straight it could have been ironed. Her name was Melinda. She had pale green eyes, translucent and eerily unyielding, the backs of them like the marbled walls of an antique swimming pool. She was a mother of three.

"They're around your age," she said. "My eldest is a lawyer. My middle son is a writer."

"It must be nice to have brothers."

"They're good support for each other."

He asked what her youngest son did.

"He's dead. He was murdered when he was fifteen."

"I'm sorry."

Melinda nodded, looking away.

A friend of Seamus's mother's had a three-year-old daughter who drowned in a river at a family reunion. Seamus remembered the woman weeping at their kitchen table, saying that losing your child was like being sliced and gutted, then made to walk around as if you were whole. His mother had taken the woman in her arms, but even then (he was only ten) he could see she didn't quite know what to do. He had watched the woman weep, wondering why his mother didn't say the things she always said when he cried: God was Love, they were all safe in His loving arms.

Melinda had bent down and was rummaging around in her carry-on. She pulled out what he thought would be a photo but turned out to be a map of Pakistan.

"This is where we're going," she said, running her finger along a region labeled *Federally Administered Tribal Areas*. "Did you do the reading?"

"I did," he said. She looked pleased and a little surprised, so he felt compelled to give her a full report. He told her how un-American the whole thing seemed: an intelligence agency killing hundreds of civilians in a noncombat zone of a country that was supposed to be an ally; the CIA director denying the existence of the program; the "double tap" policy of firing two missiles in the same spot, the second strike carefully timed to incinerate first responders—health-care workers, neighbors searching for children in their beds. Even the malicious and weirdly boyish names of the aircraft themselves—*Predator* and *Reaper drones*, the *Hellfire missiles* they carried—had unnerved him, as if the government could barely contain its glee at the prospect of murdering people by joystick.

"Seems pretty American to me," she said. "But I suppose you know that."

"There's knowing and there's *knowing*."

"That's why we're hoping for video."

Seamus made a point from one of the readings, that the civilian deaths and constant terror caused by hovering drones must be working against U.S. interests in the region.

"I hate that argument," Melinda said. "People have a right to life outside our political agenda."

He knew she was right. They passed the rest of the layover in silence.

IN ISLAMABAD THEY SPENT a few days getting ready. The sprawling flatness of the city surprised Seamus: its broad parkways and trees planted in rows, the scattering of high-rises downtown, like enormous outdated computer chips turned on their ends. Parts of the city seemed like shabbier and sweatier versions of Denver. He couldn't help feeling disappointed. On the streets people stared.

"They don't see a lot of Westerners?" he asked Melinda.

She laughed—the first time he'd heard her laugh. "Not a lot of guys your size around here."

She'd been crammed into an airplane seat next to him, but the idea of her thinking about his size felt oddly like a violation.

Melinda had arranged for them to travel illegally, with two Pakistani human-rights workers as their guides. On the second day Seamus and Melinda met the men in the hotel lobby. They were younger than Seamus expected, in their late twenties. They clearly considered Seamus the leader of the trip and directed most of their conversation to him, even after he announced that Melinda was in charge. Melinda seemed unsurprised by this state of affairs. She watched quietly as they spoke. Every now and then she asked a question that never would have occurred to Seamus. (Will we be allowed to film? *Not always*. How can we interview women if our translator is a man? *You can't*.)

The men dispensed a lot of advice: Say you're British, not American; Don't play the radio in the car; If you see a woman, turn your eyes away, and whatever you do, never touch a woman, not even to shake hands; The same man who is your enemy and intends to redress a wrong by shooting you dead is honor-bound to protect you when you set foot in his home, even at risk of harm to his family.

One of the men began explaining how to handle expensive camera equipment in such an impoverished area, and then stopped, saying to Seamus, "But you must be experienced filming in these kind of conditions." Seamus couldn't bring himself to correct him.

Later Melinda and Seamus went shopping for supplies at Jinnah Super—a two-story, open-air structure with rows of tiny stores—then stopped for a burger and fries at a food stall. While they ate, Melinda told him about women's rights in the tribal areas: honor killings, men throwing acid on young girls' faces whom they suspected of learning to read.

She had once documented an honor killing in Jordan involving a young woman whose aunts had escorted her into an open field so her little brother could shoot her in the back of the head. "The family seemed quite proud," she said.

Seamus imagined the aunts walking one on either side of the girl, stepping silently away as the boy appeared from behind.

Melinda finished off her burger and started on the fries. "It's hard to separate it all out. I'll have to remind myself we're there for the drones."

Seamus's left foot had been itching since he got off the plane, and now it ached. He leaned over and removed his hiking boot. A small red recess the size of a dime had appeared on the arch of his foot. He pressed it with his thumb, and pain rippled up his ankle.

"What's that?" Melinda asked, her green eyes on his face.

"I don't know."

"It's probably the boot."

Seamus recognized in her voice a judicial finality. Exonerated: the country, the city, the climate. At fault: Seamus—for having worn hiking boots to a city that (as she had said twice since they arrived) was one of the most cosmopolitan in South Asia.

Neither of them mentioned the foot again, and the rest of the day he limped along behind her, trying to ignore the pain. Back in the hotel room that evening, he stripped off his sock and found the infection had eaten away at his flesh; the hole in his arch was hot and red and almost twice the size it had been earlier that afternoon.

He got out his books and opened *Science and Health* to one of his favorite quotes—"Divine Love always has met and always will meet every human need." He had once believed that the material world was a dream, his own sensations and experiences shadow puppets on a curtain: projections of that infinite unknowable space where all broken things were in fact whole, where the world existed as it always had and always would, in love and infinite unity. Back then he could live in the dream, even enjoy the dream, but he knew that what he saw was not real, and he should work to recognize the harmony and perfection of all things. When he was sick or injured he prayed to know that he was healthy and whole, and then sooner or later he would become healthy and whole again.

He put down the book and lay back, closing his eyes. The pain in his foot was hot and frightening—a much bigger pain than he would have expected from a small crevice of inflamed skin. It disoriented him, as did the tiny, dank hotel room, and the knowledge that he was halfway across the world from home, his only companion a woman he hardly knew. He thought if he took a painkiller he might be able to pray without distraction, but he didn't have one and didn't want to bother Melinda. He turned out the light and lay a long time staring into the shadows. Soon the day's final call to prayer sounded over the tinny loudspeaker. While thousands of people washed their faces and forearms and feet and pulled out their mats, Seamus closed his eyes and tried to sleep.

The next morning he couldn't stand on his foot.

Later he wondered what would have happened if he hadn't agreed to let Melinda take him to the doctor. Maybe he would have been able to heal himself through prayer, as he'd been able to a number of times before, or maybe the foot would have gotten worse and he would have flown back home—back to his job and girlfriend and state of mild but workable confusion about the nature of the world and his place in it. Instead he found himself standing outside a large house, near the foothills on the edge of the city.

The doctor was a friend of Melinda's, a middle-aged Dutch expat. "You're a lucky man," he told Seamus. "I know people who'd pay good money to travel with this lady."

They followed him upstairs, past a servant on the landing, and entered a room that reminded Seamus of an ad in a magazine—a study with a leather couch, French doors, a balcony that looked out over a sparkling pool, and beyond that, the green rolling hills north of the city. The doctor sat Seamus down on the couch and gently lifted his bare foot into his lap, walking a pair of plump dry fingers along the arch.

"Is it infected?"

"No. Just the worst case of athlete's foot I've ever seen."

Melinda stood looking out over the balcony, her shoulders squared and prosaic beside the French doors. Seamus examined her back for signs of laughter.

"A topical cream and an oral antifungal should take care of it," the doctor said.

Afterward, a servant brought them tea around a small table, and the doctor and Melinda talked about their years working at an NGO together in Bangladesh. Eventually Melinda said, "We better get to the pharmacy before it closes."

Seamus had taken medication only once—antibiotics when he was a child, which he took for a chest cough that turned out to be pneumonia—and only after his mother realized that her overwhelming fear had prevented the infection from healing. Now, back in the tiny hotel room, he took out his texts and copied down a couple of his favorite lines:

*God changeth not and causeth no evil, disease, nor death;*

*That I may dwell in the house of the Lord all the days of my life, to behold the beauty of the Lord, and to inquire in His temple.*

The air conditioner sputtered beside him, pumping damp air into the room. He could hear the TV in Melinda's room next door and a bus idling heavily in the street below. He stared at the words on the page. Then he took the medicine. By the time he woke up the next morning his foot had already started to heal.

---

SUNDAY MORNING SEAMUS WOKE to find Charity sitting on the edge of the bed. "I'm running over to Virginia to pick up some work clothes," she said. "I'll be back this afternoon—unless Greg chains me to a radiator."

Seamus asked if she'd like him to go with her, and she shook her head. She was joking; she really wasn't worried. Greg was like a child; she could always stick him in a time-out if he got out of hand. As soon as she was gone, it occurred to Seamus that she might be making her escape, and he had no way to reach her; he didn't even know her last name. Still he went about his day as if he'd be seeing her in a few hours. He spent most of the morning cleaning the house, and in the afternoon he shopped for groceries, buying meat and vegetables and vodka and tonic because Charity had mentioned it was her drink—feeling sheepish and giddy at the checkout as he watched the bottles shuttle down the belt to the register.

Charity arrived at six, wearing an old sweatshirt of his that he hadn't realized she'd taken. She was carrying a large duffle.

"You're back," he said.

He must have sounded surprised because she laughed. "It looks great in here."

He put the steaks on the grill out back and came in to start on the salad. She made them both drinks and leaned on the counter, watching while he worked.

"You're a bear of a man," she said. "Do you love women?"

He'd been drinking too fast and he was sweating. He said he was raised to love everybody.

"Good. Because from what I can tell when a guy says he loves women, he just means he likes cunnilingus and feeling in control."

"Sheesh," he said, embarrassed for them both.

They stayed talking at the table long after dinner. Seamus asked about her ex-boyfriend, trying to keep his tone casual.

"It just took me a while to realize our relationship was dead," she said, "and even longer to move out. He's not an easy person. He manages a Verizon store, but he makes his real money breaking into houses. He doesn't believe in government or owning things. He says the laws are designed by people with power to protect their power. We used to fight about it. Where I come from people work hard for their shit and you're supposed to respect that. I told him stealing stuff out of a house was a violation of a person's intimate space. By then I was getting my MBA, and he said he was offended that me and my vagina were so overly privileged that we were equating taking people's property with rape." She frowned. "As if I had said that—as if not being raped is a fucking privilege."

Seamus, not knowing what to say, made them each another drink.

"In the end I managed to find a place, but on the day before I was going to sign the lease his mother broke her hip. Greg's gone a lot at night and the old lady couldn't stay home alone—and he begged me to stay around and help. So I did. I waited on her hand and foot. Then a week ago I came home early from work and caught her downstairs with her potter's wheel strapped to a dolly, dragging it across the living room." She quickly added, "It was a portable potter's wheel. God knows how she got it on the dolly. Even the portable ones weigh like fifty pounds."

"With her broken hip?"

"They faked it to keep me there. I'm telling you, that house is unhealthy."

Seamus got drunker and drunker as the evening progressed. Charity was drinking, too, but showed no signs besides two patches of pink that appeared on her cheekbones. It was as if she belonged to some other, more resilient species. At midnight he tried to do the dishes. Charity sat on the floor by the stove, hugging her knees to her chest. "Why'd the woman cross the road?" she said.

"Why?" Seamus was having trouble understanding where his wrists ended and his hands began.

"The road? Who let that bitch out of the shipping crate?"

"That's a hideous joke," he said, and she said, yes, it was. Then she said, "You know what Greg told me this morning when I went to get my clothes? He said he'd shoot himself if I left. My mom shot herself. He knows that."

The Seamus who couldn't find his hands found his anger. He came over and squatted beside her. "That asshole," he said, pulling her into his arms, her hair against his face, filled with desire and sadness and the smell of liquor on her, his body no longer struggling against his mind but taking orders from somewhere deep inside.

"It's not about me. I can see that now," she said. "All these years and I was just a foot soldier in his crusade against the world."

---

AFTER FOUR DAYS IN ISLAMABAD, Melinda, Seamus, and the human-rights workers piled into a car and went west, stopping near Peshawar to buy a burqa from a kiosk by the side of the road, and again to pick up their translator, a talkative man in a leather jacket who was soon telling them about how he would have been a doctor if the money wasn't so good in translating. The five of them spent the next couple of weeks together, traveling around the high, dusty mountains in Waziristan, staying with the families and friends of the guides, learning about the damage done by American drones and the Pakistani military. Seamus had imagined he would be out in the streets, filming strangers while they answered Melinda's questions, but now he saw how impossible that would have been. People stayed out of the streets because of the drones, and every time Seamus's party left one house it was to travel to another. The houses themselves were like fortresses, with high walls and towers lined with tiny square windows for rifles. Everywhere they went Seamus was treated as Melinda's superior. During one conversation, their host, a local chief and uncle to one of the guides, dispatched Melinda to the women's quarters to be entertained by his wife. But for the most part, men listened politely while Melinda's questions were translated, then turned to Seamus to give their answers. Seamus sometimes glanced at Melinda for a reaction, but she always looked attentively phlegmatic, giving nothing away.

Melinda wore a head scarf inside the homes, but on the road she was in full burqa, which seemed to make her more silent than usual, so that Seamus sometimes felt as if he were riding beside a bird in a cage that somebody had thrown a sheet over. He was relieved not to have to watch her watching him while he chatted with the other men, but he was also ashamed of that relief. He was always grateful to escape when the car stopped—to be away from her silence and the blue mesh of her veil, to stretch his cramped legs and spit the dust from his mouth. The men would go off in search of directions or food—one of them always staying behind, leaning against the car with the rifle while he talked to Seamus—but Melinda rarely left the back seat, a blue tent of a figure that could have been anyone.

They saw their first casualties in Miranshah, where the group toured a hospital room packed tight with cots of wounded men and children. Seamus had been given permission to film, and he walked around the room with the camera, grateful because he couldn't imagine what else to do with his hands and eyes. He filmed a man who had watched his wife die with their child in her arms, another who had lost both legs. He filmed child after child, covered in bandages, unconscious in their cots or staring into his camera with wide impassive eyes.

Afterward they found a man who identified himself as a Pashtun freedom fighter and agreed to be filmed if he could wear a scarf over his face. The translator stood at Seamus's elbow, speaking into the camera: "They murder us down to the youngest child. If they see Pashtun in a Toyota car they call them Taliban or spy. They call airstrikes onto the vehicle with innocent people in it." By "they" he meant the American and Punjabi devils.

Seamus felt the first twinges of a headache right after they had left the hospital, and it built throughout the afternoon. By evening it was jackhammering at his left eye, and his stomach rolled in his gut. Back at the house where they were staying, he threw up in a bucket and lay down on his mattress. He tried to say a few words of prayer but couldn't make sense of them, as if he were reciting a song in a language he had forgotten. He drifted off into a half-sleep and dreamt briefly that he was in the hollowed-out bone of a dead thing, where a shape he couldn't identify moved in the shadows. He had a word to describe the shape, but even dreaming he didn't know what the word meant, and when he awoke it was gone. The human-rights workers were sitting on the bed next to his, speaking in Pashto. Soon they got up and left. He dozed off again. The next time he woke up, he found Melinda sitting on the edge of his bed, holding a glass of water.

"You're not supposed to be in here," he said.

She shrugged. "I thought maybe you hadn't been drinking enough," she said coolly. "It could be altitude sickness."

He sat up and took the glass from her. "Thanks. I'll be okay."

She was watching him, and he could tell something was bothering her. After what felt like three full minutes of silence she asked, "Did you notice how few women were in that hospital today?" He nodded. "I asked one of the guides about it. He said it was becoming difficult to find female doctors to work in the region, and many female patients didn't come in because it was shameful for them to be touched by male doctors. He used that word," she said. "Shameful."

"But what if they're dying?"

"Seamus, have you ever thought about why two guys with Kalashnikovs offered to show us around Waziristan?"

"Are you saying they're not human-rights workers?"

"I'm not sure it's that simple."

The ever-present film of dust was thicker now, coating his teeth and tongue. "If we can't really know," he said, "then what's all this for?"

She stared at him, her expression unreadable. "You seem really shook up."

His ears burned, and he put the glass to his mouth and drank.

ON THEIR LAST DAY they visited a town where they had heard there'd been a number of civilian casualties. They were spending the afternoon with a family—cousins of one of the guides—and to avoid attracting attention to their visit, they parked the car a ways from the house. The day was cold, the sky a wide, hollow blue over snow-covered peaks, the streets empty except for a couple of men with rifles who turned their faces away as soon as Melinda came into sight. Seamus shivered under his heavy fleece. The translator pointed to the sky where two black dots hovered a few miles off.

"Smile," Melinda said. "Some guy in Nevada's deciding whether or not to blow your face off."

Soon they had turned a corner, but they could still see the drones and hear the humming.

"That's a sinister sound," he said.

Melinda said he might as well get used to it: "Anything you can to do somebody can be done to you."

The interview was with a father and son who gave Seamus permission to film the conversation. Melinda sipped tea, awkwardly holding the veil up with one hand. Every once in a while she interjected with a question, but mostly the men talked. Behind the video camera Seamus felt useful and strangely detached. A small group of kids gathered at his knees to stare at the machine, scattering when he moved and reconfiguring a few feet away, like minnows at low tide. At some point the men sent the children out and began talking about the latest attacks: a drone had killed ten people at a market, and then dozens more of the victims' relatives, neighbors, and friends later that same day at the funeral. They had lost two adult family members, including an uncle who was a tribal elder and supported the family, and three children. Seventy-three people were killed in all, twelve of them children. Their neighbor's wife had her nose blown right off her face.

When the interview was over, Melinda came over to Seamus and leaned in so close that he could feel her breath on his neck. "Let's get the hell out of here," she said. He looked down at her drawn face and, in a brief flash of vindication, thought, I'm not the only one who's shook up. But then he remembered her murdered son, remembered his mother's friend with the drowned child, and was ashamed.

On the way back to the car, the street was deserted, the wind kicking up dust around them. The guides and translator trailed behind; they seemed to be arguing about something. Melinda walked beside him in full burqa.

"Isn't it odd?" he said. "I mean, if a drone can read a license plate on a car from miles away, how did somebody make the mistake of hitting a funeral full of civilians?"

"Who said it was a mistake?" said Melinda sharply. Then she broke into a jog, lifting the burqa to her knees, exposing her khakis and tennis shoes. Seamus began to run also and in a second he was behind her. Together they jogged through the empty street, past the mud houses shuttered against the world. They were almost at the car when they came around a corner and found a small boy standing in the middle of the street, weeping. At his feet lay the body of a man facedown in the dirt; the back of his shirt was soaked in blood.

The interpreter appeared behind them and politely, as if he were directing them to watch for a step, said, "Please run."

"Get video," Melinda shouted, reaching over and slapping Seamus's hand, a hard, stinging slap—later he would think her hand must have slipped. He pulled the camera from his fleece and pressed record, but the guides had rounded the corner behind them and were pressing them forward with the heft of a small crowd, saying, "Hurry now, it's not safe here." Soon Seamus was running again, the camera in his hand, his breath and footsteps in his ears.

Back in D.C. he watched the footage and discovered the camera hadn't recorded sound. The boy appeared briefly onscreen—a silent flash of his figure, a small face broken with grief—followed by bumping brown hillsides, ground and sky, the high, white mountains on the horizon. Seamus was at his desk, ignoring an inbox stuffed with e-mails about hard drives and software installation. When the video was over, he went online and watched another video—Pakistani soldiers lining up Pashtun men and shooting them in the chest. On the low-quality video it looked clean, almost choreographed—the men in long shirts, standing with their shoulders touching, then dropping into the high, shifting grass. After that he found that he was done for the day, and when he got home he knew he was done for good—that he'd arrived at a jagged slab of stone at the edge of the world, with no ground ahead. He called his boss and left a message on his voice mail saying he quit.

"I lost my faith over athlete's foot," he told his girlfriend. She said he was being reductive and flip and she couldn't help him if he didn't tell her the truth. A few months later they broke up. He stopped leaving the house. His friends from church tried to support him, e-mailing him articles from the *Sentinel* on peace and spiritual thinking, stopping by Sunday mornings to offer him a ride. But after a while they seemed to sense his restlessness with their presence, or grew tired of his refusal to go to church or to share what he was thinking or feeling. He saw less and less of them, his days turning so gray and ill defined he could find no language to describe them.

---

CHARITY MOVED IN, using his towels, eating his food, riding the Metro into the city to work and in the evenings meeting him out at restaurants and bars, or returning home to the dinner he'd cooked, eating out on the back deck as the evenings grew warmer, the late-evening light fading into the trees. At one point she said she should start looking at apartment listings again, and he said, "Please don't," and they decided—quickly and together—that she should live there. She said she could pay something toward his mortgage. He said he wasn't charging her to sleep in his bed, but in the end she convinced him to let her pay. She wrote the first check on the month anniversary of their meeting and left it on the kitchen counter by the coffee pot. It was four hundred dollars over the amount they'd agreed on, and it embarrassed him so badly he had to leave the house and walk around the block. Back home he found Charity in a deck chair, taking apart the Sunday paper in her lap.

"Your check was too much."

"I hate money."

He said he felt emasculated and she said to get over it; he was living off charity now.

"What?"

"I wanted to make the joke before you did."

"I wasn't going to make that joke."

She wrote him a new check for the correct amount.

A few weeks later they drove to Arlington to pick up Charity's things. It was early evening. The rush-hour traffic was slow through the city and stopped altogether on the bridge. Charity sat in the passenger seat, snapping the door handle as if she might jump out at any moment.

"Stop," Seamus said.

"Sorry. I'm just not looking forward to dealing with Greg."

Then, as if saying his name had rattled something loose inside, she starting listing off details about her ex: he didn't drink milk because it was a quarter pus; at one time he had owned a pet ferret but abandoned it outside animal control because the smell bothered his mother; he talked constantly about climate change and had once woken Charity in the middle of the night to tell her humans were causing the end of the eleven-thousand-year-old environmentally stable Holocene epoch, and that Earth's climate had already crossed three of the nine thresholds between now and a planet that couldn't sustain widespread human civilization.

"They're like the nine rings of hell," he said, "except interlocking, so that you don't know when the whole chain will come clattering down."

She said she didn't want to discuss climate change right then, and he accused her of reckless "blindering," which she didn't think was a word. He said she'd see what he meant in a couple of decades—when the superrich bought up what was left of the inhabitable land while everyone else died of extreme weather, starvation, war, and disease.

She told Seamus how, for her birthday, Greg had driven her to an alley in Georgetown in the night, where he had scaled a fence, opened a gate for her, and led her through a backyard to a fancy old house. She was thinking there must be some kind of surprise party when he kicked down the back door. "I was stunned," she said. "I just followed him around the house while he bagged things—you know, emptied out the woman's jewelry box. I was scared we'd get caught and pissed at Greg for putting me in that situation. I kept asking him about the alarm—what if we'd triggered a silent alarm? Later I found out he had a friend at the company."

"He wanted to scare you?"

"Yeah, but I wasn't that scared," she said. "It was weird, I didn't feel that bad, either. It was this huge, spotless house and it felt good watching him fuck it up. You know they had someone waiting on them, cleaning their house every day, doing their laundry, managing their money, making their food. You know nobody in that house was working the night shift while her seven-year-old put herself to bed. And you know what? Their money's probably just as dirty as Greg's. Maybe legal, but dirty. There's a lot of that in this city. I see it all the time. If you've got enough money, you just rig the system so you don't have to break any laws."

Seamus said that watching people screw each other to get rich made it hard for him to believe in a loving, all-powerful God. "Either there's a powerful God who doesn't love us," he said, "or a loving God who has no control."

"Or no God."

"Right," said Seamus. "Or that."

Greg lived in a two-story house with a porch swing and eaves and flowering bushes around the windows. It was not what Seamus had pictured.

"There's not much to carry," Charity said. "I put most of my stuff in storage." Then she asked Seamus to wait in the car. He watched her walk up the front steps, take out a key, and let herself into the house, then he put his seat back and closed his eyes. The night was warm and still, the smell of magnolia drifting through the car window.

"Hey," somebody said near his left ear. He opened his eyes and found a face a few inches from his own. His first impression was that a puppet had popped up over the edge of the car door, all curly black beard and hair and a round, pale face.

"Are you the guy my wife's leaving me for?" Greg said. Under all the hair he looked young and slight, his slender wrists resting on the door, crossed like the paws of a cat. "She didn't tell you? Of course she didn't tell you."

"You're Greg?"

"Welcome to my world," Greg said. Seamus could smell dinner on his breath, beef and onions. "How tall are you?"

"Six five."

"What do you do for a living?"

"I'm unemployed."

Greg snorted. "Go figure. She's always looking for a big fucking project."

The screen door banged and Charity came out of the house, a trash bag in each hand. Seamus pushed the car door open, forcing Greg to step back. He walked over to Charity and took the bags from her. "You okay?" he said. She nodded, her face tight. He put the bags in the trunk, trying hard not to feel as if he'd stumbled onto the set of somebody else's life—somebody else's *marriage*.

Greg followed Charity around to her side of the car, but she climbed in, locking the door. Seamus got in, too, and started the car, but Greg ran back around to the driver's side and stuck his head in the window. "Hold on," he said, sounding so miserable that Seamus was tempted to turn off the ignition and say, Let's talk about this. It's hard but it doesn't have to be this hard. But Charity had grabbed Seamus and was digging her fingers into his elbow. He put the car in neutral and let it roll. Greg jumped back, and Seamus slid into gear.

They drove in silence until they reached the dark, empty parkway. "I'm sorry about that," Charity said. "We were common-law. I divorced him a year ago and he knows it."

"What does divorcing a common-law involve?"

"Nothing," she said. "We don't have any shared assets." Then she started to cry.

---

AS THE WEATHER GREW WARMER, they took weekend trips—hiking in the Jefferson National Forest, fishing off a rented canoe in northwestern Maryland—or walked through the woods behind the house, down to the botanical gardens. Sometimes they stopped to watch the kids on the carousel or bought tickets for the miniature train and piled in alongside the families.

During the week, Charity left early and worked late, and Seamus spent much of his day at home alone. He found himself thinking of Greg, replaying their conversation, remembering how young he looked, as if he'd been preserved by some particular rancor that flowed through the veins of people who had always known exactly what to believe and acted accordingly. Seamus was sickened by the idea of Greg and Charity as a couple, although he couldn't imagine them together at anything but a great distance—a set of small, gray figures on a barren landscape, moving far beyond his reach. When Seamus wasn't feeling panicked or jealous, he lost hours on the Internet researching topics in which he had only a peripheral interest—the latest version of the firefighter exam or details on becoming a forensic accountant—or watching old sitcoms: *Family Ties*, *Mork & Mindy*. Sometimes he got back in bed as soon as Charity left the house and spent the day sleeping, masturbating, and sleeping again, waking midafternoon when the sun hit the bedroom windows, worn out and ashamed. It was a beautiful thing, his life with Charity, but he found he had difficulty believing it was real unless she was right there beside him.

"Stand porter at the door of thought," his mother said. She meant, Changing your thinking will change your experience of the world. But he couldn't. His inertia, his *unemployment*, seemed to leak into everything, and he wondered why Charity hadn't grow tired of him yet. One evening, walking through the woods behind his house with Charity, he asked, "Am I your project?"

"Why would you say that? Do I act like I'm trying to change you?"

"No, but you haven't known me that long. What happens when you find out how depressed I am about the world?"

"The world's a fucked-up place. I can't imagine being with somebody who wasn't at least slightly depressed by it."

"Greg said I was your project."

She glanced over at him. "Why didn't you tell me?" No, she said, he wasn't her project—Greg just thought everyone had sketchy self-interested motives for what they did because that was all he could imagine. "*I* was *Greg's* project," she said.

There had been a brief thunderstorm earlier, and bits of pink sky showed through the treetops. A catbird clamored through the bushes, calling after them in a high, cranky voice. Seamus took Charity's hand.

He got worried sometimes, he said, because things seemed so good between them. In Christian Science, romantic love was supposed to bring you to divine love. "Wanting somebody this bad sets you up for trouble. You're not supposed to believe that anything beside God can make or break your happiness."

"You're not a Christian Scientist anymore," she said, her eyes on the path. She looked a little sad.

He started telling her about his trip to Pakistan, about Melinda and the guides and the hospitals—the kid he saw crying in the road over the body. He said he should have helped him: when you come across something like that, you're responsible for helping, not because you're an adult or a human-rights worker or an American, but because you—a sentient creature—happen to be there.

He expected her to say something reassuring, something about how he'd done his best in that moment, but instead she said, "I see what you mean."

He dropped her hand, picked up a stick, and swung it at a bush. He felt disgusted at himself and childishly angry; but it seemed unfair, almost sadistic, the way situations appeared out of nowhere and demanded your immediate response, then afterward provided no way of changing what you did or didn't do. "We're terrorizing families, killing old people and little kids, thousands of civilians. It's evil."

"Christian Scientists don't believe in evil, right?"

He swatted another bush, then examined the end of the stick, where an animal had chewed off the bark. Evil in Christian Science was the absence of good, he said, as darkness is the absence of light.

"My mom shot herself in a dumpster," Charity said. "Out back of the restaurant she managed. I think she was trying to be considerate, not wanting to leave a mess." She said, "Everybody's got that broken-off thing inside them, Seamus. At some point you just learn to live with it."

HE BOUGHT A PORTABLE RADIO and carried it with him all over the house, then outside to Irene's cottage, where he was doing repairs. He moved through the details of his tenants' life—a pair of child's pajamas with cows and stars, legal briefs in a pile on the kitchen floor—and listened to the news. Soldiers shot people at checkpoints; mudslides devoured towns; rebels and drug traffickers and governments tortured and killed civilians. One morning he heard a scientist talk about climate change and the planet in the decades to come: droughts, hurricanes, floods, wildfires; cities consumed by oceans and deserts. There was hope, she said. Humans already had the technology necessary to meet the world's energy needs. "At this point it's purely a political problem," she said—and Seamus saw Greg's face and felt a stab of jealousy. How unbearable it was that this thieving slip of a man, with his politics and opinions and romantic history, might be right about everything.

IN THE LATE AFTERNOONS Seamus would start making dinner, and by the time Charity arrived home from work, by the time he'd glimpsed her glossy head in the front hall, he was jittery with anticipation—would walk out, his hands covered in fat or flour or oil, to watch her as she shed her shoes and pantyhose and jacket in a little pile at the bottom of the stairs. One night she came in and stripped all the way down to her underwear. She had the expression of somebody who might punch the next person who asked something of her.

"Is everything all right?"

"Get me out of these clown clothes." She said she'd had a bad day but didn't want to rehash it. "Petty shit."

"Tell me."

She stood there in her underwear, staring at him. Then she said, "Some asshole's been bugging me at work."

Who? Seamus wanted to know. And what did she mean by bugging?

It was just somebody's stupid assistant. He'd been leaving her notes, hanging around her office, asking her out—nothing she couldn't handle. Seamus was about to ask her another question, but she shook her head in a gesture that seemed so exhausted and miserable that he put his arms around her instead. She rested her head on his chest. Then she lifted her face to him and said, "Take your pants off, please. I'd like to have an all-consuming sexual encounter."

Later that night he made her promise to tell him if the guy kept it up. "You can always call me from work," he said. "I'll come right down."

"I know."

The next week she was in Chicago for business. One afternoon he went out back in his pajama pants to water the flowers around the cottage. He was bending over to unfold a kink in the hose when he had the sudden sensation that he was being watched—not the metaphysical watching of a

Father-Mother God that he had experienced in his childhood, but a pair of human eyes on him, taking him in. He turned off the hose and checked all around the house; there was nothing. He decided the solitude must be getting to him. It occurred to him in a sort of daydream that if Charity had set up a hidden camera somewhere, if she'd seen the current state of his days, she'd have to leave; no self-respecting woman could do otherwise. He needed a job, any job.

He spent the last day of her absence cleaning the house and applying for jobs. When she came home he asked her if she'd set up a nanny cam. She laughed. "What kind of trouble did you get into while I was gone?" she asked.

"I'm scared that you'll see how depressing it is to be me without you."

Sunday evening he opened his inbox and discovered an offer for an interview. It was at the D.C. branch of a small aerospace company that manufactured plane parts and supplied some defense contractors. He called Charity over and showed her the e-mail.

She was in one of her odd, almost reckless moods that had begun appearing at the end of each weekend.

"I bet those valves are for drones. You're going to make drone valves for a living?"

"It's not entirely clear."

She was leaning on him, her elbow digging into his shoulder, breathing heavily near his ear.

"This is the world we live in," Seamus said. "If I'm going to be a part of it, I have to grow a pair."

She said he had beautiful balls, like gilded twin lapdogs guarding his asshole.

"Have you been drinking?"

"Yup."

He asked why she was drinking alone, and she said she was trying to forget that it was the start of the workweek. "It takes too much carbon to turn myself into work Charity. I'm so fucking sick of blow-drying my hair."

"I don't think anybody would mind if you stopped blow-drying your hair."

She climbed into his lap. "You're very sweet."

He could smell the alcohol on her breath. "Is it that guy, Charity? The one who was harassing you? Is that why you don't want to go to work?"

She leaned back, examining his face so carefully that he wondered if there was something on his nose. "No," she said. "Not that."

"What is it?"

"I told you I didn't want to do this shit forever," she said.

"Well, at this point I think a terrible job is better than no job. I'm doing the interview."

"You go on then," she said solemnly, as if he were announcing a birth or death.

---

A WEEK LATER Seamus was in a suit, riding the Metro into the city in the early afternoon. He found a seat in the corner, leaned his head back, and closed his eyes. The car was quiet except the hum of the wheels and the voice announcing the doors opening and closing. He was almost asleep when he felt a tap on his knee. A boy, maybe nine or ten years old, stood in front of him in a rubbery, forest-green raincoat that looked a couple of sizes too big for him. His hand was in front of him, and he was holding a fistful of paintbrushes, which stuck out of his fingers at angles, like twigs he'd scooped off the ground.

"You want to buy some brushes?" he said, staring at a spot just beyond Seamus's shoulder with eyes that looked as if they had a film of algae growing over them. "They're premium art-store quality."

Seamus wondered if the kid had been kidnapped by a criminal ring of some sort, and then, because it seemed like the least he could do, he took out his wallet.

"Three dollars," the boy said.

"All I have is a twenty."

"That's fine."

Seamus handed him a bill, and the boy took it with one hand and then opened his first.

They were, in fact, nice brushes, art-store quality. Seamus picked out a slender one with smooth, golden bristles. The boy dropped the remaining brushes in the pocket of his slicker and turned away.

"My change?"

"Sorry, man," the boy said with a shrug. "Can't change a twenty." He crossed the car and waited by the door, small and upright in the big green coat. Seamus watched him, feeling deflated, knowing he didn't have it in him to chase down a kid in a rain jacket and demand his seventeen bucks back.

The train stopped, and the boy hopped off. The doors slid closed behind him. Seamus watched as they pulled away from the station, the platform flickering to darkness. His own reflection appeared on the glass—a ghost Seamus staring back at him, woefully absurd in his suit and tie, like an oak tree dressed for dinner. He leaned his head against the window and allowed the knowledge he'd held at arm's length to settle over him—that this fantasy that he would somehow rejoin the capital's workforce, the industrial-military complex, was just that, an embarrassing fantasy.

As soon as he was above ground, he called to cancel the interview but kept landing in the wrong person's voice mail. He gave up and went inside. He couldn't bring himself to cancel at the front desk, where an older man, who smiled so sweetly that Seamus wondered if he'd mistook him for someone else, wrote down his name and directed him to a chair to wait. So Seamus waited in a small chair by a plant, growing more and more resentful as the minutes passed.

His interviewer, a middle-aged man in a suit, arrived half an hour past the scheduled time. Seamus followed him into an office and sat down on the far side of a large desk. He was feeling petulant in a way he hadn't experienced in years. If only they'd had their receptionist answer the phone, or fixed their shit phone tree, he wouldn't be there. Who thought it was a good idea to have computers answer phones anyways? What did the CIA do when it called to order more parts for their extrajudicial killing machines? Did they get the phone tree, too?

"Imagine an ideal day working for us," the man said. "What do you see yourself doing?"

"Say you get some bad press over all the kids your drones are killing," Seamus said.

The man interrupted to say they didn't manufacture drones, but Seamus couldn't have gotten off the ride if he'd wanted to: "I could design some animated Reaper drones for your splash page—some pretty little graphics of them taking out schools or ripping through family celebrations. We could set it all to an uplifting jingle."

The man sighed. "If you're here as a protester, I'm really not the guy to talk to."

For the first time, Seamus really looked at him. He was older, probably in his late sixties, with the broad, gray head of an aging mastiff. He looked exhausted, as if he'd interviewed dozens of ill-mannered applicants that day.

"I'm sorry," Seamus said. "I realized on the train over that I couldn't work for a weapons manufacturer. I didn't have the guts to cancel."

The man nodded wearily. "Sometimes things get the better of us. I understand."

Seamus said he was sorry again—and again—and then he got up and left as quickly as he could.

On the train home there was standing room only. He was sweating and uncomfortable in his suit, too miserable to be properly disgusted with himself about the interview. He just wanted to be home, curled up with Charity in bed. He anchored himself to a pole in the middle of the car and soon was wedged between another man—who could have been a congressman or a lobbyist if he hadn't been riding the Metro—and a cheerful-looking woman in a red sweater. A young couple occupied the seats below him, the girl, pregnant, resting her hands on her belly. They were arguing. "If you bring up Hitler again I'm going to scream," the girl said.

"But what's to say it won't happen again?" the boy said.

"Stalin killed twenty million people."

"Jesus, it's the Holocaust. The fucking *Holocaust*."

The woman in the red sweater turned to Seamus and told him in a hushed voice that still managed to sound cheerily informative that there was no point in having the quantity-versus-quality argument when the basic premises were flawed: Stalin killed six, not twenty, million people, but he was also responsible for the first ethnic killing campaigns in interwar Europe—something people always credited to Hitler.

Her perfume was strong and flowery; Seamus could almost taste it in his mouth. "Excuse me," he said, squeezing past her and pushing through the crowd to the nearest door, the one that divided the cars. It was locked. Panic swelled in his chest and he turned around, pushing back through the clot of people, the crowd of bodies and coats and suits and backpacks and bags, until he was at the exit doors. He stood there for minutes, bracing himself against the cool glass.

---

AN HOUR LATER he was above ground under the darkening sky. It was raining, and he walked home with the cars hissing through puddles beside him—past strip malls, Chinese and Eritrean restaurants, the park entrance, onto the dimly lit residential streets of his neighborhood. The rain was soaking through his clothes, and by the time he reached his house, he was wet and exhausted. He turned the key in the lock and swung the door inward. It connected with something on the other side. "Charity?" She was standing right behind the door, wearing her coat. She squinted as if he were slightly out of focus, her lips set in a tight line. "You okay?" he asked. She shook her head.

"I have a problem with Greg."

"Greg?"

She seemed to be vibrating, as if she were struggling to bring herself back to him. "How was your interview?" she asked.

"I'm not taking that job."

"Good," she said. "They subcontract with Halliburton. I looked it up." Then she said she had some business to take care of—she'd be back in a couple of hours. She tried to step around Seamus, but he blocked her. "Excuse me," she said. Her hand was behind her back and he reached out and unfolded her arm, bringing her fist around so the tool she held was exposed between them. It was his toilet auger, a grimy looking thing with a handle and a couple feet of coiled steel wire connected to a pole. The label read CRAFTY TITAN.

"Seamus," she said. "You don't understand."

He put his arms around her and pulled her toward him, the auger between them. "That thing's unsanitary."

She leaned her head against his chest, the smell of her hair filling his nostrils. "He's been stalking me at the office—leaving me nasty notes. I don't need this. You should be able to leave the past behind you, not track it into your new life on your shoes." She stepped back and looked up at him. "I swear I wasn't trying to lie to you, Seamus—I just didn't want to deal."

He didn't know what to say. He asked her what she was planning on doing with his toilet auger.

"There's some shit I need to unstick."

"That's not funny."

She shrugged. "It's kinda funny." Then she said she figured she could whip the shit out of the old lady's legs with the hanging bit. "It's the only way to get to him—through his mother. It used to be me or his mother. Now it's just her."

"I couldn't find a pipe," she said. She reached into her jacket, pulled out a photo, and handed it to Seamus. It was a picture of himself, wearing plaid pajama pants and a T-shirt, watering the flowers in the pots outside Claudia and Irene's cottage. Someone had written across his face in black marker, "Tell your parasitic landlord boyfriend he better watch his foie gras."

"It was on my desk at work," Charity said. Seamus stared at the photo. "See?" she said. "We can't let him get away with this. It'll only get worse."

"How does he know you're paying to live here?"

She shook her head. "He means parasite on society—as in the landlord class."

"But he's a burglar."

"Don't engage with his arguments."

"Aren't you engaging?"

"I'm not engaging, I'm escalating," she said. "I'm raising the stakes so high he can't afford to play."

He laughed a little, although he felt like he might cry. It was all wrong, he said, the photo, the break-ins, the idea of whipping an old lady to teach her son a lesson. Charity glared at the photo in his hands, looking grimly determined. He saw that his only shot at dissuading her was to go along and look for an opening.

"Wait for me," he said.

And after he had changed out of that awful suit and returned downstairs, he found her still there, waiting.

THEY DROVE ACROSS THE CITY, through the night traffic and onto the bridge, where they sat in more traffic. The Potomac was broad and black below them, the radio playing eighties hits and commercials for mattresses and blustering DJs laughing at their own ignorant jokes.

"All those months I waited on her hand and foot," Charity said. "You should have seen the way she talked to me." She was very still beside him, her face in shadow.

In Arlington they parked a block away from the house and sat in silence for a moment in the dark car. He was sick with dread and something else that it took him a second to identify as desire. He reached over and touched her face in the shadows. Her cheek was cold under his fingers, and she leaned in and pressed her mouth against his. It tasted of something bright and cold, as if she'd been running outside. "You don't have to do this for me," she said.

"I know."

They got out and walked toward the house, Charity carrying the toilet auger on her shoulder as if it were a bat. The ground was dry; the rain hadn't come this far south. At the corner of the yard she said, "I gave him back the key. We'll have to climb in. She leaves her window open, otherwise she overheats—like a pug."

He followed her through the yard to the porch, and then up one of the pillars, which was surprisingly easy to climb. He pulled himself onto the shingles and crouched next to Charity. He was about to say something about how ironic it was that they were breaking into a housebreaker's house—how it shouldn't be that easy—when she put a finger to her lips and pointed to a window.

---

HE FOUND HIMSELF STANDING in a warm little bedroom, decorated as if it were a Victorian-themed movie set: ornate wallpaper, a fireplace, a four-poster bed with a lace canopy, and a thick, oriental rug. A massive woman in a pink bathrobe sat on the edge of the bed. She was in her early sixties, with thin, reddish hair; a large, round face; and the smooth, poreless skin of a small child. Her pink terrycloth robe spread out across the bed in a mountainous landscape, falling open at her legs, exposing a pair of pale thighs. For a moment she looked surprised, but the expression quickly changed to cold amusement.

"I'm here because I won't be treated like this anymore, Mama," Charity said, twisting the auger in her hands. Her voice rose with the last word. Sweat beaded on her upper lip and she was breathing quickly, shifting her weight between feet. She didn't look like a woman who was going to whip the shit out of anyone. Seamus's gut sank.

"Show me what you got there, honey," Greg's mother said, articulating the words as if she were talking to a toddler. She put forward a plump hand.

Charity held out the tool in her hands and walked toward the bed. Greg's mother took the auger between a thumb and forefinger and dropped it onto the rug. Then she grabbed the girl's wrists and pulled her down to kneeling, pressing Charity's face into her lap, stroking her hair. Seamus saw

Charity's shoulders shaking. She was weeping in the woman's thighs. The woman raised her eyes to Seamus with a look of humorous tolerance, as if they were fond custodians and Charity their damaged little charge.

"It's okay, baby," she said. "Everything's going to be just fine." She was obscene, Seamus thought—her royal manner, the presumption of camaraderie when she met his eyes, her meaty hand on the girl's head. No, not the girl—Charity.

Charity lifted her face and said, "No, Mama, it's not okay."

And Seamus—who had finally arrived in a world where he was destined to witness but not understand—had to agree.

# Two Poems by Joshua Mehigan

## AT HOME

*"…very few are able to tell exactly what their houses cost."*
—Thoreau

This is my lawn. I planted it, I grew it,
and I work hard ensuring it's attractive.
I keep it clear of every type of pest.
I rake it and I mow it. I see to it
that no stray dogs stray here. It keeps me active.
God sends the sunshine, and I do the rest.

That is my fence, where I go lean to eavesdrop.
Outside of my own thoughts, I hear the quiet
of many smaller creatures barely moving.
In the fall, sometimes I can hear the leaves drop.
My land is mine. I have worked hard to buy it.
It's one thing I can always be improving.

In it, I find it's easier to find
the natural boundary of my heart and mind.

THE LIBRARY

We have all been there once. Some, more than that.
They forced us all to visit one September.
But that was such a long, long time ago.
There wasn't anything to marvel at.
The door was heavy. That I still remember.
Inside were many things I'll never know.

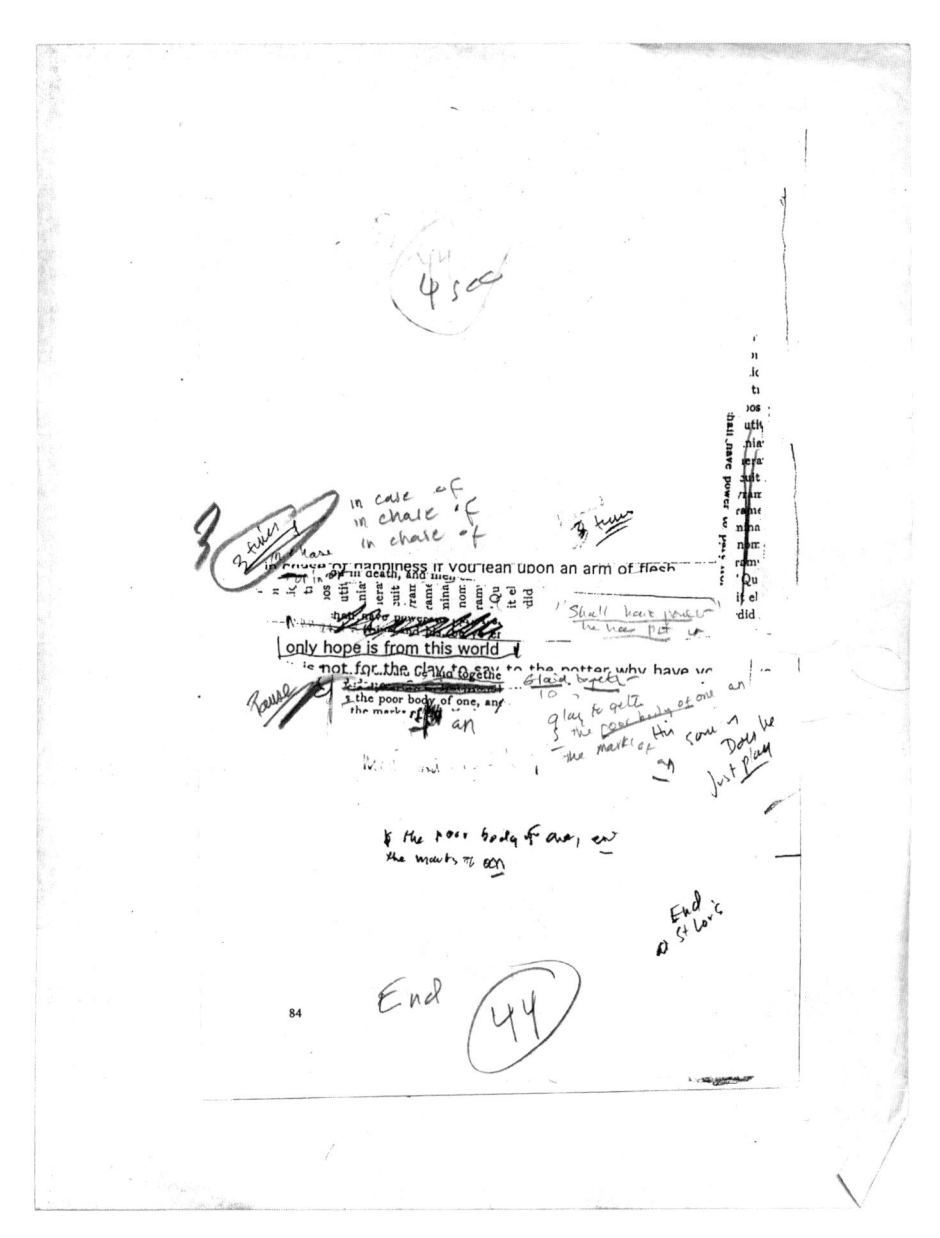

A manuscript page from *Frolic Architecture*. "What fuels the poems in the collection is the sense of epic breaking into shards."

## *The Art of Poetry No. 97*

# SUSAN HOWE

For the past four decades, Susan Howe's books have explored the word as shape, sound, and image. A haunter of archives, for whom manuscripts and marginalia and indexes are muses, she often works with the materials she finds there: among those mentioned in her 2011 Trilling Seminar at Columbia were scraps of a woman's dress, seventeenth-century diary entries on reused silk fans, and William Carlos Williams's poetic jottings on his prescription pad. The result may be a textual collage or a groundbreaking work of criticism, or both. Her *My Emily Dickinson* (1985, reissued 2007) remains a critical landmark. In the past decade, Howe has ventured into sound art and performance, collaborating with the musician David Grubbs.

Howe's work summons broad historical vistas, encompassing the violence and possibilities of the American frontier; the lost voices of Native

Americans; shunned, exiled, or captive colonial-era women; scorned preachers; the New England landscape; the Adirondack wilds; domestic intimacy; and the obscured brilliance of the linguist and philosopher Charles Sanders Peirce. She is, among other things, a serious war poet: World War II marked her earliest years—she and her mother and her sister, Fanny, traveling across a submarined Atlantic; her father absent while serving in Europe. The English Civil War (1642–51), King Philip's War (sometimes called the First Indian War, 1675–78), and the American Civil War also appear in her writing. Cities fascinate her as they did two writers she admires, William Carlos Williams and James Joyce: for her, key cities include Buffalo, Cambridge, Boston, Dublin.

As a poet, Howe has been most often associated with the experiments and rigors of the Language School, emergent in the 1970s. Yet her combination of formal invention and historical consciousness recalls modernists like Joyce, Williams, and the poet H.D. as much as her slightly younger contemporaries in the Language movement. She is less difficult than some of her admirers suggest. She occasionally flirts with the unreadable—with words crossed out or phrases collaged and typeset to interfere with one another—yet she is often quite direct. One senses that, for all her instinct for precision, Howe is impatient with confining definitions and descriptions. As she writes in *My Emily Dickinson*, "Define definition."

Most of her books contain several discrete works; her most recent, *That This*, includes a prose elegy for her recently deceased husband, the philosopher Peter Hare; a meditation on the eighteenth-century theologian Jonathan Edwards's family archives; and photograms by the artist James Welling. In her youth, Howe studied painting, and she is a visual as well as a verbal artist of the page. The page, not the line, is her unit.

Howe and I met three times this past winter and early spring in New York City for long conversations; she was living in New York for several months (leaving her home base of Guilford, Connecticut). We met in my office at NYU, a space not terribly conducive to reverie or rambunctious exchange. Yet Howe put up with the charmless environs and more than rose to the occasion, following up each session with e-mailed further thoughts and clarifications. Her many books were on my desk; we never opened them. The quality of Howe's attention is fierce yet friendly. She has a darting wit. Howe is in person both delicate and formidable; so, too, her work.

—*Maureen N. McLane*

INTERVIEWER

When did you start working on Emily Dickinson?

HOWE

Early in the seventies. Discovering Charles Olson's *Maximus Poems IV, V, VI* was crucial for the direction my work was taking at the time. He mapped the places I was familiar with—Gloucester, Boston Harbor. Olson showed me what I already knew by instinct, through being half-Irish—that spirit traces in local landscapes resound in particular words on paper.

At the same time, I was reading Richard Sewall's biography of Dickinson. I wanted to explore the cultural history of Western Massachusetts as a necessary part of her voice. My father and his sister Helen had both recently died. I read the Sewell aloud to Aunt Helen during the last week of her life, and she kept asking me to mark passages with a pencil, so that when she was better she could go back and read them again, though we both knew she wasn't going to get better. The chapter she was anxious for me to mark was on the New England Dickinsons and their heritage—Puritan character traits she recognized in herself. There she was, dying in Manhattan in a comfortable Upper East Side apartment, and she wanted to go home by a trail Dickinson provided. I inherited her copy of the book.

INTERVIEWER

Did these landscapes inhabit you as well?

HOWE

I've always felt a tremendous pull between Ireland and America, because of my parents—my mother being Irish, and my father being a New Englander from Boston. I felt torn between them—in the sense of allegiance to the word.

INTERVIEWER

Did your mother come from Dublin?

HOWE

Yes, a Dubliner through and through. Mary Manning. She didn't come over from Ireland until she was twenty-nine. I was born when she was thirty-two. Yeats directed her in a play as a young girl, and Sara Allgood was her acting teacher at the Abbey. During the twenties and thirties, she was a member of the Gate Theatre company in its early glory days, under Hilton Edwards and Micheál MacLiammóir. She edited their house magazine, *Motley*, and wrote several plays that were produced, the best known being *Youth's the Season?* She gave up her acting career when she came to Boston on a visit to her aunt and met and rather suddenly married my father, Mark DeWolfe Howe. That was in 1935.

During most of my youth he was a professor at Harvard Law School, where he was known for lecturing in perfect sentences without using notes. He believed in the American Constitution the way others believe in the Bible. Just after their marriage he visited Dublin, but that was that. He didn't like it and never went back. They were voracious readers and both loved reading aloud. Perry Miller—the Harvard professor and historian of Puritanism—dedicated *Errand into the Wilderness* to them both. I can't get over that. He and my father shared a love for Cotton Mather's preposterously baroque prose. Now I treasure my own copy of Mather's *Magnalia Christi Americana*, so it must be genetic. As for my mother, she and I read with and to each other, aloud. Shakespeare, the Brontës, Keats, Matthew Arnold, Yeats, Synge, Joyce, Tolstoy, Ibsen—reading was our vital bond.

INTERVIEWER

Was your father authoritarian?

HOWE

Heavens no, he couldn't have been gentler. But he was definitely hard on himself, self-controlled, in a Puritan sense. After graduating from law school, he was a secretary for the then-ancient Supreme Court justice Oliver Wendell Holmes and later became his official biographer, a task that in the long run hung like an albatross around his neck and probably contributed to his early death. Because of his work on the Holmes archive he was of course much involved in manuscripts. When I was young, Holmes seemed to be a stultifying figure. What did I know about his membership in the Metaphysical Club, the friendships with the James brothers, Minnie Temple, Clover Hooper— Henry Adams's wife—and Fanny Dixwell—Holmes's wife—and Charles Sanders Peirce? All these authors and their friends who mean so much to me now.

INTERVIEWER

When you say your parents had differing allegiances to the word, what do you mean?

HOWE

By the time I was thirteen, we had moved several times, but finally we bought a house in Cambridge I am sure we couldn't afford and there we stayed, and the room we called the study was its heart. My father came home from work regularly every day around six o'clock. Then my parents had cocktails in the study and we gathered with them there before supper. That's where all the books were. Two of the walls were completely lined with bookcases. On one were classics and sets, histories, and reference books—sets of histories by Parkman, and British classics like Dickens—they both loved Dickens—Trollope, George Eliot, that sort of thing. Nothing was ever alphabetically arranged. It was helter-skelter. On the other wall were my mother's books. They were almost all Irish. Poetry and plays. Yeats of course, Elizabeth Bowen, Austin Clarke, Joyce, Synge, Shaw, Ernie O'Malley, biographies of Jonathan Swift, narratives of the Easter Rebellion and the Irish Civil War—some very tattered, which gave them an air of having been carried through danger. In my imagination the divided bookshelves were separate worlds. I used to just love looking at the spines and their varieties. Wandering and looking. In my mind I divided them into sides. One was American-English—settled, true. The other was Irish-English—unsettled, secret.

INTERVIEWER

Did you spend time in Ireland?

HOWE

Yes. I was born in 1937. My mother and I spent the summer of 1938 in Dublin. I have only shadow memories under the surface of family photographs of that first visit. We returned to Boston on a ship called the *Transylvania* packed with refugees fleeing various European countries. She said you could hear weeping at night from the cabins around us.

In 1947, when it was finally safer to cross the Atlantic, my mother, my sister, Fanny, and I flew to Ireland. The flight took two days—we stopped overnight at Gander in Newfoundland, then landed at Shannon, where we boarded a tiny plane for Dublin. It bounced around violently while all the passengers vomited into paper bags. That's the first Irish summer I remember. I was ten. It was bliss. My mother was one thing in America, but here was the part of her Fanny and I didn't know. It was all infinitely rich in things connected with the ear. The soft and varied voices of my Irish relations blended with the landscape around Dublin—mountains, sea, and sky. Through her, I encountered a few surviving relics from the early days of Celtic revival. Spiritualists, actors, and authors in the Yeatsian turn-of-the-century mode were still staggering around. My God, they could be funny! I remember cross-eyed Olivia Robertson and our visits to Huntington Castle. She and her even odder brother later built a temple to Isis there, where they and others worshipped. All the emotions the landscape around Killiney and Dublin Bay and the Wicklow hills raised in me at ten came alive when, in my early teens, I read *A Portrait of the Artist as a Young Man*. I felt my soul was Irish and I belonged there, not here. When I graduated from high school I went straight back over. I followed my mother back into the Gate Theatre. In other words, I did what she wanted me to do, which was a mistake.

INTERVIEWER

To repeat and take up her missed opportunities?

HOWE

Sadly, she wanted me to repeat the life she gave up in 1935. But in 1955, the Gate was in decline. It was managed by Edward Pakenham, sixth Earl of Longford, and his wife, Christine, who wrote plays and adapted novels for the stage. Lord Longford was immensely fat, with a very red face. His minicar was specially designed so he could fit behind the steering wheel, and Christine—kind, clever, and very English—was so thin she appeared to have been squashed. They were devoted, even if Longford had a crush on an actress who, as a result, played all the leads. He was hopeless in terms of business. Actors assumed different roles every two weeks, so there were constant rehearsals, constant set and costume changes. Things were always in a state of imminent collapse. For matinees it wasn't unusual for there to be more people onstage than in the audience. Lord Longford liked to stand in the aisle at intermission rattling a wooden box with a slot for contributions. I was an unpaid apprentice and an assistant to the stage designer, so I was always either in the green room or patching together sets between productions. I guess painting sets was where I began thinking of visual art. Occasionally I played bit parts. My first was Toilet, a maid in George Colman's Restoration comedy *The Jealous Wife*, and I thought, Come on, I gave up college and here I am playing a maid called Toilet! But at that point I was proud of what I had chosen to do. In 1955, I thought of it as a bold, free gesture.

Some of the actors were wildly camp. It was all innuendos, nods and raised eyebrows, wittily barbed asides, sometimes cruel. Hilton Edwards and Micheál MacLiammóir were still living in Dublin, but they had retired from active participation in the company. During the months I was an apprentice at the Gate, Longford's company controlled the productions, while Hilton and Micheál heavily disapproved of the Longford goings-on. There were years of bad feelings I didn't understand—each faction controlled certain seasons. Hilton's glamorous, much younger, blond lover, Patrick "Bosie" McLarnon, was an actor who wasn't acting at the time. I didn't know then that Bosie was Oscar Wilde's name for Lord Alfred Douglas. Coded intercommunication like that wasn't familiar to a teenager from the Boston area. You had to be sharp to keep up.

I was also an assistant to Alpho O'Reilly, the stage designer. He was gay, but I didn't get it then and developed an intense crush on him. He was one of the funniest people I have ever known. We remained close friends, and I used to spend lots of time with him whenever I went over. He was a wonderful driver. I saw a lot of Ireland that way. But in 1996 he mysteriously disappeared. He left Sandymount in his apple-green car and was last seen heading in the direction of Wexford. They never found his body or the car.

INTERVIEWER

With whom were you living?

HOWE

I stayed as what was termed in those days "a paying guest"—or, as my mother and grandmother liked to put it, "a peeing g"—with the family of my mother's best friend from childhood, Nora Reddin. They lived in a rapidly decaying semidetached Georgian house called Ashleaf on the main street of Templeogue. In those days, farmland spread out from there to Tallaght.

Kenneth Reddin was a novelist and a notoriously eccentric district judge. He came from a Catholic middle-class family and had been schooled as a boy by Pearse and MacDonagh at St. Enda's, Pearse's radical nationalist school at Rathfarnham. He and his brother were friends of Joyce before and after he left Ireland. When Joyce died, Kenneth wrote an obituary for *The Irish Times*. Nora was Protestant, though she converted to marry him—mixed marriages were unusual at the time. Their two daughters were my age and close as sisters to me ever since. The house was filled with paintings by their contemporaries, and there were masses of books scattered everywhere, many of them dog-eared and damp. The whole family sang ballads and recited

Howe, seated at far left, with the Gate Theatre company, in 1955. Alpho O'Reilly is standing second from left.

poems, particularly Irish ones. The sense of poetry and politics as being one emotional unified force was new to me. I loved it and I drank it up, but I wasn't Irish. I couldn't change my voice. Though I may have been happier in Dublin, I knew I had to come back to America.

INTERVIEWER

So you came back and did what?

#### HOWE

I was accepted into the Neighborhood Playhouse in New York, which was considered a big deal. I was brought up in the repertory tradition and this was method acting at its height. I was at sea. I have never been so lonely nor felt so abandoned in my life as I did during those six or eight months I lasted. The noise and rush of Manhattan. It seemed impossibly huge.

The legendary Sanford Meisner was my teacher. Method acting is great for some people, but I was hopeless. Improvisation sessions scared me. The written script didn't seem to matter to Meisner, but it did to me. I was hopelessly uptight. Martha Graham taught a class in stage movement, and she was magnificent. She was an old woman then, or so I thought. Probably younger than I am now, but fierce and inspiring. I remember her toes. The tights under her practice skirt ended and there was the bare foot and both her big toes turned in at a solid angle from so much hard use.

After a few months I realized I was far too nervous to be an actor and returned to Boston feeling a total failure. I knew then, and I still do, that the biggest mistake I made in life was not going to a university.

#### INTERVIEWER

Really? Why?

#### HOWE

Because I love history, I love scholarship, but I'm an autodidact. I have never touched down in a disciplined way. I get these obsessions and follow trails that often end up being squirrel paths. There are huge blanks.

#### INTERVIEWER

How did you find your way from theater to visual art and then poetry?

#### HOWE

From start to finish in my work, I've been involved with images. The porous border between visual and verbal is always there. When I came back to Boston, I went to the School of the Museum of Fine Arts for four years. A couple of years after graduating in 1961, Harvey Quaytman and I moved with our small daughter, Rebecca, to New York. I was making stained color-field paintings at the time. I started making lists of single words, usually nouns, bird names, or place-names, often cut from books and collaged with pencil lines and watercolor washes. I began incorporating old engineering instruction manuals, maps, and charts. Single words and the letters that formed them were what attracted me. Gradually I came to make books of watercolor stains, photographs, and words. After a time I just used words on drawing paper, or pasted on walls. It was as though I had a book of the wall.

INTERVIEWER

Were they cutouts?

HOWE

They were both typewritten and cutout. I hadn't solved the problem of the font size, or of what you might do in terms of surface size, but that was because, in the long run, words and their sound, meaning, and letter shapes were what mattered. I remember seeing word drawings by John Cage and Carl Andre. I knew Duchamp's notes and studies for *The Large Glass*, of course, and was familiar with the concrete poets' minimalist use of page space and typography. At some point I decided to take a poetry workshop at St. Marks's Poetry Project. Ted Greenwald, the poet who was running it, came over to the studio I was sharing with the painter Marcia Hafif. He saw what I was doing around the walls, and said, Why don't you put these into a book? And so I did.

INTERVIEWER

That's fantastic!

HOWE

The book became *Hinge Picture*. The editor of *Telephone* magazine and press, the poet Maureen Owen, published it as a mimeo book. At the time I was writing art reviews for *Art in America* and a few other journals. One was crucial to my transitioning from visual art to writing essays and poems—"The End of Art," a piece for the *Archives of American Art Journal,* based on the correspondence of the painter Ad Reinhardt with Ian Hamilton Finlay and Robert Lax. This began a long correspondence between Finlay and me. Finlay started out as a poet, then became a concrete poet, then a sculptor. He always wrote on a particular kind of notepaper. There would be a carefully printed aphorism at the foot, along with the address "Committee of Public Safety, Little Sparta, Dunsyre, Lanark, Scotland." His humor was barbed, and there was never an unnecessary word. He expended such care on each letter he wrote me, though I was an unknown artist-poet at the time. He sent me pictures and pamphlets. Single words and aphorisms, many of which had been cut into stones placed around his garden in hidden spots. They often concerned boats or the sea. He loved the sea and boats and so did my husband David von Schlegell, who was a sculptor and a great sailor as well. I sometimes felt Finlay was writing to David through me.

INTERVIEWER

Do you think of the work you do in libraries and archives as research? As telepathy? As spelunking?

HOWE

Because of my outsider status—until 1988, when I went to SUNY Buffalo as a visiting fellow—gaining access to the stacks of a university library has always seemed to me an adventure verging on trespass. I am quite agoraphobic. I don't travel easily. If I can get into a library—public libraries or even a bookstore—I feel safe, and that probably goes back to our library at home. What I love about university libraries is that they always seem slightly off-limits, therefore forbidden. I feel I've been allowed in with my little identity card and now I'm going to be bad. I have the sense of lurking rather than looking. You came in search of a particular volume, but right away you feel the pull of others.

INTERVIEWER

Don't you quote Dickinson, "Luck is not chance"?

HOWE

That's right. "Luck is not chance—/ it's Toil—/ ... the Father of / the Mine / is that old-fashioned Coin / we spurned." That sense of the spurned book, the hidden one, is intuitive. It's a sense of self-identification and trust that widens to delight—discovering accidental originals or feeling that you're pulling something back. You're rescuing or bringing them into the light. You could call it civilly disobedient telepathy.

INTERVIEWER

What are the discoveries or rescues that have meant the most to you?

HOWE

When I was a visiting poet at Temple, I encountered two huge volumes called *Melville's Marginalia*. Its editor, Wilson Walker Cowen, had collected and printed all the passages Melville had marked in his personal library. At first glance, this alphabetically arranged collection of quotations from numerous authors resembled a giant Charles Olson poem. The preface said Cowen died young. All this immense labor had been for his graduate-student degree. I thought of the pale usher and the sub-sub-librarian in *Moby-Dick*. Then, as I was going over the material, I came upon Melville's notes in his copy of the Irish poet James Clarence Mangan's collected works. I remembered singing Mangan's "Róisín Dubh" with the Reddins. I looked into Mangan's life and work, and by following Mangan—God! I couldn't believe it—I found that he may have been a source for the character of Bartleby.

Earlier, when I was writing the poems that would become *Frame Structures*, I stumbled on Longfellow's wife Frances Appleton, who died by fire in their home library. She was trying to paste locks of her children's hair into an album, using a candle to melt the wax, when a spark fell on her dress. His beard you see in the famous photograph was grown to cover the scars on his face, which was badly burned when he tried to save her. The Longfellow House is now a National Historic Site, and when I took the tour I asked the guide which was the room she burned in. He brushed the question aside as if such a thing had never happened. It doesn't fit the sunny portrait of the author they are hired to exhibit.

In the same way, I came upon Jonathan Edwards's sister Hannah by chance when I slipped her "private writings" out of a folder in the Beinecke Reading Room at Yale.

I don't want to be so arrogant as to say these are recoveries. Maybe certain people find me.

---

Howe, ca. 1990. "Gaining access to the stacks of a university library has always seemed to me an adventure verging on trespass. You come in search of a particular volume, but right away you feel the pull of others."

DER THE SIEUR HERTEL DE
RMING IN O          ADES ON THE D
RPRISED              THE SLEE
       AND              CAPTU
HE GRE                ITS INHA

                        either hand
orded in lo      erence by th
are the            GES of
who

INTERVIEWER

A kind of mediumship through the archive?

HOWE

William James says that in times of trauma and crisis a door is opened to a place where facts and apparitions mix. I wrote *Frolic Architecture* shortly after my husband Peter Hare's sudden death from a pulmonary embolism in 2008. I was constructing what I thought was a collaged text, often while listening to Morton Feldman's music and John Adams's *Shaker Loops*. As I moved between computer screen, printer, and copier, scissoring and reattaching words and scraps of letters, I thought, I've never gone as far or felt as free.

INTERVIEWER

It's a willingness to be taken up by materials, voices, spirits.

HOWE

It's far more acoustic than visual. That's the strange thing. I honestly don't think that Hannah telepathically spoke to me, but something is odd there. I mean, the material—the fragment, the piece of paper—is all we have to connect with the dead. That's why I have this passage in *That This* where a page from her "private writings" is laid open on a light table at the Beinecke to be photographed. Pinioned under the lights, she is Narcissus, reflecting and reflected. There's a level at which words are spirit and paper is skin. That's the fascination of archives. There's still a bodily trace.

INTERVIEWER

That makes a lot of sense—the importance of paper as a medium for a trace. As you say, it becomes a flyleaf, a permeable barrier.

HOWE

Trying to describe the allure of now-obsolete interleaves in old books helped me to connect the elements that went into *Bed Hangings*. Interleaves used to separate the title page from the engraved portrait or color illustration following. The interleaf is a relic, fragile but tough. It's blank and semitransparent at once, like a scrim—always between. A bridge between intuition and the law. The paper relic rustles when turned. It could almost be a wing.

*Relic* is itself a beautiful word. The archaic *relict*—a widow, a survivor—from Latin *relictus* is even sharper.

INTERVIEWER

Your sense of composition is so materially attuned.

HOWE

And I hope sonically, too, because phonic measure is everything in poetry, or in the kind of prose I write. I always have my mother's copy of *Finnegans Wake* near at hand. I can't read the whole book—I can't read the whole Bible, either. If I'm stuck, I'll just open *Finnegan* anywhere and look at a sentence or paragraph. It's all based on wordplay and punning. The ear and the eye. Chance, luck, and logic.

INTERVIEWER

Many of the traces you've recovered were left by women—Mary Rowlandson, Anne Hutchinson, Emily Dickinson. To what extent do you think of yourself as a feminist?

HOWE

I don't like the idea of feminist poetry anthologies. Or anthologies of any kind of work in the arts by women. It's isolating and reductive. However, I can't pretend that there aren't a lot of problems we face. In early American literary history, the question of who is telling whose story and why is horribly vexed. Rowlandson's violent narrative is preceded by an anonymous preface, as if to bring it under control. It was rumored to have been penned by Increase Mather. His son, Cotton, wrote Mercy Short's narrative of possession and Hannah Duston's account of her captivity. Anne Hutchinson's voice only exists in trial records written by men. I am grateful we have these narratives. On the other hand, I wonder. During the 1980s, I was angry about male editorial meddling even in the work of twentieth-century poets such as H.D. and Lorine Niedecker. The editorial history of Emily Dickinson's manuscripts was an issue that especially troubled me, and still does.

INTERVIEWER

Can you say more about that?

Emily Dickinson is one of the greatest poets we have, and I don't mean "we" merely in America. I mean she is one of the greatest of poets. It's important to remember, in the case of editing her work, that in the beginning almost all the collecting, editing, and transcribing was accomplished by Mabel Loomis Todd with the help of Lavinia Dickinson and, to some degree, Susan Gilbert Dickinson. Dickinson died in 1886, but the variorum edition of her collected poems remains under the control of Harvard University Press. The authorized editing of her extraordinarily complex manuscripts has basically been in the charge of two men. First, Thomas H. Johnson's edition in 1951. Then Ralph Franklin's edition replaced it in 1998. Franklin's facsimile edition of the manuscript books in the early eighties should have radically changed the nature of Dickinson scholarship—at last her line breaks were visible, and so was her increasing use of variant word lists.

Seeing the facsimile edition for the first time should have raised questions about her final intentions, about her use of the page as a field and about the possibility that groups she gathered and sewed together in fascicles might have been series works. But a majority of critical studies and biographies didn't ask them. That may have been because Franklin didn't provide transcriptions, as other collaborative editorial projects did, such as the Cornell edition of Yeats's manuscripts, or the Garland Shelley.

I grew up on the Johnson edition. That's how I first knew and loved Dickinson. The capitals and dashes, the removed variants, the arbitrary line breaks, with chronological and other changes by Franklin. It is what her work has come to represent to general readers. In 2012, this outdated and rigid approach is a problem, to say the least. Thankfully, digitalized images of the manuscripts are beginning to change the direction scholars and general readers can go in. Marta Werner, who worked on the late fragments and drafts for years, has collaborated with the visual artist Jen Bervin to produce a limited edition of Dickinson's work on pieces of envelopes. Their collaboration on just these envelope fragments is a promise of wonderful changes to come.

I'm not saying there is any correct way to clear this entangled primal paper forest. Maybe this is her triumph. She has taken her secret to the grave and will not give up the ghost.

INTERVIEWER

What do you make of Dickinson's so-called Master letters?

HOWE

Dickinson's three Master letters may represent the conversion experience she was going through—a Calvinist nature's secular conversion, its needs and demands. Yes, this experience had an erotic push, but the constant need of some scholars to decode in these letters a flesh-and-blood lover belittles the ferocity of her poetic calling.

I think she realized her vocation, and it was terrifying. She wasn't playing around anymore.

INTERVIEWER

Do you think you had an appetite for conversion before you encountered these renderings of conversion?

HOWE

I don't know. Although I'm not a religious convert, I believe in the sacramental nature of poetry. Jonathan Edwards's manuscripts announce the coming of Dickinson's. When you see the material objects, in all their variety of shapes and surfaces, it's like coming on unexplained spirits singing into air.

INTERVIEWER

You have been so invested in the materiality of archives and in collaging practice—what is your relation to digitization and new media?

HOWE

I would love to be able to use Photoshop, and wonder as to what I might be able to experiment with in terms of page space. But I just can't, I'm too old. I already lived through the crisis of going from the typewriter to the computer in my poetry, and that was a major step.

INTERVIEWER

When was that?

INTERVIEWER

Most of *My Emily Dickinson* was written by literally cutting and pasting. Then I shifted to a computer at the end of the eighties. It was clear there was no going back in terms of prose. The cut-and-paste mode for an eraserhead like me seemed heaven-sent. But it took a long, long time for me to get my poetry off of the typewriter, probably up to the midnineties. It's still partly there.

Howe, 1990.

INTERVIEWER

Did shifting to the computer change your rhythm of composition or your techniques?

HOWE

The funny thing is, I still cut and paste. Anything in my books that looks as if the computer has done it—it didn't. All of that was all done by me cutting, taping, going to Xerox machines, coming back, doing it again. I found that to do any splaying of words across the page or anything like that was absolutely impossible on the computer, because I wasn't adept enough. If I could use Photoshop or whatever the new ones are that are cooler than Photoshop, I probably would never get anything accomplished. I would be endlessly cutting and tweaking. When you look at the typescripts of, say, Pound, H.D., Williams, or whomever, they're just different. You press a key, the key hits the platen. It's a different rhythm. I must have a printer to begin to see what I am doing on paper. I believe what's on the paper, not on the screen. I always think that what I see on the monitor is going to suddenly vanish. Sometimes it does!

INTERVIEWER

Do you ever write longhand?

HOWE

I make a few notes longhand. I have a little black sketchbook, the same brand for years. I make notes first, and then I type them into the computer and I start working. I have endless little black books, like commonplace books, where I have quotations and beginnings of poems.

INTERVIEWER

Many people might first encounter you as, say, "poet and professor, Susan Howe," and it might be hard for somebody to understand that, for you, the native place isn't the university.

HOWE

People often tell me my work is "difficult." I have the sinking feeling they mean "difficult" as in "hopeless."

INTERVIEWER

Do you say that to people?

HOWE

Paul Valéry once said, "The mollusk does not know its shell until it lives it," so I curl up inside and work and wait. In my shell are books from all worlds.

It's a tychic encounter, as Charles Sanders Peirce might say—I read them and use them as alignments, and conjunctions appear.

This is what attracts me so strongly to the ideas of Peirce, the philosopher and logician. I don't begin to understand logic, but I see things through the visual quality of his manuscripts that a professional Peircian might miss or ignore. They present some of the problems or joys Edwards's and Dickinson's manuscripts raise. Peirce's ideas of the Categories—Firstness, Secondness, Thirdness as a way to explain the process of artistic inspiration—are dear to me. I love him for his titles—*Man's Glassy Essence, How to Make Our Ideas Clear, Evolutionary Love*—and for the fantastic words he invents or adopts—*ideoscopy, tychism, abduction, synechism. Synechism* is the tendency to regard everything as continuous in the way no "scholarly interpretation can be." It suggests the linkage of like and like-in-chance contiguities and alignments. That idea is in my writing generally. He was willing to carry the doctrine so far as to maintain that continuity governs the domain of experience, every part of it. Synechism denies there are any immeasurable differences between phenomena, not even between sleeping and waking. This comforts an insomniac.

INTERVIEWER

In the library you feel like an interloper, but what is your relation to the academy?

HOWE

My entrance into academia was similar to a child's being thrown into deep water to see if she will sink or swim. I spent two years at Buffalo and then was at Temple for two semesters. In 1991, I was suddenly made a full professor with tenure at Buffalo, largely due to the efforts of Robert Creeley, who wanted to establish something called the Poetics Program. They needed to hire poets who had produced some criticism. Charles Bernstein had written *Content's Dream*, and I had written *My Emily Dickinson*. Neither book could be described as a standard scholarly production, but they were allowed to pass. To this day I'm not sure what the term *poetics* signifies, but I am grateful for it.

So I was incredibly lucky. I didn't have to go through the hell of the usual academic career trajectory. I taught graduate seminars and the occassional undergraduate workshop. It was absolutely wonderful for me, for my writing—partly because I was so frightened. I had to cover bases I wasn't sure of. This moment was the high tide of critical theory. It was very strong in Buffalo, and it was thrilling, but I felt as if I was moving through a fog of jargon. I was both mystified and fascinated.

INTERVIEWER

You're talking about post-structuralism?

HOWE

I never approached Barthes, Foucault, Kristeva, Irigaray, Lyotard, or Derrida on a systematic basis. In magpie fashion, I went for the bits and the pieces, the fragment and usable quotation. The essays in Foucault's *Language, Counter-Memory, Practice*—particularly "What Is an Author?"—were crucial to my thinking about Dickinson's editorial history and much else. The marginal marks all over "Nietzsche, Genealogy, History" show how much that chapter once meant to me, even if I never look at it now. When it came to poets, the emphasis in the Poetics Program during the nineties was on Stein, Williams, Spicer, Riding, Mac Low, Zukofsky, and other Objectivists.

INTERVIEWER

So there was a striking poetic and intellectual ferment at Buffalo.

HOWE

The mix of theory, psychoanalysis, and poetry—with strong Americanists such as Leslie Fiedler—sometimes working in tandem with the cutting-edge media and music departments was what made Buffalo unique, years before Charles and I arrived. I hope we were a continuation. Robert Creeley was the presiding spirit of the Poetics Program. He was the bridge between poets like Pound, Duncan, Zukofsky, and Olson, while Charles Bernstein—coming from a more Marxist approach—was the sign of the future. Creeley was the grand master. I suppose Black Mountain was his model. Without his ability to work the political system at UB, and his poetic reach, the program would have been inconceivable. Charles worked harder than anyone else to build a successful program that would also embrace our digital future. His manic energy and dedication were unbelievable. He was immensely helpful to me, even if, when it came to the twentieth century, I went somewhat against the Buffalo grain. I was more interested in teaching twentieth-century American authors. I liked teaching Eliot's *Four Quartets* rather than *The Waste Land*, as well as H.D.'s *Trilogy* and *Tribute to Freud*. Charles and I worked in tandem, and I think we each needed the other for balance.

### INTERVIEWER

Many people encounter your work through the grid of Language poetry. Is that useful?

### HOWE

I'm not a hard-core Language poet. But some of the individuals involved in that group provided inspiration, encouragement, and even a readership for my work when I badly needed it. *L=A=N=G=U=A=G=E* magazine, edited by Bruce Andrews and Charles Bernstein, was like a blast of fresh air. And Lyn Hejinian's Tuumba Press was exemplary in its simplicity and intellectual reach. I shared their distaste for certain aspects of American poetry, but being from an older generation, I have always been attracted by modernism rather than postmodernism and its anti-Romantic high theory.

### INTERVIEWER

You seem to have a really different relation to Williams than to, say, Olson. You don't insist that there be some huge project governing everything, à la Olson's *Maximus Poems*, or even Williams's *Paterson*.

### HOWE

I should insert here that my favorite twentieth-century poet is Wallace Stevens, and he doesn't really fit into this company. Neither does John Ashbery, whose poems I adore. Poems in *The Tennis Court Oath* were as important as *Maximus* to me when I was beginning to write, and every new collection since then is a wonder. Stevens and Ashbery are American but are without governing projects, apart from the most important one—nobly riding the sound of words.

### INTERVIEWER

"Spontaneous Particulars of Sound," as you called your Trilling Seminar at Columbia.

In New York, 2011. "From start to finish in my work, I've been involved with images. The porous border between visual and verbal is always there."

HOWE

Yes, I set out to give a lecture on Stevens's late work in *The Rock*, but I am so much in awe of his power—he is the father figure, if you like—that Williams and the library section of *Paterson* seemed more humanly possible to discuss, because the work is both fallible and fabulous. I feel guilty. I've got to go back to the poet whose work I meant to write about, Stevens, but when I try, out comes Williams disguised as a mother.

INTERVIEWER

The obstetrician. It's like you don't get to know in advance what you're going to give birth to.

HOWE

Maybe it's because the epic push isn't there in Stevens. The reason I started "Spontaneous Particulars of Sound" with Williams's quotations—from *Paterson III*—is Williams's ambivalence, his attraction and repulsion toward

167

letters. Some of his most gorgeous lyric poetry seems fueled by diatribes *against*. There are incredibly beautiful passages in there.

INTERVIEWER

Do you think ambivalence is a good muse?

HOWE

Maybe it is. In *Paterson* Williams tries to continue in an epic tradition, influenced heavily by Joyce's *Ulysses,* Pound's *Cantos,* and Crane's *The Bridge,* but always with an American difference. In spite of myself, I share this screwed-up magpie ambivalence. I mean, I am an Americanist. There's something that we do, a Romantic, utopian ideal of poetry as revelation at the same instant it's a fall into fracture and trespass. *Frolic Architecture* cuts itself to bits. It could be that because I am a woman, bullets are more like blanks. What fuels the poems in that collection is the sense of epic breaking into shards.

INTERVIEWER

I've heard the recording of your performance of *Frolic*, and you actually speak—sound out—its fragments and phonemes, those shards. You treat your work as a score.

HOWE

Collaborating with the musician-composer David Grubbs has brought vividly home to me how acoustic a seemingly collaged and visual work can be. Several years ago our first collaboration was for a performance at the Fondation Cartier in Paris, and was based around an early poem of mine called "Thorow." We collaborated again to produce *Souls of the Labadie Tract.* The work I have done with David has influenced the course of my later poetry by showing me a range of contemporary music with which I was unfamiliar. It also restored my earlier interest in Charles Ives. I love the way Ives's musical use of quotation throws connectives to the winds. His work is Romantic and iconoclastic at once.

INTERVIEWER

Is that a fair point of entry into your work, thinking of you as both a Romantic and an iconoclast?

HOWE

Thinking about the miracle of Emily Dickinson's poetry, prose, word drawings, and drafts in all their iconoclastic and Romantic variety brought out the buried New England Puritan antinomian in me. Here, you can be both things at once.

INTERVIEWER

Do you still paint and draw?

HOWE

No, I don't. But I often think of the space of a page as a stage, with words, letters, syllable characters moving across. In a certain way you can also say the poems in *Frolic* might be some sort of drawing. I started with words on the wall, and now I've framed some of the page proofs from *Frolic*. And I love to look at them as if they are drawings. I look and say to myself, Oh my God, that one works! Which I can't say about any real painting I ever did. So when I say I've broken everything open, maybe I've been moving in a circle.

# Regan Good

## THE WASPS' HOUSE

Mortared by macerated wood-pulp effluvium,
                       a paper palace hangs.

The young queen spun her eggs and hatched her grunts.

The wasps drag paralytic legs through the air,
those long wisps most weeping, strange, and ill.

They build a giant house, a birch-like comb of paste,
lifted high to dangle by the rotation of their wings.

Inside it is vast asylum, Escher-like stairways.
A center staircase curves like a nautilus's turn.

The workers build. The house is heavy, though papery,
like curling birch or sloughing human skin—

it is a lantern with no light. A white balloon,
a papier-mâché head with a dirty mouth hole
jammed under the eaves of the foursquare.

A clown face with collapsed and lopsided mouth
                       sucking in living balls of light.

They hover, rise, hang, crawl continually into the corners
                       of the sunken lips.

They built by instinct this paper pleasure dome,
                       this chambered domicile

of blacks and grays, then the stained opening, that lipless mouth—

the entrance now the portal for a nozzle of poison smoke.

Toothless, stinking piehole. Look now: your busy head is black.

*Blanks*

---

# RACHEL KUSHNER

When I had first moved to New York from Reno, I found an apartment on Mulberry Street and planned to make films with the camera I never returned to the art department at the University of Nevada, a Bolex Pro. I arrived with the camera, my savings from selling my motorcycle, and a phone number for Chris Kelly, my single contact. I was twenty-one. I figured I'd wait to call mythical Chris Kelly, a UNR student I had known only slightly. He had been shot in the arm by Nina Simone when he tried to make a film about her. I'll get situated first, I thought. I'll have some sense of what I'm doing, a way to make an impression on him. Then I'll call. I knew no one else, but downtown New York was so alive with people my age, and so thoroughly abandoned by most others, that the energy of the young seeped out of the ground. I figured it was only a matter of time before I met people, was part of something.

My apartment was about as blank and empty as my new life, with its layers upon layers of white paint, like a plaster death mask of the two rooms, giving them an ancient urban feeling, and I didn't want to mute that effect with furniture and clutter. The floor was an interlocking map of various unmatched linoleum pieces in faded floral reds, like a cracked and soiled Matisse. It was almost bare, except for a trunk that held my clothes, a few books, the stolen or borrowed Bolex, a Nikon F (my own), and a man's brown felt hat, owner unknown. I had no cups, no table, nothing of that sort. The mattress I slept on had been there when I rented. I had one faded pink towel, on its edge machine embroidered PICKWICK. It was from a hotel in San Francisco. I knew a girl who had cleaned rooms there and I somehow ended up with the towel, which seemed fancier than a regular towel because it had a provenance, like shoes from Spain or perfume from France. A towel from the Pickwick. The hat was a Borsalino I'd found in the bathroom of a bar. I wrapped my jacket around it, rather than giving it to the bartender. It decorated the empty apartment. Each morning I went to a coffee shop near my apartment, the Trust E on Lafayette, and sat at the counter. The same waitress was always there. The men who came into that coffee shop tried to pick her up. She was pretty and, perhaps more importantly, had large breasts framed in a low-cut waitressing smock.

"Hey, what's your name?" a man in a yellow hard hat said to her one morning as he stared at her breasts and dug in the pocket of his work overalls to pay his check.

She glanced at the radio behind the counter. "My name is … Zenith," she said, smiling at him with her slightly crooked teeth.

That was the precise moment I wanted to be friends with Giddle—her actual name, or at least the one I knew her by.

THERE ARE NO PALM TREES on Fourteenth Street, but I remember them there, black palm fronds against indigo dusk, the night I met the people with the gun.

That was how I thought of them, before I knew who any of them were. *The people with the gun.*

I had been in New York a month, and the city to me seemed strange and wondrous and lonely. The July air was damp and hot. It was late afternoon.

The overcrowded sidewalk, with young girls standing along Union Square in shorts and halters the size of popped balloons, electronics stores with salsa blaring, the Papaya King and its mangoes and bananas piled up in the window, all made Fourteenth Street feel like the main thoroughfare of a tropical city, someplace in the Caribbean or South America, though I had never been to the Caribbean or South America, and I'm not sure where I saw palm fronds. Once it became familiar, Fourteenth Street never looked that way to me again.

I remember a rainbow spectrum of men's wing tips parked in rows, triple-A narrow, the leather dyed snake green, lemon yellow, and unstable shades of vermilion and Ditto-ink blue. All of humanity dresses in uniforms of one sort or another, and these shoes were for pimps. I was on the west end of Fourteenth. My feet, swollen from the heat, were starting to hurt. I heard music from the doorway of a bar, soft piano notes, and then a singer who flung her voice over a horn section. *What difference does it make, which one I choose? Either way I lose.* A voice so low it sounded like a female voice artificially slowed. It was Nina Simone's. A piano note and a man's baritone voice percussed together, and then higher piano notes came tumbling down to meet the low ones. I went in.

The music was loud and distorted by the echoing room, where a man and woman sat close together at the far end of a bar, the sole customers. The woman had the kind of beauty I associated with the pedigreed rich. A pale complexion, cuticle thin, stretched over high cheekbones, and thick, wavy hair that was the warm, reddish blonde of cherrywood. The man conducted the song with the tiny straw from his drink, jerking his arm in the air to the saxophone and the cartwheeling piano notes, which fell down over us as if from the perforations in the bar's paneled ceiling. The horns and strings and piano and the woman's voice all rode along together and then came to an abrupt halt. The room fell into drafty silence.

The woman sniffled, her head down, hair flopped over her face, curtains drawn for a moment of private sorrow, although I sensed she was faking.

"Why don't you sit down," the man called to me in a nasal and Southern voice. "You're making us nervous." He wore a suit and tie but there was something derelict about him, not detectable in his fine clothes.

The woman looked up at me, a glisten of wet on her cheeks.

"She's not making anybody *nervous*," she said, and wiped under her eyes with the pads of her fingers, careful not to scratch herself with long nails painted glossy red. I realized I'd been wrong. She was not the pedigreed rich. He was and she was not. Sometimes all the information is there in the first five minutes, laid out for inspection. Then it goes away, gets suppressed as a matter of pragmatism. It's too much to know a lot about strangers. But some don't end up strangers. They end up closer, and you had your five minutes to see what they were really like and you missed it.

"Come on, honey," she said to me in a voice like a soft bell, "sit down and shithead will buy you a drink."

I'D THOUGHT THIS WAS HOW artists moved to New York, alone, that the city was a mecca of individual points, longings, all merging into one great light-pulsing mesh, and you simply found your pulse, your place. The art in the galleries had nothing to do with what I'd studied as fine art. My concentration had been film, but the only films the galleries seemed to be showing were films scratched beyond recognition, and in one case, a ten-minute-long film of a clock as it moved from ten o'clock to ten minutes after ten, and then the film ended. Dance was very popular, as was most performance, especially the kind that was of a nature so subtle—a person walking through a gallery, and then turning and walking out of the gallery—that one was left unsure if the thing observed was performance or plain life. There was a man in my neighborhood who carried a long pole painted with barber stripes over his shoulder. I would see him at dusk as I sat in the little park on the corner of Mulberry and Spring. He, too, liked to sit in the little park in the evening, in his bell-bottoms and a striped sailor's shirt. We both watched the neighborhood boys in their gold chains and football jerseys as they taunted the Puerto Rican kids who passed by. They were practicing for the future war. The Italians were going to exterminate the Puerto Ricans with the sheer force of their hatred. Or maybe they would just remove all the Italian-ice pushcarts and the pizza parlors, and the Puerto Ricans would starve. The man sat there with his striped pole jutting over his shoulder like an outrigger, one leg crossed over the other, his sunbrowned toes exposed in battered leather sandals. He smiled foolishly when the Italian kids asked what his pole was for. When he didn't answer, they flicked cigarette butts at him. He kept smiling at them. Once, he walked past the Trust E, holding the pole over his shoulder as if carrying construction materials to a work site. "There goes Henri-Jean," Giddle said.

"You know him?"

"Yeah. He lives in the neighborhood. It's his thing, that pole. No sellable works, just disruption. Goes to gallery openings, bonks people on the head by accident."

The children who taunted him in the playground all had fathers in the Mafia. Every Sunday, the fathers exited their social club on Mulberry, next door to my building, and got into black limousines. There were so many limousines they took up the entire block, lined up like bars of obsidian-black soap, double-parked along Mulberry so that no traffic could pass. The chauffeurs stood next to the open passenger-side doors all afternoon. It was summer, and sweat rolled down their faces as they waited for the men to emerge from the social club.

Every morning I sat at the counter of the Trust E on Lafayette, hoping Giddle and I might talk, and if business was slow, we did. I paid my rent to a Mr. Pong, who said I should contact him only if I was moving out or if the city showed up to inspect. I spent each day looking at the want ads and walking around. As I came and went from my apartment, I would say hello to the two teenage girls who cut and styled each other's hair in the hallway. Sometimes they were in the courtyard between the two buildings— one building was behind the other, and I lived in the front—working out dance routines under the wet flags of hung laundry. Each night I went to a pizza place on Prince. The kind of young people I hoped to know, women and men in ripped, self-styled clothes, smoking and passionately discussing art and music and ideas, were all there. I didn't interact with them except for once, when one of the men called me *cutie*, he said, "Hey, cutie," and a woman near him became upset, telling him that the street was not his pickup joint, and the other women laughed, and none of them asked if I needed friends. Which was something people never would ask. I ate my pizza and went to lie in bed with all the windows wide open. The trucks rumbling down Kenmare, the honking, an occasional breaking of glass, made me feel that I was not separate and alone in my solitude, because the city was flowing through my apartment and its sounds were a kind of companionship.

I had met Giddle, but she was of little real help. The stream of New York, at least the one I imagined, moved around her as it did around me. She seemed as isolated as I was, which was troubling, because she'd been in New York, as far as I could tell, for many, many years. She would tell me about herself, but it often contradicted something she'd said on a different day. Once she said she was raised in a Midwestern Catholic orphanage. We wore green skirts, she told me, white blouses, white bobby socks, saddle shoes, green jackets. We watched the nuns shower. But then, on another quiet morning at the diner, she told me her father sold appliances. They'd lived in Montreal. Her mother stayed home, was always there when Giddle returned from school. She had three brothers. Got an F in French. And I looked at her and nodded and realized she had forgotten she'd told me about the nuns a few days earlier.

Something would happen, I was sure. A job, which I needed, but that could isolate a person even further. No. Some kind of event. "Tonight is the night," I later believed I'd told myself on that particular night when I heard the music and Nina Simone's voice, walked into the bar on Fourteenth Street, and met the people with the gun. But in truth I had not told myself anything. I had simply left my apartment to stroll, as I did every night. What occurred did so because I was open to it, and not because fate and I met at a certain angle. I had plenty of time to think about this later. I thought about it so much that the events of that evening sometimes ran along under my mood like a secret river, in the way that all buried truths rushed along quietly in some hidden place.

"THIS IS MY WIFE," the nasal man in elegant clothes said as I sat down next to them at the bar. "Nadine."

He said it again. "Nay-*deeen*," and looked searchingly at her.

She ignored him, as if she were used to this audible pondering of her Nadine-ness in bars, for the benefit of strangers.

"We were at a wedding," Nadine said, turning to me. "They asked us to leave. They asked Thurman to leave, I mean. But I don't like weddings anyway? They make my face hurt?"

That was how she spoke.

"Why did they want you to leave?" I asked, but I could sense why. Something about their presence in an empty bar many levels below what the man's clothes might suggest.

"Because Thurman lay down in the grass?" Nadine said. "He started taking pictures of the sky. Just blue sky, instead of bride and groom. He'd had a few too—"

"I did not have *a few too*. I was looking for something decent to photograph. Something worth keeping. For posterity."

"Oh, posterity," Nadine said. "Sure. Great. If you can afford it. You could have just told Lester you didn't want to be the picture taker."

There was a camera sitting in front of him on the bar, an expensive-looking Leica.

"You're a photographer?" I asked him.

"Nope." He smiled, revealing a tar stain between his two front teeth.

"But the camera—" I couldn't think of how to say it. You have a camera but you aren't a photographer. I sensed he would only keep meandering away, like something you are trying to catch that continually evades your grasp.

"Better to say yes," Thurman said, "and then disappoint people. I mean really let them down."

"Lord knows you're good at that," Nadine said in a quiet voice.

"I'm talking about building a reputation."

"So am I," she said.

"All I want," Thurman said, "is for people to stop asking me to come to their weddings. And funerals."

"I don't mind funerals?" Nadine said. "Except when they buried my daddy in a purple casket. That was awful." She turned to me. "Thurman knew my daddy? Daddy was a mentor to him? A teacher?"

"A mentor," I repeated, hoping this might lead somewhere, to some explanation of who she and Thurman were. Because they were someone or something, I was sure of it.

"Well, my daddy was a ... I guess you could say pimp. Pimp is acceptable—I mean now that he's dead. And you know what? It's 1975 and people just don't say *procurer* anymore."

I thought of the narrow wing tips in tropical-bird colors. Who knew what was true.

"And my mother was a whore, so they got along perfect."

Probably nothing was true, but I liked the challenge of trying to talk to them. I had spoken to so few people since arriving that it felt logical to interact in this manner. It was direct and also evasive, each in a way that made sense to me.

"May he rest in peace," Thurman said. "A gentleman. I wanted to ask him for your hand in marriage. You were fourteen and goddamn. I wanted to just marry the pants off you." He grinned and showed the ugly stain on his teeth. "But then there was no point. It wasn't marrying to get in your pants, since you were allowing it. Not with me. That motherfucker you did marry, later on."

Nadine frowned. "Do you want a purple casket, Thurman? Because Blossom might have one all picked out for you. With a copper millennial vault, to preserve your—"

He got up, walked to the end of the bar, and aimed his camera at a sign above the register. SORRY, NO CREDIT.

Three or four drinks in, still they hadn't asked me anything. But what interesting thing did I have to tell? I was content to listen to their stream of half-reports on people I'd never heard of, stories I could not follow, one about a baby named Kotch. "This lady was nursing him," Nadine said, "and then another lady and you begin to think, wait a minute, whose baby *is* Kotch? I don't know who was his mother and who was a wet nurse—"

"I'll make you a *wet nurse*," Thurman said as he grabbed Nadine and cupped one of her breasts. She twisted away and then she was prattling about a McDonald's she once went to in Mexico. I had been in a McDonald's commercial when I was in high school, and I thought, as Nadine spoke, that it might be a story I could share with them.

"McDonald's is supposed to be the same everywhere, right? Well, not in Mexico. They Mexicanize it. *Hamburguesa con chile*. No fries—*fri-jo-les*. I was with my ex. We were starving and I was ready to eat beans. We're at the counter and find out we have no money. He had lost his wallet."

She went on about this ex, the revolution he had been fomenting that never took place and had led to their harsh and vagrant life in the mountains of northern Mexico, the hole in his pocket that his wallet had wriggled through, leading to his inability to provide for her the most fundamental thing—a McDonald's hamburger. That was how she put it, that he couldn't provide *even a hamburger*. After which she left him and went to Hollywood, where the nightmare really began, a series of episodes and hard luck that involved rape, prostitution, and an addiction to Freon, the gas from the cooling element in refrigerators.

"What you get," Thurman said, when she was finally finished, "for marrying a motherfucker."

"I don't want to talk about him. And stop calling him that, would you?"

"You brought him up."

"Only to tell her about the Mexican McDonald's."

"I was in a McDonald's commercial," I said.

"Oh, you're an actress!"

"No, I just did the one thing, I was sixteen and it was just something, an ad our coach answered and—"

"Thurman, she's an actress."

"Well, I … we did act, I guess. But that's not … they needed a girl who could ski, and so I—"

"You're an actress and a skier! I never meet anyone who skis."

"Do you ski?" I asked, only vaguely hopeful.

"Do I ski. No, honey."

The commercial's director and crew had come to Mount Rose, where we trained. They talked to our coach and ended up choosing me and a racer named Lisa, a quiet girl no one really knew. There was a long day of takes and retakes. They wanted two girls with hair flying, snow bunnies on a brisk sunny afternoon. A week later they flew us both to Los Angeles, to a strange McDonald's in the City of Industry where they only filmed commercials. It looked like a regular McDonald's, with cashiers in paper hats, a menu board, the plastic bench tables where Lisa and I sat across from each other and smiled as if we were friends although we weren't, each of us holding a hamburger in our fingers with hot lights on us, in this fake restaurant that looked real except they didn't serve customers. I tried to explain this to Nadine, but she kept interrupting me.

When we finished shooting the ad, I flew home to Reno. Lisa was supposed to be on the flight but she wasn't. She was eighteen, an adult, and I didn't wonder. She had apparently gone to a bar near the fake McDonald's in the City of Industry. No one ever heard from her again.

"Freaky," Nadine said. "There's no telling. Once I met the serial killer Ted Bundy. Can you believe it? He was real handsome. Real smooth. I was on a beach and here comes this hunky college guy. I was *this* close from ending up like the gal in that commercial with you."

It hadn't occurred to me that Lisa had been murdered. I assumed she'd been impatient to meet her future and had just fled into it and never bothered to let anyone know where she was and what she was doing. The representative who paid me could not track her down. He called to ask if I knew anything, and I'd said no.

"I miss Los Angeles," Nadine said. "Don't you?"

"I was only there the one night," I said. "In the City of Industry, which isn't really Los Angeles, and so—"

"The way the palm trees shake around," she went on, "and it sounds like rain but everything is sun reflecting on metal. I once went to a house in the Hollywood Hills that was a glass dome on a pole, its elevator shaft. Belonged to a pervert bachelor and he had peepholes everywhere. He was watching me in the toilet. Same guy drugged me without asking first. Angel dust. I was on roller skates, which presented a whole extra challenge."

Thurman was laughing. I understood she was his airy nonsense-maker, a bubble machine, and occasionally he would be in the mood for that.

"How the hell did you manage, drugged, on skates?" he asked her.

"Like I said, there was an elevator. Anyhow, there's some use in being doped against your will. Before it happened I didn't have my natural defenses. Some people don't get the whole boundaries thing until they've had their mind raped by another person. It helped me to establish some kind of minimum standard."

She turned to me. "Did you see *Klute*?"

"Yes," I said, "I did, I—"

"I liked it," she said. "He didn't." She gestured at Thurman. She wasn't curious what I thought of *Klute*. But that very film had been on my mind, this portrait of a woman who is so alone in the dense and crowded city. In my empty apartment I'd been thinking of the scenes where her phone rings. She answers and no one is there.

PERHAPS BECAUSE I WAS SO ISOLATED, as darkness fell outside that Fourteenth Street bar, and more drinks were ordered, and a sense of possession over time faded away, a sense of the evening as mine loosened, one in which I would eat my habitual pizza slice and lie down alone, I began to cling in some subtle way to these people Thurman and Nadine, even as they were drunk and bizarre and didn't listen to a word I said.

I heard the sound of a motorcycle pulling up on the sidewalk in front of the bar.

A man walked in wearing jeans tucked into engineer boots and a faded T-shirt that said MARSDEN HARTLEY on it. He was good-looking and I guessed he knew it, this friend of Thurman and Nadine's whose name I did not catch. He walked in knowing he was beautiful, with his hard gaze and slightly feminine mouth, and I was struck. He had the Marsden Hartley T-shirt and I loved Marsden Hartley. He rode a motorcycle. These commonalities felt like a miracle to me. I realized when he sat down that he had made his T-shirt logo with a pen. It was not silk screened. He'd simply written MARSDEN HARTLEY. He could have written anything and that was what he wrote.

Compared to Thurman and Nadine it was like reason had stepped through the door. He didn't speak in rambling non sequiturs or take pictures of the ceiling. Thurman started acting a bit more normally himself, and he and this friend of his had a coherent exchange about classical music, Thurman demonstrating a passage of Bach by running his hands over the bar as though it were a piano, his fingers sounding pretend notes with a delicate care and exactitude that the rest of him seemed to lack. There were several rounds of drinks. Their friend asked if I was an art student. "Let me guess," he said. "Either Cooper or SVA. Except if you were at Cooper your enlightened good sense would keep you away from dirty old men like Thurman Johnson."

I said I'd just moved to New York.

"You had a college sweetheart who is joining the military. He was also in fine arts. He'll use his training to paint portraits of army colonels. You'll write letters back and forth until you fall in love with someone else, which is what you moved here to do."

These people seemed to want to have already located the general idea of the stranger in their company, and to feel they were good guessers. It was somehow preferable to actually trying to get to know me.

"I didn't move here to fall in love."

But as I said it, I felt he'd set a trap of some kind. Because I didn't move here not to fall in love. The desire for love is universal but that has never meant it's worthy of respect. It's not admirable to want love, it just is.

The truth was that I'd loved Chris Kelly, who'd gone to the South of France to find Nina Simone, only to be shot at with a gun she'd lifted from the pocket of her robe. We were in an Italian film class together. He looked at Monica Vitti like he wanted to eat her, and I looked at her like I wanted to be her. I started cutting and arranging my hair like hers, a tousled mess with a few loose bangs, and I even found a green wool coat like she clutched to her chin in *Red Desert*, but Chris Kelly did not seem to notice. He was graduated and gone by my second semester at UNR and mostly an impression by this point, a lingering image of a tall guy who wore black turtlenecks, a cowlick over one eye, a person who had risked himself for art, had been shot in the arm, and then moved to New York City.

A few days earlier, I'd finally tried the number I had for him, from a pay phone on Mulberry Street. I'd gone downstairs, passing the teenage girls styling each other's hair in the hallway, trying not to breathe because the Chinese family one floor below me slaughtered chickens in their apartment and the smell of warm blood filled the hallway. I'd dialed the number from the phone booth, nervous but happy. Someone was yelling, "*Babbo*, throw down the key!" It was the morning of the Fourth of July and kids were lighting smoke bombs, sulfurous coils of red and green, the colors dense and bright like concentrated dye blooming through water. I was wearing Chinese shoes I'd bought for two dollars on Canal Street. The buckles had immediately fallen off, and the straps were now attached with safety pins. Sweaty feet in cheap cotton shoes, black like Chris Kelly's clothes. It was sweltering hot, children cutting into the powerful spray from an uncapped fire hydrant. As the phone began to ring, I watched an enormous flying cockroach land on the sidewalk. A woman came after it and crushed it under the bottom of her slipper.

The phone was ringing. Now there was a huge mangled stain on the sidewalk, with still-moving parts, long, wispy antennae swiping around for signs of its own life. A second ring of the telephone. Mythical Chris Kelly. Third ring. I was rehearsing what I would say. An explosion echoed from down the block. An M-80 in a garbage can. The key sailed from a window, inside a tube sock, and landed near the garbage, piling up because of the strike.

A voice came through the phone: "I'm sorry. The number you have dialed is no longer in service."

It was true: I didn't move here not to fall in love. That night, after I attempted to call Chris Kelly, I watched from my roof as the neighborhood blew itself to smithereens, scattering bits of red paper everywhere, the humid air tinged with magnesium. It seemed a miracle that nothing caught fire that wasn't meant to. Men and boys overturned crates of explosives of various sorts in the middle of Mulberry Street. They hid behind a metal dumpster as one lit a cigarette, gave it a short puffing inhale, and then tossed it onto the pile, which began to send showers and sprays and flashes in all directions.

A show for the residents of Little Italy, who watched from high above. No one went down to the street, only the stewards of this event. My neighbors and I lined our rooftop, black tar gummy from the day's heat. Pink and red fireworks burst upward, exploded overhead, and then fell and melted into the dark, and how could it be that the telephone number for the only person I knew in New York City did not work?

I had asked Giddle if she knew an artist by that name and she'd said, "I think so. Chris. Yeah."

We were on Lafayette, outside the Trust E Coffee Shop.

"I can't believe it," I said excitedly. "Where is he? Do you know what he's up to?"

She tugged the foil apron from a new pack of North Pole cigarettes and tossed it on the sidewalk. I watched it skitter.

"I don't know," she said. "He's around. He's on the scene."

The wind blew the discarded foil sideways.

"What scene?" I asked, and then Giddle became cryptic, like, if you don't already know, I can't spell it out. That was when I first sensed, but then almost as quickly suppressed, something about Giddle, which was that there might be reason to doubt everything she said.

I TOLD THIS FRIEND of Nadine and Thurman's that I was from Nevada and he started calling me Reno. It was a nice word, he said, like the name of a Roman god or goddess. Juno or Nero. Reno. I told him it was on the neon archway into town, four big red letters, R-E-N-O. I made a film about it, I said. I set up a tripod and filmed cars as they came to a stop at the traffic light under the archway.

"Spiritual America," he said. "That's Thurman's thing, too. Diner coffee. Unflushed toilets. Salesmen. Shopping carts. He's about to become famous. He's having a show at the Museum of Modern Art."

Thurman was not listening to us. He was nibbling on Nadine's ear.

The friend said, "He's a great artist."

"And what are you?" I asked.

"I turn the hands on the big clock in the lobby of the Time-Life Building. Twice a year it has to be reset, to daylight savings and then back to standard time. They call me. It's a very specialized job. If you push too hard, you can bend the hands of the clock."

There were tacit rules with these people, and all the people like them I later met: you weren't supposed to ask basic questions. "What do you do?" "Where are you from?" "What kind of art do you make?" Because I understood he was an artist, but you weren't allowed to ask that. Not even "What is your name?" You pretended you knew, or didn't need to know. Asking an obvious question, even if there were no obvious answer, was a way of indicating to them that they should jettison you as soon as they could.

"I was in Nevada once," he said. "To see something a guy I knew made, the *Spiral Jetty*. The artist, Smithson, had just died. He was a friend, or something like one. Actually, he was an asshole. A sci-fi turkey, but brilliant—"

I said excitedly that I'd been there, too, that I had read his obituary, I knew who he was, but he didn't seem to think it was a remarkable coincidence.

"He had a hilarious riff about the 'real authentic West,' pretending he's Billy Al Bengston, you know, gearhead who makes paintings, and he'd say, 'You New York artists need to stop thinking and *feel*. You're always trying to make concepts, systems. It's bullshit. I was out there chrome-plating my motorcycle and you're, like, in skyscrapers, reading books.' Smithson was a genius. There are two great artists of my generation," he said. "Smithson is one and my friend Sammy is the other."

"What does he make?"

"Nothing. He makes nothing. He's living outside this year. He doesn't enter any structures. Right now he's camped in a park in Little Italy. He had been out in the Bronx sleeping on a construction scaffold and they were shooting at him."

There was another man, besides Henri-Jean with his pole, who was often in my little park at Mulberry and Spring. He slept there sometimes and I figured he was homeless but he didn't quite look it, this young Asian man with shoulder-length hair. There was something too careful and precise about him. I asked if his friend Sammy was Asian and he nodded and said Taiwanese, and I told him I thought I'd seen his friend. He said Sammy had come to New York as a stowaway on a merchant vessel, and that whenever this came up people assumed it was an art project, a performance he had done, and Sammy would have to explain the obvious, that he did it like millions of others, to come to New York. To be an American. And people would laugh as if there were a deep irony under the words.

AT SOME POINT Thurman and Nadine decided we were going to another bar. "You're coming?" I asked the friend. I sensed his hesitation before he nodded sure. Under it, *Why not? There's nothing better to do.* He left his motorcycle in front of the bar because it turned out Thurman had a car. Not just a car but a car and driver—a mid-1950s black and brushed-metal Cadillac Eldorado with a chauffeur who looked about fourteen years old, in a formal driver's jacket that was several sizes too large and white gloves, also too large. I thought of the drivers on Mulberry. I said it was like Little Italy on a Sunday but no one heard me or they didn't care.

We piled into the car with drinks in our hands. Nadine had picked hers up and carried it toward the bar's exit, and following behind I thought, Yes, of course. This is how it's done. Thurman paid our tab, and I was with them, in a Cadillac Eldorado, heavy rocks glasses in our hands, damp cocktail napkins underneath, the ice in our glasses ta-tinking as the car turned slow corners, honking so people would get out of our way, because we were important in that car, me on their handsome friend's lap, our drinks going ta-*tink,* ta-*tink*.

"This is my favorite," the friend said, pulling a leather datebook from a pocket in the door. "It actually comes with the car: the 1957 Brougham's own datebook. And this," he said, pulling out a perfume bottle from a little cubby in the armrest. "The cologne atomizer with Lanvin Arpège perfume. You could order this stuff at the GM dealership when these models were new. Thurman, what else is this thing loaded with?"

"Beats me," Thurman said. "Blossom was willed the car. It belonged to Lady von Doyle."

This Blossom had been mentioned several times now. I didn't ask who she was, who any of the people they mentioned were. I wanted to study the way they spoke. Not interrupt the flow, be the person they had to stop and explain things to.

Their friend reached back into the armrest and retrieved a leather-bound flask with a big GM symbol on it, opened it, and sniffed.

"Scotch," he said. "This is true post-Calvinist delirium. Like the Jews at Sammy's Roumanian, eating steaks that hang off the plates, a big pitcher of chicken schmaltz on the table. It's all about never going hungry again."

He poured from the flask into our glasses. I felt the presence of his body as he leaned.

"I think Lady von Doyle was Jewish," Nadine said. "Thurman, wasn't she Jewish?"

The friend said that seemed about right, for a Jew to drive a Cadillac. "In a sense," he said, "there is simply this axis of General Motors and Volkswagen. I myself have a VW Bug, a car we associate with Eugene McCarthy and flower power and not with Hitler, who created it. The VW doesn't make you think of Hitler and genocide. It's a breast on wheels, a puffy little dream. The Cadillac, now, that's a different dream. Of the two, you'd expect the Cadillac would represent some unspeakable horror, crimes against humanity. Look, here's the Brougham powder puff. The lipstick case. The pill dispenser. The Evans pocket mirror. All that's missing is the Tiffany cocaine vial and a chrome-plated .44 Magnum."

"Keep looking," Thurman said.

"Ha-ha. Right. But you would never be tempted to chrome a .44 Magnum, Thurm. That's strictly for rednecks and off-duty cops. My point is that compared to the humble little folks-wagon, the GM seems guiltier, more dissolute, and yet there's no genocide or forced labor camps under this leather upholstery. Just cotton-wool batting—itself, unlike the beautiful car, not built to last. But these days, only people in the ghetto think it's uptown to drive a Cadillac. In fact, only people in the ghetto think in terms of uptown and downtown. Are you aware there's an oil crisis? I don't even drive my Bug anymore, with the price of gas," the friend said. "I got my little Harley."

"I ride motorcycles," I said. "I mean I used to, but I sold mine."

He looked at me. I was seated sideways on his lap.

"You do have a kind of tomboy allure, I might call it. Yeah."

Okay, I told myself. Something is starting to happen.

"What kind?"

"What?" I asked.

"What kind of bike did you ride?"

"Oh, a Moto Valera."

"See? This fits in with my general thesis. It just so happens I know one of them, though he's not involved with the company. I like to rib him about those sexy calendars they print. They pretend this name, Valera, is about firm Italian tits and desmodromic valves, but actually, they used Polish slave labor to make killing machines for the Nazis. Perhaps not specifically. Not exactly.

But they used some kind of $x$ to make a $y$; fill in your human cost and slick modern contraption of choice."

"Mine was a '65," I said. "Way after the war."

"Which makes it innocent," he said. "Just like you." He touched his hand to my cheek, quick and glancing. "You don't have it anymore? The Moto Valera?"

"I sold it to move here."

"$X$ for $y$."

He had placed his hand on my waist, and I felt heat issue from it, and with that heat, something else, something sincere flowing from him to me, a message or meaning that was different in tone from the way he spoke.

I turned toward him.

"Do you want to know something funny?" I said quietly, not wanting Nadine and Thurman to hear.

"Yes," he whispered back, and moved his hand from my waist to my leg. There wasn't really any other place for him to put it in that crowded backseat. And yet I read the gesture of his hand on my leg as exactly that. A man's hand on a woman's leg, and not a hand that had no other place to rest itself.

"I don't remember your name," I whispered.

"That is funny," he whispered back.

IT SEEMED WE'D BEEN DRIVING for quite a while, the teenage chauffeur working the wheel smoothly, readjusting the comb that was wedged in his Afro like a knife in a cake, as if he'd trained his whole life to drive an enormous Cadillac and retouch his hair simultaneously, and in white gloves whose fingers sagged at the tips, too large for his young hands. We must have been traveling in circles. Only later did I realize we were on Twenty-Third Street in Chelsea, just a few blocks north of where we'd started.

We carried our drinks into a crowded bar, a Spanish place on the ground floor of a hotel, full of color and noise and people they knew. A man called Duke, with root beer–colored chandelier lusters hooked onto his shirt, came rushing toward us. He said the lusters were from the Hotel Earle.

"You're the Duke of Earle," Nadine said.

"I'm the Duke of Earle," he said and shimmied his crystals.

People crowded around them to say hello. I had the sudden feeling they would shed me. I was a stranger they had picked up in an empty bar, and I was irrelevant now that they'd found their place in a familiar scene. I scanned the faces, wondering if this were the sort of place I might find Chris Kelly. I wasn't completely sure I'd recognize him. Pale skin, dark hair over one eye. This might be a bar he'd go to. I asked Thurman and Nadine's friend if he knew an artist named Chris Kelly. "Who?" he said, cupping his ear. I repeated the name. "Oh, right," he said. "Sure, Chris."

"You know him? He's from Reno. I've been trying to find him."

"Chris the artist, right?"

It took me a moment to realize he was joking. As I did, I felt that he and his friends were unraveling any sense of order I was trying to build in my new life. And yet I also felt that he and his friends were possibly my only chance to ravel my new life into something.

He steered us to an empty booth. I slid in next to him. The Duke of Earle joined us. We ordered drinks and the friend punched in selections on the remote jukebox console. Roy Orbison's voice entered the room like a floating silk ribbon.

"My mother had his records," I said to the friend.

"Your mother had good taste, Reno. That voice. And the hair. Black as melted-down record vinyl."

Someone passed the duke a big bottle of soap solution, and he and Nadine took turns dragging on their cigarettes and then blowing huge, organ-shaped bubbles. The bubbles were filled with milk-white smoke from their cigarettes, quivering and luminous, floating downward as Thurman photographed them. The next table over wanted the soap. The duke blew one final bubble of plain lung air. It was clear and shiny, and everyone watched it as it drifted and sank, popping to nothing on the edge of our table.

"You chose this, didn't you," Thurman said to their friend as a new song came on.

It was "Green Onions" by Booker T. and the M.G.'s.

"It's still a good song," the friend said. "Even if it was stuck in my head for almost a decade." He turned to me and said he'd been in jail. Not a decade, just thirty days.

I asked what for. He said for transporting a woman across state lines, and Nadine erupted in laughter. I smiled but had no sense of the coordinates, of what was funny and why.

"The Mann Act," he said. "*Impure intent*: what is impure intent? I did some time. And then I was free but my head was jailed in this song, so it was like I did a lot more time."

He hummed along with "Green Onions," nodding his head.

"At first, it wasn't so bad. 'Green Onions' was this special secret. Something I was hiding, like a pizza cutter up my sleeve. I was pulling one over on them, jamming out to 'Green Onions' while my fellow inmates were getting their cold shower, eating their pimento loaf, reading letters from women who wanted husbands on a short leash. A really short leash. The men wrote back to these lonely women and did push-ups and waited for the women to come a-courting on visitors day, with their fried chickens and their plucked eyebrows."

He had helped the other inmates write their letters to the women. "'Reach out to your loved ones, thirty-nine cents,' a sign in the common room said. You got an envelope, paper, and a stamp. These guys would be working away with a little pencil like they give you for writing down call numbers at the public library. 'How do you spell *pussy*?' they'd ask. 'How do you spell *breasts*?' 'Does *penis* have an *i* in it?'"

"What was the pizza cutter for?" Nadine asked.

"For cutting pizza, sweet Nadine." He gave her a puppy-dog smile. "When I got out, I thought, Okay, unlike a lot of my friends, I know what the inside of a prison is like. Most people don't even know what the outside of a prison is like. They're kept so out of sight. You only know signs on the highway warning you in certain areas not to pick up hitchers. While I know about confinement and boredom and midnight fire drills. Amplified orders banging around the prison yard like the evening prayer call from the mosques along Atlantic Avenue. I know pimento loaf. Powdered eggs. Riots. The experience of being hosed down with bleach and disinfectant like a garbage can. I know about an erotics of necessity."

"Oh, baby," the Duke of Earle said.

"There's something in that. You think you're one way—you know, strictly into women. But it turns out you're into making do."

"I am going to melt," the duke said, "just puddle right in this booth. I had no *idea*—"

"I don't want to disappoint you, Duke," the friend said, "but I'd have to be in prison, and I don't plan on going back."

His arm was around me. I was in the stream that had moved around me since I'd arrived. It had moved around me and not let me in and suddenly here I was, at this table, plunged into a world, everything moving swiftly but not passing me by. I was with the current, part of it, regardless of whether I understood the codes, the shorthand, of the people around me. Not asking or needing to know kept me with them, moving at their pace.

"When you get released, they dump you in Queens Plaza at four A.M. Guys are darting in and out of the doughnut shop, wedded in some deep way to prison cafeteria code, drinking coffee, holding a doughnut in a greasy bag like they've got a bomb, strutting, but unsure who they're strutting *for*, now that there's no guard, no warden, no cell mate. They are just random dudes in Queens Plaza, wonderfully, horribly free. That same hour of the night women and children line up in midtown to get bused out to Rikers for visitors' day. Buses letting out felons here, collecting visiting-day passengers there, while most people are sleeping. The prisons must stay hidden geographically, and hidden in time, too.

"After I got out," he said, "I was incredibly happy. Freedom after confinement is different from plain freedom, which can sometimes be its own sort of prison. The problem was 'Green Onions.' Weeks turned to months and it hung around. That surging rhythm was always in my head and I mean always."

He hummed it. "It woke me up in the middle of the night, like someone had turned up the volume and there I was, lying in the dark listening to the tweedling 'Green Onions' organ riff, waiting for the guitar parts to cut in, stuck inside its driving rhythm, this groovy song boring out the canals of my brain. It was so unfair, because I had paid my debt to society."

"Green Onions" came on again, for I think the third time, and it felt to me that the whole room was conspiring in some kind of hoax. The friend hummed enthusiastically.

"If you had to hear it for ten whole years," I said, laughing, figuring if I laughed openly, he would stop putting me on, "how can you stand to listen to it now?"

"Because you have to know your enemies," he said. "How can you fight if you don't know what you're up against? Who are *your* enemies?"

I said I didn't know.

"See? Exactly."

LATER WE DANCED. My arms were around his neck, his Marsden Hartley T-shirt clinging to his broad shoulders in the heat and sweat of the bar. I had not kissed him but knew I would, and he knew that I knew, and there was a kind of mutual joy in this slide into inevitability, never mind that I didn't know his name or if anything he said was true.

"You're pretty," he said, brushing my hair away from my face.

How did you find people in New York City? I hadn't known this would be how.

"They could put your face on cake boxes," he said.

I smiled.

"Until you show that gap between your teeth. Jesus. It sort of ruins your cake-box appeal. But actually, it enhances a different sort of appeal."

Some women wouldn't want a man to speak to them that way. They'd say, "What kind of appeal do you mean?" or "Go fuck yourself." But I'm not those women, and when he said it, my heart surged a little.

The hotel, it turned out, was the Chelsea. I don't know whose room it was, maybe it was Nadine's, a room that Thurman got for her. There was the sense that Thurman helped her out when he felt like it and that perhaps she was out on the street when he didn't. We were drinking from a bottle of Cutty Sark, and Nadine was not, it turned out, Thurman's wife. From a phone pulled into the hallway he spoke with his actual wife, Blossom, or maybe he just called her that, not at all tenderly, a nasal "Blossom, I will call you in the morning." He enunciated each word like the sentence was a lesson the wife was meant to memorize and repeat. "In the morning. I will call you tomorrow, after I've had my Sanka." Which sent Nadine into hysterics. "*Sanka*! After he's had his *Sanka*!"

After he got off the phone, Thurman seemed energized by a new wildness, as if the compromise of the phone call had to be undone with behavior that Blossom, wherever she was, might not approve of. He put on a Bo Diddley record with the volume turned all the way up, and when it began to skip he pulled it from the turntable and threw it out the window. He put on another record, a song that went "There is something on your mind," over and over, with this clumsy but sexy saxophone hook. At the friend's suggestion, I danced with Thurman. He smelled like aftershave and cigarettes and hair tonic. There was something synthetic and unnatural about him, the way his hair formed a perfect wave and the crispness of his fitted suit, clothing that kept him who he was, a person of some kind of privilege, through whatever degraded environment or level of drunkenness.

*There is something on your mind*
*By the way you look at me*

The friend was dancing with Nadine. Her arms were slung around his neck, her strawberry hair over his shoulder. She pressed her hips against him, and he pressed back.

*There is something on your mind, honey*
*By the way you look at me*

Watching their bodies make contact, I wished we could trade partners.
"Well, look at that," Thurman said. "Take your eye off her for just a minute—"
I felt him fumble for something in his suit jacket. Nadine and their friend turned as a unit, slowly one way and then the other.
Before I understood what it was Thurman had retrieved from his coat pocket, something body-warm, heavy, he was aiming it at them, at the friend and Nadine, who danced to the slow rhythm of the song, pressed together and unaware. I heard a click. He was pointing it at them. A deafening bang ripped through me.
The friend laughed and asked for the gun and Thurman tossed it in his direction. The friend opened it and took out the bullets and inspected them.
"Blanks," he said, and gave it back to Thurman, who grabbed Nadine by the neck in mock violence and stroked the front of her dress up and down with the gun barrel. It seemed a stupid and ridiculous gesture, but she took it seriously and even moaned a little like it turned her on.
I remembered hearing someone back in Reno say that blanks could kill a person. Thurman put the gun in a cabinet and brought out a new bottle of Cutty Sark. He poured us fresh drinks and then played "Will the Circle Be Unbroken" on the little electric piano that was in the room. The friend took me up to the roof of the building and narrated the New York skyline. "It's up here on roofs where all the good stuff is taking place," he said.

"Women walking up the sides of buildings, scaling vertical facades with block and tackle," he said. "They dress like cat burglars, feminist cat burglars. Who knows? You might become one, even though you're sweet and young. *Because* you're sweet and young."

"What are you, some kind of reactionary?" I said.

"No," he said. "I'm giving you tips. But actually, the roofs are somewhat last year. Gordon Matta-Clark just cut an entire house in half. It's going to be tough to beat that. What now, Reno? What now?"

Back downstairs, Thurman barged into the bathroom while Nadine was peeing, for some reason not in the toilet but in the bathtub. He looked at her, sitting on the edge of the tub with her minidress pushed up.

"You know what I love more than anything?" he said.

"What?" she asked, with quiet reverence, as if the whole evening were a ritual enacted in order to arrive at this moment, when he would finally tell her what he really loved.

"I love crazy little girls." He grabbed her and hoisted her over his shoulder, her underpants still around her ankles. Carried her into the bedroom and shut the door.

"You know what they do?" the friend said. "They shoot each other with that gun. In the crotch. Bang. Pow. It makes your eardrums feel ripped in half the next day."

"Isn't that dangerous?" I asked.

"Of course. That's why they do it."

The gun went off. Nadine shrieked with laughter. The telephone in the room began ringing.

The friend and I sat quietly, either waiting for the next gunshot or for the phone to stop ringing, or for something else.

"Hey," he said. "Hey, Reno. Come here."

But I was already right next to him.

We kissed, his pretty mouth soft and warm against mine, as the phone kept ringing.

WHEN WE'D FINALLY LAIN DOWN on my bed, the early sun over the East River filling my apartment with gold light, I told him I didn't want to know his name. I didn't think much about it. I just said it. "I don't even want to know your name."

He was wearing the brown Borsalino I'd found at the bar near my house. He took it off and put it on the floor next to my mattress, peeled off his homemade Marsden Hartley T-shirt, and pinned me down gently.

My heart was pounding away.

"I don't want to know yours, either," he said, scanning my face intently.

What was he looking for? What did he see?

What transpired between us felt real. It *was* real: it took place. The things I'd heard and witnessed that evening, their absurdity, were somehow acknowledged in his dimples, his smirk, his gaze. The way he comically balled up the Marsden Hartley T-shirt and lobbed it across the room like a man fed up with shirts once and for all. Surveyed the minimal room, nodding, as if it were no surprise, but information nonetheless that he was taking in, cataloguing. And then surveying me, my body, nodding again, all things confirmed, understood, approved of. And us, two people without names but as entwined as two people could be.

I had followed the signs with care and diligence: from Nina Simone's voice, to the motorcycle, to the Marsden Hartley shirt. All the way through the night, to the gun and now this: a man in my room who seemed to hold keys to things I'd imagined Chris Kelly would unlock had I found him. I never did.

WHEN I WOKE UP IN THE LATE MORNING, he was gone. The day was mid stride, full heat, full sun. My head pounded weakly. I was tired, hungover, disoriented. The brown felt Borsalino was gone, and I remembered that I had wanted him to have it, had told him to have it.

I sat on the fire escape. It was Sunday. Down below, the limousine drivers were in front of the little Mafia clubhouse, waiting next to a long line of black cars. They looked sweaty and miserable and I envied them. To wait by a car and know with certainty that your passenger would appear. To have such purpose on that day.

I had said something embarrassing about the Borsalino being *already* his, that it had been waiting for him in my apartment. I was doing that thing the infatuated do, stitching destiny onto the person we want stitched to us. But all of that—me as Reno, he as nameless, his derelict friends against whom we bonded, and yet without whom I never would have met him—all of it was gone.

I had said I didn't want to know his name and it wasn't a lie. I had wanted to pass over names and go right to the deeper thing.

RAIN FELL. Every day, heavy rain, and I sat in my apartment and waited for sirens. Just after the rain began, there were always sirens. Rain and then sirens. In a rush to get to where life was happening, life and its emergencies.

Do you understand that I'm alone? I thought at the unnamed friend as I stood in the phone booth on Mulberry Street, the sky gray and heavy, the street dirty and quiet and bleak, as a woman's voice declared once more that I'd reached a number that had been disconnected.

It was just one night of drinking and chance. I'd known it the moment I met him, which was surely why I was enchanted in the first place. Enchantment means to want something and also to know, somewhere inside yourself, not an obvious place, that you aren't going to get it.

Jack Goldstein, *The Murder*, 1977, 33 ⅓ rpm, 12 minutes.

This twelve-minute record is a montage of sound effects—mostly breaking glass, pouring rain, and thunder. Goldstein had all the right ingredients for myth: brilliant, cool, mysterious. He was hugely influential but ended up living in a trailer in East L.A., selling ice cream from a truck; the ice cream once melted completely when he had to wait in line for methadone, but he refroze it and sold it anyway. He died in 2003, and so his body of work is now, sadly, a bounded set.

# THE FLAMETHROWERS

*curated by*

*Rachel Kushner*

---

The first image I pinned up to spark inspiration for what would eventually be my novel *The Flamethrowers* was of a woman with tape over her mouth. She floated above my desk with a grave, almost murderous look, war paint on her cheeks, blonde braids framing her face, the braids a frolicsome countertone to her intensity. The paint on her cheeks, not frolicsome. The streaks of it, dripping down, were cold, white shards, as if her face were faceted in icicles. I didn't think much about the tape over her mouth (which is actually Band-Aids over the photograph, and not over her lips themselves). This image ended up on the jacket of *The Flamethrowers*, whose first-person narrator, introduced in this issue, in the story "Blanks," is a young blonde woman. A creature of language, silenced.

The second image was of Ducati engineer Fabio Taglioni standing behind a 1971 750 GT. The Ducati is in metal-flake orange; Taglioni in double-knit Brioni. I didn't have an image of a girl on a motorcycle, although the book opens with the narrator riding one in the Bonneville land speed trials. *Girl on a Motorcycle* was the title of a film starring Marianne Faithfull and Alain Delon (which was released in certain European markets, such as Italy, as *Naked Under Leather*). In the trickiest riding scene, Marianne Faithfull has a double, a hulking man in a honey-blonde wig, as you'll see if you play it on slow.

The young woman in war paint was from an archival document of 1970s Italy, and she symbolized for me the insurrectionary foment that overtook the country in that decade. "Autonomia" was the term for this foment, the movement of the 1970s, a loose wave of people, all over Italy, who came together for various reason at various times to engage in illegality and play, and to find a way to act, to build forms of togetherness in a country whose working class was impotent and whose sub-working class was fed up with work, by turns joyous and full of rage, ready to revolt, which they did. There were various layers, of which the most violent, shadowy, and clandestine (and yet, paradoxically, the most visible and sensational) were the Red Brigades. The Italian seventies had seemed a logical subject for fiction, on account of the fact that I kept stumbling upon its lore. It all began when I met a mysterious and magnetic Italian woman who didn't say much, and who, when I naively asked her what she did, what she was interested in, stared at me and said, "Niente." She had been the girlfriend of a Red Brigades terrorist, I learned. Her "niente" did not mean "nothing." It meant, I don't engage in what you'd call work. Or interests. I might add that I met this woman in a house on Lake Como that was filled with someone's mother's Fascist memorabilia, busts of Mussolini, D'Annunzian slogans chiseled into marble.

Which connects to the third image I pinned up as I wrote, of two proper-looking gentlemen in a World War 1–era motorized contraption, an arcane cycle and bullet-shaped sidecar. Of the pair, the man in the sidecar, if passively at the mercy of the one over the handlebars, looks more self-possessed. He looks, actually, like F. T. Marinetti. I pretended that he was, and asked myself, Why did those guys never actually build anything? They drew vehicles on paper. They called war the world's only hygiene. But they had no relation to engineering and factories, to machines or munitions—except that a few of them lost limbs, or lives, in the war. But so did a lot of regular, non-Futurists.

There are two central threads to *The Flamethrowers*: Italy in 1977, the crest of the movement, and New York at that time, a period that has long fascinated me, when the city had a Detroit-like feel, was drained of money and its manufacturing base, and piled up with garbage. Parts of downtown became liberated zones of abandonment, populated by artists and criminals. The blackout of 1977 has a special place in my heart—the "bad" blackout, compared to 1965, the "good" blackout, when everyone in the housing projects behaved, an event whose textures DeLillo rendered so memorably in *Underworld*.

I wanted to conjure New York as an environment of energies, sounds, sensations. Not as a backdrop, a place that could resolve into history and sociology and urbanism, but rather as an entity that could not be reduced because it had become a character, in the manner that a fully complex character in fiction isn't reducible to cause, reasons, event. I looked at a lot of photographs and other evidentiary traces of downtown New York and art of the mid-1970s. Maybe a person is a tainted magnet and nothing is by chance, but what I kept finding were nude women and guns. The group Up Against the Wall Motherfuckers, who figure in the novel, papered the Lower East Side, in the late 1960s, with posters that said, LOOKING FOR PEOPLE WHO LIKE TO DRAW, with an image of a revolver. I had already encountered plenty of guns in researching Italy—the more militant elements of the Autonomist movement had an official weapon, the Walther P38, which could be blithely denoted with the thumb out, pointer finger angled up. I would scan the images of rallies in Rome, a hundred thousand people, among whom a tenth, I was told by people who had been there, were armed. Ten thousand individuals on the streets of Rome with guns in their pockets. But among New York artists, I hadn't expected guns, and yet that's what I encountered: lots of guns, and as I said, lots of nude women. Occasionally in the same image, Hannah Wilke in strappy heels holding a petite purse pistol—like Honey West, except naked. But mostly it was men posing with the guns: William Burroughs, William Eggleston, Sandro Chia, Richard Serra. Warhol's gun drawings. Chris Burden out in Los Angeles having a friend shoot him. And women with their clothes off: Carolee Schneemann, Hannah Wilke, Francesca Woodman, Ana Mendieta, Marina Abramović, who was both nude and with a loaded gun pointed at her head (by a man). What does all this mean? Many things, I'm sure, but for starters, it means people were getting out of the studio. Art was now about acts not sellable; it was about gestures and bodies. It was freedom, a realm where a guy could shoot off his rifle. Ride his motorcycle over a dry lakebed. Put a bunch of stuff on the floor—dirt, for instance, or lumber. Drive a forklift into a museum, or a functional racecar. But that's art history. For the purposes of a novel, what did it mean? I was faced with the pleasure and headache of somehow stitching together the pistols and the nude women as defining features of a fictional realm, and one in which the female narrator, who has the last word, and technically all words, is nevertheless continually overrun, effaced, and silenced by the very masculine world of the novel she inhabits—a contradiction I had to navigate, just as I had to find a way to merge what were by nature static and iconic images into a stream of life, real narrative life.

As I wrote, events from my time, my life, began to echo those in the book, as if I were inside a game of call and response. While I wrote about ultraleft subversives, *The Coming Insurrection*, a book written by an anonymous French collective, was published in the United States, and its authors were arrested in France. As I wrote about riots, they were exploding in Greece. As I wrote about looting, it was rampant in London. The Occupy movement was born on the University of California campuses, and then reborn as a worldwide phenomenon, and by the time I needed to describe the effects of tear gas for a novel about the 1970s, all I had to do was watch live feeds from Oakland, California.

In 1978, the Red Brigades killed the leader of the Christian Democrats and former prime minister of Italy Aldo Moro. That same year, Guy Debord made his final film, *In girum imus nocte et consumimur igni*, its title a famous Latin palindrome, translatable as "we turn in the night in a circle of fire." A film that includes many still images, which I looked at and into as I wrote. Debord's relationship to women and girls is so strange. He's suggesting they've been used for banal consumer culture, to sell soap, for instance, and yet surely he enjoys seeing them in their bikinis, their young flesh and sweet smiles, as he edits them into the frame. As I was working on the novel, I encountered a woman who was friends with the only Situationist not expelled by Debord, the enigmatic, infamous Gianfranco Sanguinetti. "What is he up to?" I excitedly asked. "What does he do now?" She shrugged, and coolly, disdainfully, said, "He lives."

A few more films besides Debord's that were important sources: Barbara Loden's *Wanda*, about a young woman who isn't afraid to throw her life away. Chantal Akerman's *News from Home*, in which the camera wanders the deserted streets of Lower Manhattan. Alberto Grifi and Massimo Sarchielli's *Anna*, the mother of all films about Italy in the 1970s. Also, a filmic fact: that *Taxi Driver* was rerated from X to R after the producers scaled back the brightness of reds in the film. Michel Auder's *The Feature*, which I saw at Anthology Film Archives, just me and one old man crinkling a paper bag as Auder spent Cindy Sherman's money on prostitutes, playing himself in a despicable but brilliant game. Before he was married to Sherman, Auder had been with Viva, the Warhol superstar. Viva later dated the photographer William Eggleston, when she was living at the Chelsea Hotel, just after he made *Stranded in Canton*, in which his Memphis friends waggle guns and hold forth in Quaalude slurs.

An appeal to images is a demand for love. We want something more than just their mute glory. We want them to give up a clue, a key, a way to cut open a space, cut into a register, locate a tone, without which the novelist is lost.

It was with images that I began *The Flamethrowers*. By the time I finished, I found myself with a large stash.

William Eggleston, *Stranded in Canton*, 1974, still from a black-and-white videotape, 77 minutes.

Larry Fink, *Black Mask*, 1967, black-and-white photograph, 11" x 14".

Black Mask was a Dada-inspired antiwar movement that intervened in culture and politics and later morphed into Up Against the Wall Motherfuckers, "a street gang with an analysis." They ran soup kitchens and a free store and tried to empower and motivate the disenfranchised. Their legacy made way for the great culture of East Village artists' squats like the Gas Station on Avenue B and the Rivington School sculpture garden.

Right: Danny Lyon, *88 Gold Street* (detail), 1967, black-and-white photograph, dimensions variable. From the series "The Destruction of Lower Manhattan," 1967.

The same year that Larry Fink photographed Black Mask on Wall Street, Danny Lyon methodically captured with a view camera the vast demolition of Lower Manhattan, much of it coming down for the construction of the Twin Towers. Factories and warehouses to be replaced by finance, which gives literal shape to a significant transformation of the seventies: the death of American manufacturing.

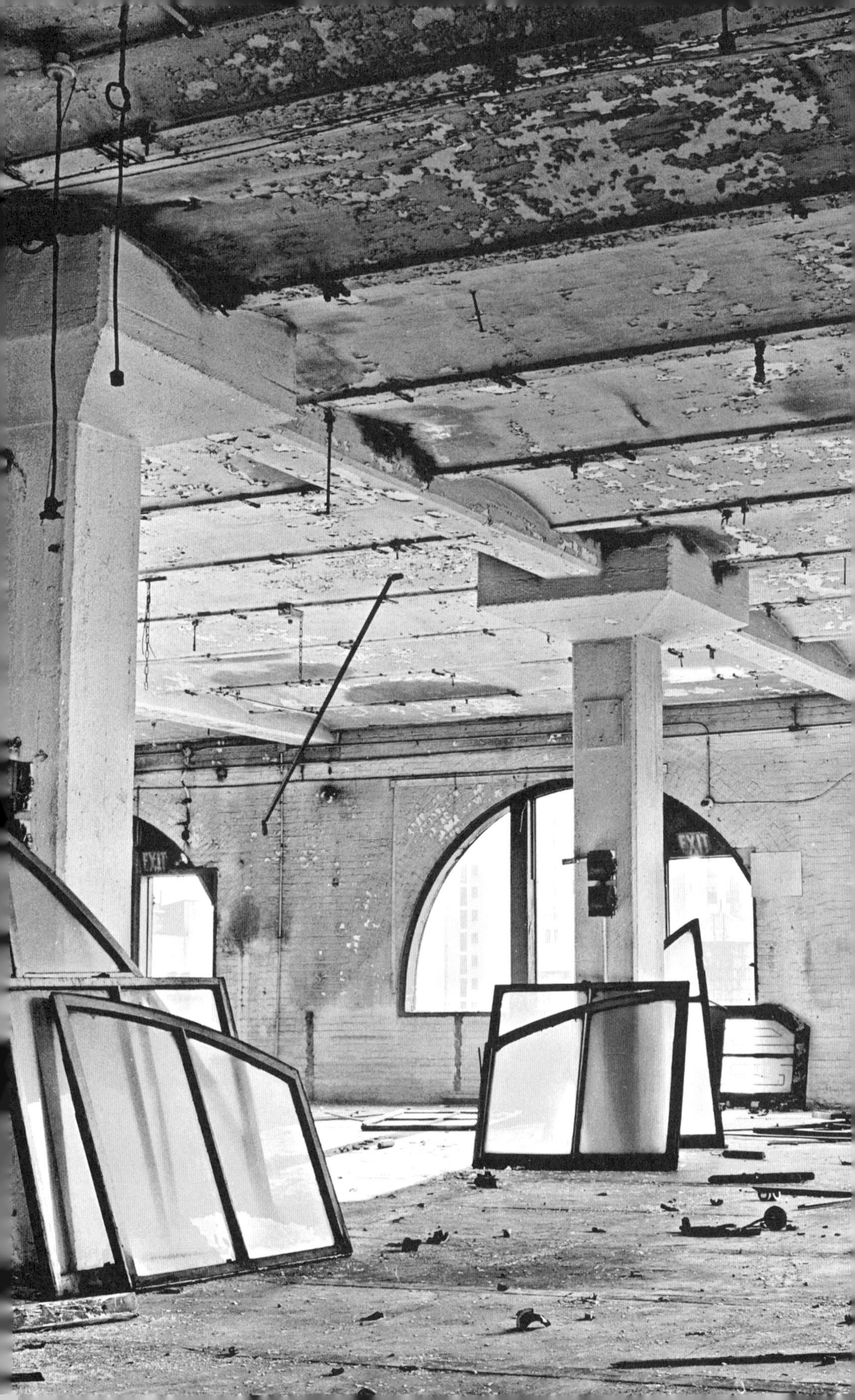
EXIT
EXIT

Andy Warhol, *Screen Test: Virginia Tusi*, 1965, still from a silent black-and-white film in 16mm, 4 minutes at 16 frames per second.

Who is she? No one seems to know. "A young woman identified only as Virginia Tusi," according to the catalogue raisonné. She was included in Warhol's *Thirteen Most Beautiful Women* along with Susanne De Maria and Julie Judd—the exceptionally pretty wives of Walter De Maria and Donald Judd. Warhol's two favorite kinds of people were beautiful people and the American upper classes. When those were combined into one person, such as Edie Sedgwick, bliss. One of the more striking men that Warhol filmed in 1965 was in the audience when I saw a program of *Screen Tests* last year. This man, a beard now tumbling down his chin, big belly protruding from his open blazer, shared anecdotes. "Warhol wanted me to flex my jaw," he said. And, "Edie was a real bitch." It might be better if Virginia Tusi just keeps beaming resplendently from her *Screen Test*, a mystery of mute loveliness.

Julie Buck and Karin Segal, *China Girl #56*, 2005, digital print from a color film, 12" x 15".
From the series "Girls on Film," 2005.

China girls, whose faces were used to adjust color densities in film processing, were mostly secretaries who worked in the film labs—regular women who appeared on leader that was distributed all over the world. It's not clear why they had that rather racist moniker; some say the original ones were Asian, and others speculate that a particular secretary who posed for film leader was a habitual server of tea (which makes the name seem even more problematic). In France, they were "les lillis." If the projectionist loaded the film correctly, you didn't see the China girl. And if you did see her, she flashed by so quickly she was only a quick blur. They were ubiquitous and yet invisible, a thing in the margin that was central to each film, these nameless women that, as legend has it, were traded among film technicians and projectionists like baseball cards.

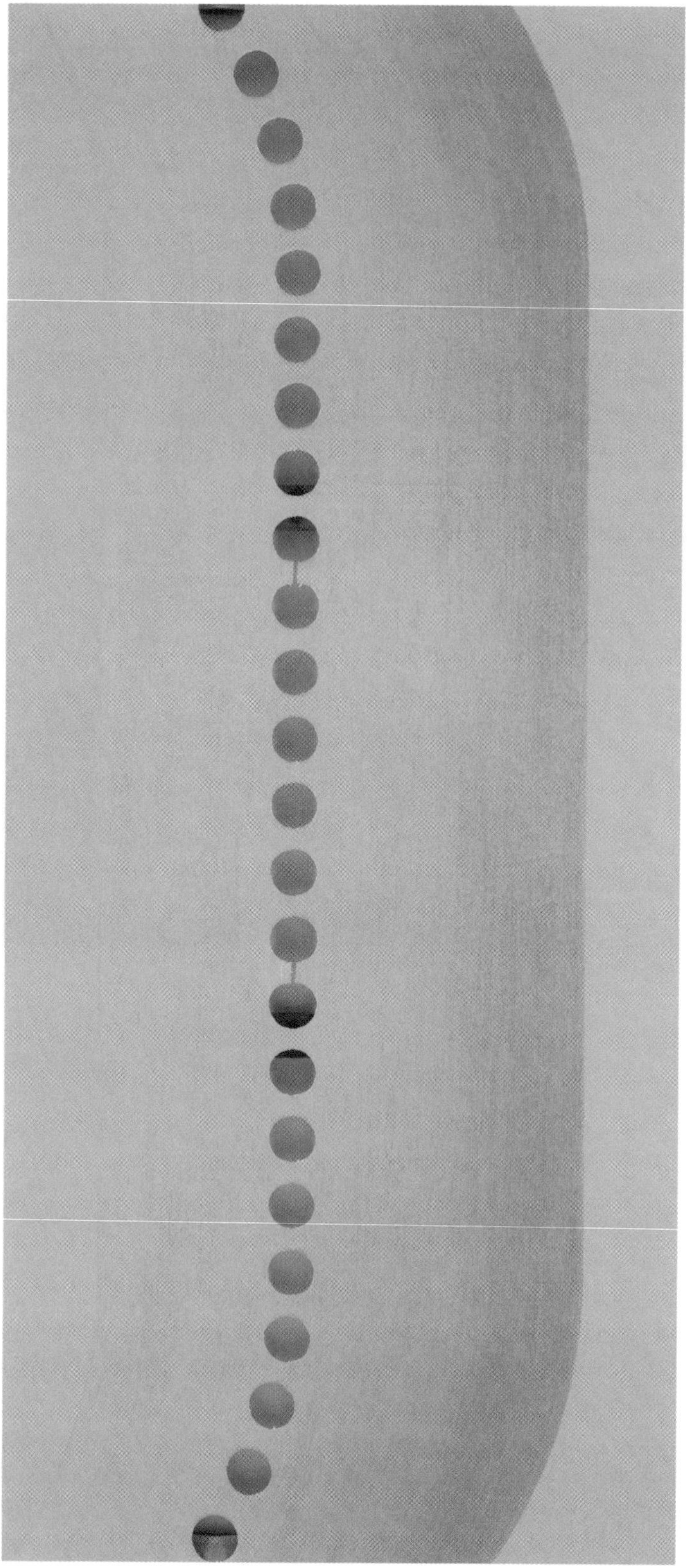

Allen Ginsberg, *Sandro Chia* (detail), 1985, black-and-white photograph, 11" x 14".

"In a serious confrontation, I'd take a shotgun any day. It's a much more formidable and effective weapon than a handgun, unless it's a hand shotgun. I'd like to see more of those," wrote William Burroughs. The artist Sandro Chia had been firing at targets with Burroughs in Rhinebeck, New York, when this photograph was taken.


Left: Lee Lozano, *Punch, Peek & Feel*, 1967–70, oil on canvas with perforations, 95 ⅝" x 42 ⅛" x 1 ⅝".

Lozano was a tough and uncompromising person, celebrated by her male contemporaries for her conceptually driven paintings and the way she collapsed art into life. She had a solo show at the Whitney in 1970. In 1971, for her piece *Decide to Boycott Women,* she did just that: she didn't speak to women for the next twenty-eight years, right up until her death.

Robert Heinecken, *Cliché Vary: Autoeroticism*, 1974,
photographic emulsion on canvas and pastel chalk, 39 ½" x 39 ½".

The sweet innocence of the McLuhan seventies. By the 1980s, when I was a teenager, I carried around a copy of *Subliminal Seduction: Are You Being Sexually Aroused by This Picture?* and thought I was being very ironic and clever. The culture by that point was already using the ability to decode to sell us to ourselves in even more effective ways. Selling us sex. Even as sex was, is, and will be one of the few things people can do to each other for free.

David Salle, *The Coffee Drinkers*, 1973, black-and-white photograph with affixed product advertisement, one of four panels, each 20" x 16".

She's having a quiet, contemplative moment in morning light. She's selling coffee. Or coffee's selling her, as her, or as … lifestyle? Something feminine, calming, pure? "Images that understand us" was a phrase coined by Salle and James Welling. Salle, as a twenty-one-year-old student, made a prescient series of images—well before we came to know work by Richard Prince or Cindy Sherman—by photographing four women in his life (among them his girlfriend and mother) and gluing on the Nescafé label.

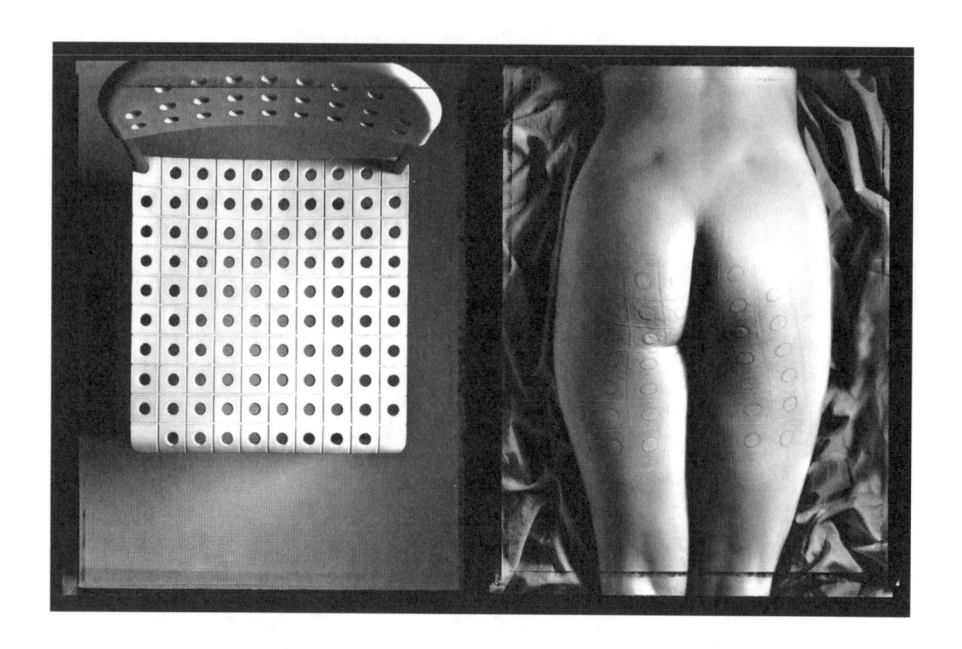

Gabriele Basilico, *Contact*, 1984, two black-and-white photographs, 23 ⅝" x 31 ⅞".

"Putting together chairs and bottoms was very enjoyable for me," Basilico has said of his series *Contact*. He calls the residual marks from this process "provisional relief tattoos." But tattoos of what? Modernism, as painless as modernism looks but never is. The link between violence and modernism is everywhere but too broad to get into in the form of a caption. It's something more like a life's work. Someone's, anyhow, if not mine.

Enrico Castellani, *Superficie*, 2008, resin on canvas, 19 ¾" x 31 ½".

Enrico Castellani, a younger contemporary of Lucio Fontana and Alberto Burri, was the first person in Italy targeted in the massive sweep of arrests in the seventies. Castellani seems to have circulated among leftists. A recent catalogue of his work includes an essay by Adriano Sofri, former leader of the leftist group Lotta Continua, who spent twenty-two years in prison for instigating the assassination of a police captain (Sofri vehemently maintains his innocence).

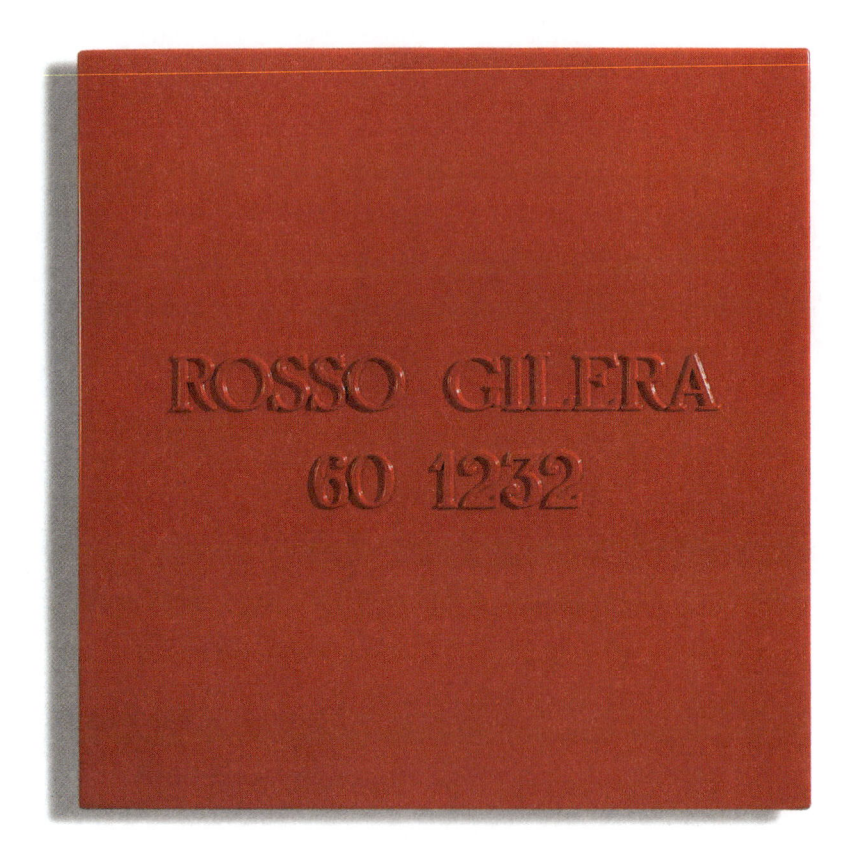

Alighiero Boetti, *Rosso Gilera, Rosso Guzzi*, 1971,
enamel paint on two iron panels, each 27 9/16" x 27 9/16".

Boetti made a series of works using industrial paints, like in this case, colors used for motorcycle makes Gilera and Moto Guzzi. The point wasn't merely that colors had been branded. Factory politics in Italy were about to erupt, in the "hot autumn" of 1969. Meanwhile the fastest bikes in the world were being produced in Northern Italy, where Boetti was from. In *Rosso Gilera, Rosso Guzzi*, speed, racing, conceptual and formal precepts, and an industrialized but not yet subjectivized class of workers collide and simmer, all in a work that looks so friendly, uncomplicated, and Pop.

Tano D'Amico, *At the Gates of the University*, 1977, black-and-white photograph, 7" x 9 ⅜".

Go to Italy and no one talks about the 1970s, when their country literally almost had a revolution. That explosive era and its joys, traumas, and failures have been all but erased. Luckily, there are some remainders, like the amazing photographs of Tano D'Amico. Here, he captures students at the gates of Sapienza University in Rome on February 17, 1977, when it was occupied by students, as Luciana Lama, leader of the biggest labor union in Italy, came to pay them a visit and was heckled and expelled.

Right: Ida Faré and Franca Spirito's *Mara e Le Altre*, 1979.

"Mara" is Mara Cagol, a former leader of Italy's leftist-militant Brigate Rosse (BR). "Le altre" are the militant women in Italy in the 1970s, whose Leninism and bombs were only one small and contested facet of a vast and complex wave of feminist actions that transformed the landscape of Italy and are of great interest still to feminist theorists for their sophistication and lucidity. It's curious that for the cover of this book an image from Godard's 1967 film *La Chinoise* was chosen. Not an image of a real female terrorist, of which Italy produced many, but a still from a film where an actress (Juliet Berto) *plays* a terrorist, crouching behind a machine-gun turret built of stacked copies of Mao's little red book. The real terrorist, Mara Cagol, successfully broke her husband from prison, fellow BR leader Renato Curcio, in 1975. The same year, she was gunned down in a shoot-out with carabinieri. The founder of Feltrinelli, the press that published this book, had died accidentally in 1972, attempting to sabotage Milan's power supply.

# I NUOVI TESTI  FELTRINELLI ECONOMICA

IDA FARÉ / FRANCA SPIRITO

# MARA E LE ALTRE

LE DONNE E LA LOTTA ARMATA:
STORIE INTERVISTE RIFLESSIONI

# Three Poems by Geoffrey Hill

## FROM 'EXPOSTULATIONS ON THE VOLCANO'

*8*

Fantastic to be Lowry by proxy,
Confabulating him; to stand tongue-tied
In awe of yourself; to hold epoxy-
Resin postures rather than be thought dead;

To ape his helpless vamping and to fall,
Face down, upon Dollarton's tide-machine,
Among odd jetsam to posture and flail,
Stark in the shallows, laved with soapy brine.

Who has not totted his black bile, Consul,
Where *Qliphoth* is wet coal and gritstone setts,
Spackled and wintry with hoary moonspill?
As vile an intro as the spirit gets.

Matter stubborn to be legendary
In situ: I fear they are off the beam,
Those masters who could break and brand fury,
Turning things back upon themselves for shame.

For shame my riposte here not better made
Than, picked from underlip, shreds of *Gold Flake*.
And I no smoker. Let it be; upgrade
Folie à deux to singular double-take.

*49*

Time and light move simultaneously
In either direction: such is my view
Based on a vision that came painlessly
And liquorless as mostly I am now.

I say *painlessly*; but there stands belief
With which you are familiar. Time, great
Laden shuttle reduced to its begriff,
In which you and I, love, rue with Wyatt,

Against the whinge of pulsars; a pressure
Unimaginable; here recognized
And with charts to prove them. I am less sure
Of other measures anarchs have devised.

Clue me as to how we are immortal
Yet again. Yet again impulsive flares
From lourd sophistry, of misrequital;
Much as this causeless spin our lords and heirs

Have not forefashioned. Must we end with him,
This mortifying old man, his bent wits,
With the slow-dying spiral of his rhyme;
And with whatever else in judgment sits?

54

Who sacrificed our young daughters to win
Compensation and our sons to gain time;
Whose loves were implicate with rites obscene,
Whose beauty was of light, angle, and frame:

How shall we expel a new birth? My age
Tells against me in a speech not my own
But familiar. Face raddled with rouge
Cast me as Quentin Crisp not as Timon;

A tenured special adviser to life.
Could have wished confirmation while all slept.
I would not curse to redefine belief,
Disfigure telling rhyme of the adept.

Calvinist-Papist, stuck with a basic
Flaw in deportment. Note: I am still owed
For the lost memory stick. *Take physic,
Pomp*, ill-rehearsed by voices well-endowed.

Grand zero Wurlitzer tops all in this,
Its co-ordinates late Nemo's. No man's
Certitude my servitude. Nothingness
Mates infinity. There are no demons.

*Letter from Kentucky*

## J. D. DANIELS

John C. Skaggs was born in Green County in 1805, thirteen years after Kentucky became our fifteenth state. His son, Ben Skaggs, was born in 1835 in Bald Hollow and married Missouri Ann Carter.

Their second eldest boy, Will Franklin Skaggs, had his pick of Pleasant Poteet's granddaughters: he could have had Delilah or Myrtie Scripture, but he chose Ella Green Poteet; and their third child, after Carter C. and Elvie Omen, was Sylvia May.

Meanwhile, in Larue County, Elmina G. Dixon married Bryant Young Miller's boy, and they bore a girl they called Mary Bothena Doctor Bohanan Sarah Lucritia Miller Rock, who, mercifully, named her own son Charlie.

And Thomas Jefferson Quinley's daughter Sefronia married Edwin Russell Wheatley, and begat Mildred Lucille, who married Robert

Raymond Salisbury, who called himself Butch Daniels—of whom we will not speak.

Their son married Charlie and Sylvia's daughter, and begat me: "His Majesty the Ego," as Freud wrote in 1908, "the hero of all daydreams and all novels."

This happened in Kentucky, except for the Freud part. That happened in Austria.

I WAS BORN IN KENTUCKY and lived there for the better part of three decades.

As schoolchildren we were taught that the word *Kaintuckee* came from *Ka-ten-ta-teh*, which meant, in Cherokee, "the dark and bloody ground."

Later they said *Ken-tah-ten* meant "future land" in Iroquois. In high school, they claimed it was Wyandot for "land of tomorrow," and I recall a field trip to see a documentary with that name.

Before long historians were telling us it could be Seneca for "place of meadows," or it might be a Mohawk word, *Kentah-ke*, meaning "meadow."

And from time to time there was an expert, often but not always on a barstool, who argued that the region in its pristine state had seemed to its settlers to be nothing but wild turkeys and river canebrakes: *Kaneturkee*.

It was clear that no one had any idea what he was talking about—and, in this manner, the most valuable part of our education was received.

I FLEW BACK TO KENTUCKY on a cold spring day aboard a paper airplane that every sneeze of wind knocked sideways. Next time I'll swim. Everyone hates flying. Even birds hate flying.

A sign in the airport said LOUISVILLE WELCOMES TOGETHER FOR THE GOSPEL NAZARENE YOUTH INTERNATIONAL 2012 PENTECOSTAL FIRE YOUTH CONFERENCE. There was nowhere to sleep. The many hotel rooms of downtown Louisville were occupied by boys and men in red T-shirts with white crucifixes ironed on. They stood in traffic, gawking.

Someone had cut down the peach tree in the front yard of my old Preston Street house. There was a scrap of vinyl siding across the front step, and plastic wrap on the inside windows to keep out the draft, and wax paper fluttering under a gap in the door.

Across the street from that house had once been the only bar where they had known what I wanted, a shot of Jim Beam and a bottle of Sterling, and Bill set it up every time he saw me coming. It was called B & B Bar, said to have been named for its owner Bill and then for Bill again, because what kind of name is the B-Bar.

I had seen an old man get shot in front of that bar because he wouldn't give two kids his bicycle. I snorted pills off the back of the toilet in that bar with a woman I didn't understand was a prostitute: but later it became clear to me.

Blind John, still dripping rain from his trip to the ATM, offered me a hundred dollars to let him go down on me. "I think you're in the wrong bar," I said. "Maybe you are," he said.

I lost a lot of money shooting nine ball in that bar. Listen to your uncle Tim-Tom and never play pool for money against a man called Doc.

I saw a little man stab a big man with a carving knife on that bar's front steps. Later the wet knife glimmered under the streetlight on the hood of a prowl car. The big man went to the hospital; the little man went to the penitentiary. I don't know where the bar went.

I DROVE DOWN to the tractor-trailer plant where my father had managed the repair shop, but the plant had closed. I had worked there twice.

The first time was in the touch-up shop with Orville, soldering brake-light wires and repainting trailers Andrew had banged his forklift into, as a summer job and as a warning from my father: this was the kind of job I was going to wind up with if I didn't straighten up and fly right. I was the only man in that garage with ten fingers.

The second time was in the decal shop as a college dropout. I had not straightened up, I had not flown right, this was the kind of job I had wound up with.

By day, Mayflower trailers, Frito-Lay trailers, Budweiser and Bud Light trailers, Allied trailers; by night, drinking Colt 45 with Allen down by the train trestles, and later Boyd crawling around on the floor with a cardboard box on his head, insisting that he was a Christmas present. I read *The Faerie Queene*—counting syllables, thinking about the number seven—and thought: One of these days I am going to jump off the Second Street Bridge.

FINLEY'S WAS GONE, TOO, nothing but a pile of bricks. At Indi's, eating the rib tips with red sauce and macaroni and cheese and mashed potatoes and gravy, I listened: "You never know. That's what I told them at his funeral this morning. I said *all right, see you later*. But I was wrong."

And I remembered my friend Allen asking me if I saw a plain white van parked across from his house down by the racetrack.

Allen said, "Tell me something, man. The van is real? I'm not paranoid? It's been parked there for days. Three days."

"I am sure that is true."

"Listen—am I crazy? Could it be the FBI?"

"Allen," I said, seated in his forest of pot plants, "let me ask you a question. What amount of drugs and paraphernalia is in your house, do you think? And what is it the FBI gets paid to do all day? I am one hundred percent certain it is the FBI. I will see you later."

I said *see you later*, but I was wrong. I did not see Allen later. Allen went to jail.

I TOOK THE GENE SNYDER FREEWAY out to the Bible College and got off at Beulah Church and drove past AMF Derby Lanes ("all you can bowl") and Highview Church of God and Highview Baptist Church and Victory Baptist Church Camp.

An old woman with a long gray ponytail was doing yard work, cutting back bushes I had planted in front of the house where I had grown up, where I had tried to grow up. A tired black dog lay in the yard, her yard now, not mine.

It's an old story. The horse knows the way to carry the sleigh: you go back to the place, but the place isn't there any more.

I drove out of Fern Creek down Bardstown Road toward Buechel, past Cash Xpress and Mister Money, past Xtreme Auto Sounds and Ventura's Used Tires and Global Auto Glass, and past the Heart of Fire City Church, the pastor of which had once helped us move some furniture and when it came time for my mother to write him a check for his services he said, "Don't cheat a blind man, sister, I can't read."

I drove to my uncle Charles's house out in Okolona, past Latino Auto Service and the Godfather (the strip joint that once had on its marquee THE MAYOR IS GAY PLEASE SUE SO I CAN PROVE IT), past Liquor Palace 5 and Discount Medical Supplies, past Furniture Liquidators Home Center, past Cash America Pawn and Cashland, past the Mower Shop, past Los Mezcales and El Molcajete, past Big Ron's Bingo and Cashtyme Cash Advance ("You're Good For It!"), past Moore's Sewing & Learning Center, and DePrez Quality Jewelry & Loan, and Floors Unlimited, and Chain Saw World.

I turned on the rental car's radio and the man on the radio said, "Your gift right now, just twenty dollars a month, could help. Seventy-three more gifts needed. People like you, doing their part. One song left in this challenge. Standing in the gap for those who need it. We here believe in the infallible Word of God. Unchanging principles for changing times."

I drove past something. Then I drove past something else.

"THERE IS AN AWFUL LOT OF DRUGS NOW in these small towns and big towns both," my uncle Charles said. "You may not know the police shot that boy you all used to play with. Said he was cooking meth down there in his shed. They had him surrounded and he came out alone with his pistol. Found thirty-seven shell casings when it was all done with. What was his name?" But Charles couldn't remember the dead man's name.

"You'll stay with us tonight," my aunt Alice Carol said.

"I have a hotel room near the airport."

"Honey, everything in this town is near the airport."

"I guess I made a foolish decision."

"You've always been foolish."

My aunt was teasing me. She didn't think I was so bad. One Thanksgiving—we were listening to the old boys jaw for hours about hiding up a tree with my grandfather's shotgun in order to shoot a neighbor's brown dog that had killed two of their chickens, and after both barrels were empty there was nothing left but the dog's collar and its tail, which they'd helped the neighbor bury—she had turned to me and said, "If you want to be a writer, why don't you go get a pen and paper and write down all these lies?"

STANDIFORD FIELD WAS NOW CALLED Louisville International Airport and the Executive West hotel was the Crowne Plaza, but Executive

Strike & Spare still stood on the other side of Phillips Lane. I walked across the street and shot nine-ball for a couple of lazy hours. It turns out it's like riding a bike—you never forget how, and especially not if you never knew how in the first place.

Overheard at the bar: "He and his friends see this old man take his wallet out at the liquor store, so they know he's got money, and they follow him home. But his wife's there. Now that's two counts. I called him and his mother says, He ain't here. I called back. I said, Santino, I heard you cut your monitor off. You know you got court this Friday? You coming? You know that's another felony? Do not shave your head again, I told him."

"It's funny what order we all remember the salad dressings in."

"My youngest daughter has excellent upper-body strength."

"I sleep very well on the floor."

I TOOK 64 EAST OUT OF LOUISVILLE through the junction. Panels of cars and blown-out tires were scattered in the breakdown lane. I passed Exit 8, the off-ramp to the Southern Baptist Theological Seminary, such as Southern Baptist theology is. The speed limit rose to seventy, and mangled deer, coon, possum, turkeys, and skunks began to appear.

Over the Kentucky River in Fayette County, I stopped and for three dollars I ate a plate of biscuits and sausage gravy that would almost have fit into a football stadium.

"Here comes Rex. Today's to-do list: raise hell with the waitresses."

"That ain't on his list. That's just normal."

I did not change to the Bert T. Combs Mountain Parkway, which is the way I would have gone fifteen years earlier if I'd been drinking beer with my friend Gary on our way to Red River Gorge before he went crazy and they put him away in Central State for the first time, but not the last.

Gary was a big boy, ugly and pale, with a nose like a peeled potato. I'm not just saying that because my ex-wife slept with him once. We all slept around. She slept with Larry, too, but I don't have anything bad to say about Larry. I myself almost slept with Larry, he was irresistible, a beautiful man. *Gary* and *Larry*—these names have been changed to protect the innocent, but not mine: I am guilty.

But before any of that happened Gary and I were good friends, and we were together in the pro-Martin faction when Lawyer Jack pulled a knife on

Big Martin one night in the kitchen of the Highland House and Martin just shrugged and picked up the kitchen table and hit Jack with it.

Gary and I agreed on that dispute and on other important matters, we camped out together, we got high and talked about numerology, and it was in this way that I became important enough to him to lash out at when he fell ill.

"You blue-eyed Jew," he said to me as his mind disappeared. "You dumb piece of fuck. I'm going to stuff six dollars and ninety cents in pennies up your ass and staple it shut."

Six-ninety was 138—which was 23 times 6 (the 2 and 3 of 23 multiplied)—times 5 (the 2 and 3 of 23 added). Gary could go on for hours about the significance of these numbers to him. He had infinite bad luck, he would say, because of 138: an unlucky 13 conjoined with the sideways Möbius strip of an 8.

They wheeled him away, strapped to a stretcher.

GARY HAD WRITTEN, "Jack looks like your dad! Whew! Happy reading!" in the copy of *On The Road* he'd given me for Christmas in 1992. I don't remember if I read it or not. It's about a road.

I didn't have a Dean Moriarty for my long car trip, but I had the man on the car radio. And the man on the radio said: "Pieces of the Divine puzzle will be played out in the coming economic Armageddon. From crisis to consolidation. I want you to pray for me today."

WE SANG ABOUT THE BLOOD Wednesday nights at church suppers, Thursday nights at choir practices, mornings and evenings on Sundays, and every summer at a peacock-ridden revival camp in Alabama.

The old rugged cross, stained with blood so divine. There is a fountain filled with blood. I must needs go on the blood-sprinkled way. He bled, He died to save me. How I love to proclaim it, redeemed by the blood.

*They vainly purify themselves,* said Heraclitus, *by defiling themselves with blood, just as if one who had stepped into the mud were to wash his feet in mud. Any man who marked him doing thus would deem him mad.*

Our pastor had a method. After his sermon, we sang "Just As I Am" over and over again—without one plea, but that Thy blood was shed for me, and so on. We would sing until someone gave in. We sang all day.

It was the same unrelenting method of the middle school phys-ed coach who, perceiving that Weak Henry was weak, hit on the technique of making the whole class do extra push-ups until Henry finished his allotted twenty. Henry couldn't make it happen. We did twenty more, thirty more, forty; and after class, Demetrius and Alonzo beat Henry in the locker room until he peed.

One morning, after an hour of "Just As I Am," my mother shrieked and fell into the aisle. My father helped her stand. His face was strange. The two of them knelt and prayed at the altar. A nice old lady wearing a white gauze eye patch smiled. I waited to see what the people who told me what to do were going to tell me to do next.

It was this child grown into a man, then, if anyone ever grows up, who now drove past Lynn Camp Baptist Church, who drove past Hazel Fork Holiness Church and Living Waters Pentecostal Church, who drove past Faith Tabernacle Pentecostal Church and Turkey Creek Baptist Church short of breath, sweating like a sinner, drowning in blood.

I PLAYED JESUS ONE YEAR and Judas the next in the passion play. I taught Vacation Bible School, and visited and sang hymns to the homebound, and, all that rigamarole having been accomplished, I chased the preacher's daughter through the cornfield after Sunday evening services until I caught her.

And my father mowed the field out back of our church. He helped Deacon Jack repaint the sanctuary and he helped Deacon Willy reshingle the roof. He cooked and served at the Wednesday night church suppers and was happy to do it. But he didn't have much time for what he called *churchified* people.

"I find it difficult to believe that the Creator of the universe gives a fuck if I drink a cold beer on a sunny day," my father said. "These people can't say *sugar*, they just got to say *sucrose*. Meanwhile they don't have no more idea what God wants from me than the man in the moon. It's my own dick I'm talking about, and I can jump up and down on it like a pogo stick if I want to."

I THOUGHT I WAS BACK in Kentucky to write a magazine story about a TV show set in Harlan County. That isn't how things worked out. I wrote this letter instead.

Harlan is not *nowhere*. What you want to do is this: You drive to nowhere, then you turn left. You keep going until page eighty-eight, the last page of the atlas and gazetteer with its detailed topographical maps, which has apparently been paginated on the assumption that Harlan is the last place you're going to want to go.

In Harlan, in the morning, a woman walked across a restaurant and closed my notebook and said, "You can work all day, honey. Eat your biscuits while they're hot."

And the woman at the hotel's front desk said, "If you're like those other people, you're going to want a zero balance."

"I guess I am like other people."

"I know all you government men like to keep a zero balance."

I came out of Harlan bewildered on the Kingdom Come Parkway headed back toward Pineville, with its massive floodgates.

The man on the radio said: "I'm going to have a multitude of nations come forth from my loins. And as part of my covenant, You are asking me to mutilate the very part of myself through which You are going to fulfill Your promise. I mean, Abraham, he didn't have the biological insight that we have in our modern medical world, but Abraham knew well where babies come from. And here's God—"

I passed Daniels Mountain and Manito Hill. Out past Tin Can Hollow, I turned south on 25E. I passed Clear Creek Baptist Bible College and John's Tire Discount and an immense sign that said ARE YOU ADDICTED TO PAIN MEDICATION?

I bore south through Meldrum and Middlesboro (home of the actor Lee Majors, aka Harvey Lee Yeary, aka Colonel Steve Austin, "The Six Million Dollar Man") all the way to the corner of Virginia, Kentucky, and Tennessee, aka the Cumberland Gap.

Pale pink-and-white dogwoods and purple wildflowers lined the ascent to Pinnacle Overlook. At the gap Boone had penetrated a wall of rock and forest 600 miles long and 150 miles wide. He saw a new world, where all the old mistakes waited to be made again.

When Boone was asked if he had gotten lost in that forest, he said: I can't say as ever I was lost, but I was bewildered once for three days.

BACK ON 25E, HEADING NORTH, I drove through crumbling hills past West Roger Hollow through Corbin into Laurel County. I drove past Magic Vapor Shop and Tri-State Flooring. I took 192 East to the Hal Rogers Parkway out past Lick Fork.

Soon I saw a barn I remembered. I saw horses and cows, trailers up on broken cinder blocks, front yards full of table legs and coffee cans. I passed Urban Creek Holiness Church. I passed Jimbo's 4-Lane Tobacco and the Federal Correctional Institution.

At Burning Springs I turned on 472 to head toward Fogertown, where barns had been reclaimed by the land, overgrown with tall trees poking through holes in their roofs. At Muncey Fork was a burnt-down house. Creeping vines were pulling down telephone poles and billboards.

All at once and with no fanfare I passed Cornett Charolais, where I had spent many pleasant Sunday afternoons with old Joe Dale and Dale Junior and Linda and Bessie—*pleasant* is a pious lie—more like bored, *bored*, not knowing what all of this would one day mean, what I would one day want to pretend it had all meant.

I wanted it to mean to me what it meant to my father: home and happiness with his foster family. I liked being sent to slop out the hogs after dinner, listening to the rustling in the dark along the fence line. I liked hiking in the rocky hills with my father, seeing that he was calm and pleased, seeing the shale and sandstone and limestone and schist and slate. I liked walking across fields and hearing him holler, "Sookie! Sook calf!"

Apart from those pleasures I had been bored and sullen, reading photocopied pages of *The Antichrist* folded inside *Sports Illustrated,* waiting to escape from that army of hayseeds. But twenty years later my father's foster mother is dead, as anyone but me might have foreseen, because she was a person and not a tree; and I would eat a photocopier in exchange for two more bowls of her soup beans and cornbread—one for me, and one for my father, to whom it would mean the world made young again.

Instead I name these places. I throw my song into the mouth of death. I break his teeth. There is no death, there is no hell.

I DROVE PAST the old Russell House Grocery, and there was what I wanted to find: the Pleasant Grove Baptist Church, established 1860. I have seen my father cry three times, and one of those times was in this church, at his foster father's funeral.

The second time I saw my father cry was while he was strangling me. He had said my friends, Scott and Allen and Gary, were no-good weirdos and long-haired faggots, and I was on the verge of becoming one too, and that if I didn't act right he was going to cut my hair himself with the lawnmower.

I dared him to, more than a little frightened that he would try it. That was just the sort of thing he was always doing: kicking in a locked door, or pushing around a far-too-young panhandler with a sign that claimed he had been a VIETNAM VETERAN.

"Step around the corner, John Henry," my father said, "I'd like to have a word with this young man in private." He nudged the kid with his boot. "Yes, I do mean you—you dilapidated cocksucker."

And afterwards, in the cab of his truck, trembling, beating his fists against the steering wheel, he said, "What's the matter with these people, Johnny? I'm a Vietnam veteran. And just look at me. I'm fine. I'm fine!"

I dared my father to cut my hair, and he picked me up by my throat and smashed me against the wall, then threw me through the doorway into my bedroom and leapt on top of me, and he was strangling me with both hands and shaking me and cursing and shouting at me before he came to his senses and started to cry.

"My family is falling apart," he said, and it was true, I was destroying our family, why couldn't I do as I was told without having impulses and desires of my own.

That is the second time I saw my father cry. The third time is private.

IT'S NOT AS IF MY FRIENDS *weren't* no-good weirdos. Big Scott had come over earlier that afternoon, and my father had said, "Hey, gorilla." Then: "Scotty, come here, boy, you're hurt."

My father had glimpsed a bloody letter *s* above the collar of Scott's T-shirt. He pulled the collar down and saw the still-bleeding word PUSSY, which Big Scott had cut into his chest with a razorblade moments before sprinting over to show me.

"Who did this to you, boy?" my father said. "You can tell me."

Scott looked at my father.

"I don't believe that," my father said. "No."

I DIDN'T WANT TO WRITE about my father, but I don't seem to have much choice. There is no such thing as a repressed impulse: the inside and the outside are the same side.

What serpent's-tooth-sharp story is this to tell about the man who helped to give me life, who saved my life when I was choking on shish kebab (thereby earning, certain tribesmen might argue, the right to choke me himself), who sacrificed his body at punishing jobs in order that I might have shish kebab to choke on?

*Take, eat: this is my body, which is broken for you*—and I hope you choke on it.

I visit my father in the Florida Everglades and I see a nice old man. Just this week, he mailed me his sausage-gravy recipe. ("Step Five: Buy helmet, put on, tongue smacking top of mouth may cause injury.") I am deceived: Where has this nice old man hidden the menacing ogre of my childhood?

His aim was to protect me from the darkness all around us, using the darkness inside himself. All that darkness had to be *good for something*, didn't it? That was what the darkness was *for*, wasn't it?—not only for tormenting him and, using him as its instrument, everyone he loved?

It's nothing to get upset about, it isn't even me it happened to, that person died in 1995, he died again in 2003 and again at the beginning of this sentence. He's been dying for most of act 5, scene 2. Maybe someone ought to stab him again.

THE MAN ON THE RADIO SAID, "Four famine scenarios. How to prepare for an economic crisis of Biblical proportions. The salt plan: how to turn adversity into advantage."

"Whence comest thou, Deceiver?" I said. "From going to and fro in the earth, and from walking up and down in it?"

"Be a blessing to others in times of economic turndown. This book will help you get your head straight about what is happening in the world today, and it's very personal and practical at one hundred and forty-two pages."

"Leave me alone," I said to the man on the radio. "That's just the word

*God*, the word the conjure man uses to wring hot tears out of the wet rag of your heart. I don't want the word *God*, but the Word of God."

The man on the radio said to me: *I ordained thee a prophet unto the nations.*

I said, "Ah, Lord God, I cannot speak, for I am a child."

But the man on the radio said: *Say not, I am a child: for thou shalt go to all that I shall send thee, and whatsoever I command thee thou shalt speak. Behold, I have put my words in thy mouth.*

I wept until I had to pull over. God had laid His burning hand on me. If you don't turn the radio off, you can't drive anywhere in this country.

# *Yasiin Bey*

ONE CALLED TRILL

Beasts
At the threshold
Rats
At your feet
Mansions
Madness&murder
In the streets
Fire to the leaf
Dogs
At the heel
Layers
To the rhythm
And spokes on the wheel
Trill

Trill.
Trill.   Trill
Trill  trill
Trill
This is what
Death can't
Kill

WINNER OF THE NPR
THREE-MINUTE FICTION CONTEST

# *The Dauphin*

## MARC SHEEHAN

*Three times a year, the National Public Radio show* Weekends on All Things Considered *holds a fiction contest in which listeners from across the country submit stories that can be read aloud in less than three minutes. This fall's judge was the novelist Brad Meltzer, who asked for stories that revolve around a U.S. president. "Three-Minute Fiction" winners appear in* The Paris Review *by special arrangement with NPR.*

President Agnew is tired after his daily briefing and ready to watch a rerun of *The Love Boat*. Next to his glass of jug wine on the kitchen table rests the Football, an old, scuffed Detroit Lions model. He refuses to go anywhere without it. He often complains about the responsibility of knowing the nuclear codes.

It's a mystery how, when my father's dementia struck, it took the form of his belief that he is President Spiro T. Agnew. Father was never political. He did get upset when Gerald Ford, the representative of our West Michigan district, became president without being elected, but not enough to even write a letter to *The Grand Rapids Press*.

Now it's 1984, after what would have been the Agnew administration, and long after I gave up athletics for chasing girls and smoking pot. Back in junior high I was a second-string quarterback, and Dad, already in his fifties, used to jog across the yard with his arms outstretched for a catch as I practiced my spiral.

In the spring, when I got laid off from my injection-molding job, I moved back in to spend time with him and give Mom a rest. The wine and *Love Boat* are everyone's rewards for getting through another afternoon cabinet meeting.

"Are we doing all we can to further relations with China?" he asks. "After everything that's happened to Dick, I think it's the least we can do."

"Yes, Mr. President," I say, "although Chairman Mao is unpredictable as always."

"Would the president like Salisbury steak or turkey and peas for dinner?" asks my mother, the secretary of the interior.

President Agnew ponders, a finger stroking the pebbly surface of the football. "Turkey and peas," he announces.

"Then the vice president is having Salisbury steak," she says, looking at me. "The White House kitchen has only one turkey and peas."

We've had frozen dinners most nights since an X-ray found a tumor, inoperable and fast growing, in the president's lung. The doctor said we could try radiation and chemo but thought the cure would kill him faster than the disease. Before the X-ray, we had gently tried to convince him he is not President Agnew.

Summer drags on. We survive the fall of Saigon, the *Mayaguez* incident, and Hoffa's disappearance. His breath becomes shallow and labored, even with the flow from the oxygen tank cranked up high. By mid-September it's just mother and me sitting at the kitchen table, drinking rosé and watching ocean-borne romance with the sound turned low, while the president drowses in his recliner.

One night, after eating our microwave dinners on TV trays in the living room, I help get the president dressed in his pajamas and tucked into bed. I ask him if he wants to keep up with events. He nods and I turn on the portable Magnavox perched on my parents' dresser. Father cradles the football next to him, atop the chenille bedspread. He has the little nozzle portion of the plastic tubing from the green tank in his nose. The oxygen makes a hissing sound as he stares blankly at a man shaving his thickly foamed face with a disposable razor.

"You'll make sure everything is okay when I'm gone, won't you?" he wheezes. I don't know who's asking me this—my father, or Spiro Agnew.

"Yes, I will, Mr. President. Dad," I say. He smiles. Then he nudges the football up onto his stomach where he can grab it firmly, and hands it off to me.

# The *Paris Review* App

New issues in full

Rare back issues

The *Paris Review* Daily

New collections

---

Look for us in the App Store, or visit

www.theparisreview.org

# ISA

WWW.ISA.GG

# Have you heard Willis Earl Beal?

# WILLIS EARL BEAL
## ACOUSMATIC SORCERY
### Out Now

XLRECORDINGS.COM
WILLISEARLBEAL.COM

- NEPENENOYKA
- TAKE ME AWAY
- COSMIC QUERIES
- EVENING'S KISS
- SAMBO JOE FROM THE RAINBOW
- GHOST ROBOT
- SWING ON LOW
- MONOTONY
- BRIGHT COPPER NOON
- AWAY MY SILENT LOVER
- ANGEL CHORUS

CONTRIBUTORS

YASIIN BEY, formerly known as Mos Def, is an artist from Brooklyn, New York, and the founder, with Talib Kweli, of Black Star.

STEVEN CRAMER's new poetry collection is *Clangings*. He directs the M.F.A. Program in Creative Writing at Lesley University.

J. D. DANIELS lives in Massachusetts.

SARAH FRISCH is a lecturer in creative writing at Stanford University, where she recently completed a Stegner Fellowship.

REGAN GOOD's first book of poems, *The Atlantic House*, was published in 2011. She lives in Brooklyn, New York.

GEOFFREY HILL is Oxford Professor of Poetry.

DEVIN JOHNSTON is the author of several collections of poetry, the most recent of which is *Traveler*.

RACHEL KUSHNER's second novel, *The Flamethrowers*, is forthcoming in April.

BEN LERNER's most recent books are the novel *Leaving the Atocha Station* and *Mean Free Path*, a book of poems.

MAUREEN N. MCLANE is the author of two books of poems, *Same Life* and *World Enough*, and a book of experimental prose, *My Poets*.

JOSHUA MEHIGAN's second book, *Accepting the Disaster*, is forthcoming in 2013.

PETER ORNER is the author of two novels, including *Love and Shame and Love*. His second story collection, *Last Car Over the Sagamore Bridge*, is forthcoming next year.

LINDA PASTAN's latest book is *Traveling Light*. She received the Ruth Lilly Prize in 2003 and is a former Poet Laureate of Maryland.

JAMES SALTER's sixth novel, *All That Is*, will be published in April. In 2011, he received *The Paris Review*'s Hadada Prize and in 2012 the PEN/Faulkner Malamud Award.

MARC SHEEHAN, the winner of NPR's Three-Minute Fiction Contest, is the author of two collections of poetry, *Greatest Hits* and *Vengeful Hymns*.

IMAGE CREDITS *Cover: The Everett Collection. Page 64: From* 300 000 mennesker i døgnet *(1973), director: Espen Thorstenson. Copyright Oslo City Archives. Page 162: Sylvia Plachy © 2012. Page 167: Lawrence Schwartzwald © 2012. Page 196: Copyright © The Estate of Jack Goldstein. Courtesy Galerie Daniel Buchholz, Cologne/Berlin, and the Estate of Jack Goldstein. Page 201: Courtesy of the Eggleston Artistic Trust and Jerry McGill. Page 203: Courtesy Danny Lyon/Magnum Photos, Edwynn Houk Gallery, and dektol.wordpress.com. Page 204: Courtesy Warhol Museum, Pittsburgh, PA. Page 204: ©2012 The Andy Warhol Museum, Pittsburgh, PA, a museum of Carnegie Institute. All rights reserved. Film still courtesy of The Andy Warhol Museum. Page 205: Courtesy Julie Buck and Karin Segal. Page 206: Courtesy © The Estate of Lee Lozano; Moderna Museet, Stockholm; and Stefan Altenburger Photography Zürich. Page 207: Copyright © Allen Ginsberg Estate. Page 208: Copyright © The Robert F. Heinecken Trust. Page 209: Collection of the Metropolitan Museum of Art, New York, ART copyright David Salle/Licensed by VAGA, NY. Page 211: Courtesy of the artist and Haunch of Venison. Pages 212–213: Courtesy © 2012 Artists Rights Society (ARS), New York / SIAE, Rome and Archivio Alighiero Boetti. Page 214: Courtesy of Tano D'Amico and the General Collection, Beinecke Rare Book and Manuscript Library, Yale University.*

### STATEMENT OF OWNERSHIP, MANAGEMENT, AND CIRCULATION

Publication Title: The Paris Review. Publication No.: 0420-720. Filing Date: October 1, 2012. Issue Frequency: Quarterly. Number of issues published annually: 4. Annual Subscription Price: $40. Complete Mailing Address of Known Office of Publication: 62 White St., New York, NY 10013-3593. Complete Mailing Address of Headquarters of General Business Office of Publisher: 62 White St., New York, NY 10013-3593. Full Names and Complete Mailing Addresses of Publisher, Editor, and Managing Editor: Publisher: Antonio Weiss, 62 White St., New York, NY 10013-3593; Editor: Lorin Stein, 62 White St., New York, NY 10013-3593; Managing Editor: Nicole Rudick, 62 White St., New York, NY 10013-3593. Owner: Full Name: The Paris Review Foundation, Inc.; Complete Mailing Address: 62 White St., New York, NY 10013-3593. Known Bondholders, Mortgages, and Other Security Holders: None. Tax Status: Has Not Changed During Preceding 12 Months. Publication Title: The Paris Review. Issue Date for Circulation Data: Issue 202, Fall 2012. Extent and Nature of Circulation: Average Number of Copies Each Issue During Preceding 12 Months (Number of Copies of Single Issue Published Nearest to Filing Date): Total Number of Copies: 20,296 (20,599); Mailed Outside-County Paid Subscriptions Stated on Form 3541: 7,841 (7,447); Mailed In-County Paid Subscriptions Stated on Form 3541: 0 (0); Paid Distribution Outside the Mails Including Sales Through Dealers and Carriers, Street Vendors, Counter Sales, and Other Paid Distribution Outside USPS: 9,213 (89,297); Paid Distribution Through Other Classes of Mail Through the USPS: 0 (0); Total Paid distribution: 17,054 (17,444); Free or Nominal Rate Distribution: Free or Nominal Rate Outside-County included on Form 3541: 0 (0), Free or Nominal Rate In-County included on Form 3541: 0 (0), Free or Nominal Rate Copies Mailed at Other Classes Through the USPS: 0 (0); Free or Nominal Rate Distribution Outside the Mail: 49 (49); Total Free or Nominal Rate Distribution: 49 (49); Total Distribution: 17,103 (17,493); Copies Not Distributed: 3,193 (3,806); Total: 20,296 (20,599); Percent Paid: 99.7% (99.7%); Publication of Statement of Ownership Will be Printed in Issue 203 of this publication; Signature and Title of Editor, Publisher, Business Manager, or Owner: I certify that all information furnished on this form is true and complete. Nicole Rudick, Managing Editor.

# VEDA

THISISVEDA.COM

# 92ND STREET Y
# UNTERBERG POETRY CENTER
## THE VOICE OF LITERATURE
### 12/13 SEASON
+ literary readings + performances + seminars + writing workshops

Kincaid    Yehoshua    Hemon    Herzog    Karr    Cox

## WINTER/SPRING EVENTS

### FEBRUARY
- **11 Mon** Words & Music: **Charles Ives** and **American Transcendentalism** with **Jeremy Denk**
- **25 Mon** Jamaica Kincaid: A Live *Paris Review* Writers-At-Work Interview with **Darryl Pinckney**

### MARCH
- **14 Thu** A. B. Yehoshua
- **28 Thu** Aleksandar Hemon and Wenguang Huang

### APRIL
- **4 Thu** Will Eno and Amy Herzog
- **8 Mon** *Poetry* at 100: An Anniversary Reading with Frank Bidart, Mary Karr, Christian Wiman, Charles Wright and others
- **15 Mon** *Living with Shakespeare*: An Anthology Reading with Brian Cox, Eamonn Walker, Harriet Walter and others
- **18 Thu** Bob Hicok and Heather McHugh
- **22 Mon** Brecht in the 21st Century with Classic Stage Company

**Great seats available!**
For a full listing of events and to purchase tickets, visit 92Y.org/Review | 212.415.5500
Limited number of **$10 tickets** available for patrons age 35 and Under.

**92Y** AN OPEN DOOR TO EXTRAORDINARY WORLDS™

92nd Street Y | Lexington Avenue at 92nd Street Federation    An agency of UJA-Federation

The Plimpton Circle is a remarkable group of individuals and organizations whose contributions of $1,000 or more help advance the work of The Paris Review Foundation. The Foundation gratefully acknowledges:

---

Donna Jo and William R. Acquavella • Keith and Peggy Anderson • Lisa Capozzi and Dave Anderson • Jeff Antebi • Winsome Brown and Claude Arpels • R. Scott Asen • Amanda Urban and Ken Auletta • René-Pierre and Alexis Azria • André Balazs • Mahnaz Ispahani Bartos and Adam Bartos • Alexandra Styron and Edward Beason • Patricia Birch Becker and William Becker • Helen and William Beekman • Robert Bell • Kate Bellin • Liz and Rod Berens • Kathryn and David Berg • Clara Bingham • Joan Bingham • The Blackstone Group • Leslie Tcheyan and Monty Blanchard • Emily Blavatnik • Ross Bleckner • Bloomberg • Lauren Schuker and Jason Blum • Livio M. Borghese • Luke Parker Bowles • Alison and George Brokaw • Stephen M. Brown • Winthrop Brown • Timothy Browne • Anne and Russell Byers • Heather Kilpatrick and Stephen Byers • Ariadne and Mario Calvo-Platero • Maria B. and Woodrow W. Campbell • Dr. Sally Peterson and Michael V. Carlisle • Lisa and Dick Cashin • Kathy Cerullo • Molly and Walter Channing • Allan Chapin • Sarah Teale and Gordon W. Chaplin • Michael Chon • City National Bank • Stephen Clark • Susanna Porter and James Clarke • Cassius Marcellus Clay • Stacy and Eric Cochran • Gifford Combs • Conde Nast Traveler • Bernard F. Conners • Marianna Cook and Hans Kraus • Wendy Mackenzie and Alexander Cortesi • Georgia Cool and Christopher Cox • Hilary Cooper and Chris Crowley • Celerie Kemble and R. Boykin Curry IV • Michel David-Weill • Don DeLillo • Robert de Rothschild • Raymond Debbane • Gayatri Devi • Michelle and Thomas Dewey • Leonardo DiCaprio • Diane von Furstenberg and Barry Diller • Abigail E. Disney • Jane C. Dudley • Disney Publishing Worldwide • EBSCO Publishing • Janet Ecker • Kelly and Randolph Post Eddy III • Gwen Edelman • Inger McCabe Elliott and Osborn Elliott • Rachel Cobb and Morgan Entrekin • ESPN • Harold Evans • Lise and Michael Evans • Farrar, Straus and Giroux • Jeanne Donovan Fisher • Estate of Richard B. Fisher • Wendy Stein and Bart Friedman • Arlene Hogan Fuller • Minnie Mortimer and Stephen Gaghan • Mr. and Mrs. Rowan Gaither IV • Tara Gallagher and Luke Mitchell • Martin Garbus • The David Geffen Foundation • Slavka B. Glaser • Barbara Goldsmith • Toni K. and James C. Goodale • Noah and Maria Gottdiener • Jane M. Gould • Stephen and Cathy Graham • Francine Gray • Sol Greenbaum • Michael Greenberg • The William & Mary Greve Foundation • Grubman Indursky Shire & Meiselas, P.C. • Lawrence H. and Lucy Guffey • Mala Gaonkar • HBO • Hachette Book Group • Christina Lewis and Dan Halpern • Peter Harf • Alexander Hecker • Drue Heinz • Kathryn and John Heminway • Ken Hirsh • Franklin W. Hobbs • Christopher Hockett • Susan Levine and Wade Hooker • Sean Eldridge and Chris Hughes • Ala and Ralph Isham • Kathleen Begala and Yves-André Istel • Joele Frank, Wilkinson Brimmer Katcher • Mary Karr • Katheryn C. Patterson and Thomas L. Kempner, Jr. • Lisa Atkins and Tony Kiser • Alfred A. Knopf • Nina Köprülü • John and Duff Lambros • Fabienne and Michael Lamont • Mr. and Mrs. Stephen Langman • Sherry Lansing • Jenny Lee • Elizabeth and Jeffrey T. Leeds • Bokara Legendre • Dan Levine • Anne Kerr Kennedy and Matthew G. L'Heureux • Barbara and Robert Liberman • Gary Lippman • Hilary Mills Loomis and Robert Loomis • Renee Khatami and John R. MacArthur • Macmillan and Holtzbrinck Publishers • Chris and Kevin Madden • Alexandra and Terrence Malick • Shelby and Anthony E. Malkin • Ellen Chesler and Matt Mallow • Mr. and Mrs. Donald Marron • Peter Matthiessen • Tatiana Maxwell • Ellen and Frank McCourt • Jeanne McCulloch • Joanie McDonell • Stacey and Terry McDonell • Anne Hearst and Jay McInerney • Clare E. and Robert B. McKeon • Keith and Jon Meacham • Sandy Gotham Meehan • Peter Melhado • Michael Werner Gallery • Lorrie Moore • Robert and Bethany Millard •

Alexander B. Miller • Charlotte Morgan • Gary Mueller • Amy Loyd Grace and Chris Napolitano • Henry and Cathy Nassau • Bruce S. Nelson • Lynn Nesbit • Mr. and Mrs. Arthur Newbold • The New York Review of Books • The New Yorker • Francesca and Richard Nye • Euelyn J. Offenbach • Abdim M. Okanovic • Anita Braker and Dave Olsen • Ron and Jane Olson • Linda Ong • Open Road Integrated Media • Other Press • Hannah C. Pakula • Eunice and Jay Panetta • Park Pictures • Elena and Michael Patterson • Deborah S. Pease • Radhika Jones and Max Petersen • Joan Ganz Cooney and Peter G. Peterson • Marnie S. Pillsbury • Sarah Dudley Plimpton • Annie and Edward Pressman • Random House • Regele Builders, Inc. • Manuel Reis • Esther B. Fein and David Remnick • Mr. and Mrs. Oscar de la Renta • Betsy von Furstenberg Reynolds • Frederic C. Rich • Valerie Riftkin • Matthew Roberts • Sage Mehta and Michael Robinson • Elizabeth and Felix Rohatyn • Emmanuel Roman • Lauri Romanzi • Joanna and Dan Rose • Laura Love Rose • Marjorie and Jeffrey A. Rosen • Mr. and Mrs. Benjamin Rosen • Gerald Rosenfield and Judith Zarin • Mary Lee Stein and Mark Rosenman • Mr. and Mrs. William Rosoff • Sumner Rulon-Miller • Perri Peltz and Eric Ruttenberg • David Salle • Mr. and Mrs. Forrest Sawyer • Schlosstein-Hartley Family Foundation • Elisabeth Schmitz • Irene and Bernard Schwartz • Stephen A. Schwarzman • Andrea Schulz • Marie Semple • Lynn Povich and Stephen Shepard • Georgia Shreve • Stanley and Sydney Shuman • Gloria and Alan Siegel • Robert Silvers • Skadden, Arps, Slate, Meagher and Flom LLP • Sarah and Henry Slack • Lawrence Slaughter • Ashley Baker and Davin Staats • Jean Stein • Joan and Michael Steinberg • Antoinette Delruelle and Joshua Steiner • Christine Taylor Stiller and Ben Stiller • Rose Styron • Sullivan and Cromwell LLP • Nan and Gay Talese • Marcia and Mark Thomas • Tibor de Nagy Gallery • Time Inc. • Bardyl and Anne Bell Tirana • Kyra Tirana • Joseph Tomkiewicz • Wolfgang and Catherine Traber • Judson Traphagen • Jamie Trowbridge • Sandra and Bruce Tully • Gordon Veneklasen • Liza and Paul Wachter • John and Amanda Waldron • Barbara Walters • Michele Smith and David Weinberg • Harvey Weinstein • Tali and Boaz Weinstein • James Crichton and Adam Weiss • Susannah Hunnewell and Antonio Weiss • Leslie Marshall and William Weld • Wenner Media • Tom Werner • Emile Westergaard • Priscilla Rattazzi and Christopher Whittle • William Morris Endeavor Entertainment • Stuart Woods • The Wylie Agency • Dylan Yaeger • Virginia and Donald Zilkha • Mortimer Zuckerman

*The Paris Review* is grateful for the support of its friends. Please send your tax-deductible contribution to The Paris Review Foundation, 62 White Street, New York, NY 10013. Contact Emily Cole-Kelly at 212.343.1333 or ecolekelly@theparisreview.org.

EDITORIAL ASSOCIATES

Nelson Aldrich, Robert Antoni, Sara Barrett, Adam Begley, Andy Bellin, Larry Bensky, Adrienne Brodeur, Charles Buice, Jamie Byng, Chris Calhoun, Christopher Cerf, Stephen Clarke, Penny Dante, Jonathan Dee, Beth Drenning, Morgan Entrekin, Robert Faggen, Sarah Fay, Anne Fulenwider, Rowan Gaither, Tara Gallagher, Dan Glover, Dana Goodyear, Francine du Plessix Gray, Eliza Griswold, Anthony Haden-Guest, Fayette Hickox, Edward Hirsch, Mavis Humes, Tom Jenks, Radhika Jones, Gordon Knox, Daniel Kunitz, James Linville, Jack Livings, Larissa MacFarquhar, Lucas Matthiessen, Dan Max, Joanie McDonell, Molly McGrann, Molly McKaughan, David Michaelis, Jonathan Miller, Thomas Moffett, Lillian von Nickern, Meg O'Rourke, Ron Padgett, Maggie Paley, Elise Paschen, Gilles Peress, Robert Phillips, Nathaniel Rich, David Robbins, Philip Roth, Elissa Schappell, Frederick Seidel, Elisabeth Sifton, Mona Simpson, Ben Sonnenberg, Sarah Stein, Remar Sutton, William Wadsworth, Hallie Gay Walden

*Fivestory New York.*

*Curated Fashions. Timeless treasures.*

*Endless stories await*

*in the heart of Madison Avenue.*

**FIVESTORY**
NEW YORK

*18 EAST 69TH STREET*

*NEW YORK, NY 10021*

*212 288 1338*

*FIVESTORYNY.COM*

*twitter @FIVESTORY | instagram @CLAIRE_FIVESTORY*

# The *Paris Review* Print Series
## Born, 1964. Revived, 2012.

*Donald Baechler, 2012, limited edition, $3,500.*

In 1964, a gift from Drue Heinz enabled *The Paris Review* to commission a series of prints by major contemporary artists. The purpose was to encourage works in the print medium while publicizing and providing financial support for the magazine. Among the early contributors were Andy Warhol, Robert Rauschenberg, Helen Frankenthaler, and Robert Motherwell. Later contributions were made by Louise Bourgeois, Ed Ruscha, William Bailey, and others. Many of the original prints are still available for purchase.

Suspended in 2004, the print series was revived this year with a print by Donald Baechler.

*To inquire, visit us online at*
www.theparisreview.org *or* call 212.343.1333

# GRANTA

THE MAGAZINE OF NEW WRITING

'An indispensable part of
the intellectual landscape' – *Observer*

A spectacular gift for the curious mind

Every issue of *Granta* is a feast of the best new writing from around the world. In our pages you'll find stories, reportage, poetry and photography from the acclaimed and the infamous, the prizewinners and the ones to watch.

This Christmas, buy a gift subscription to *Granta* and receive a 25% DISCOUNT. Four issues for just $36 – that's a saving of $31 on the cover price.

Visit GRANTA.COM/PARISGIFT
or call 866-438-6150 and
quote 'PARIS GIFT'

# MICHAEL GENOVESE
*Lines and Cracks and Zebras and Horses*

January 12 - February 09

# OHWOW
937 N. La Cienega Blvd., Los Angeles, CA 90069
oh-wow.com